PÁRÍS SQ

The Archives of BFF Vol. 1

35 Reasons Why You Shouldn't Idolize Us.

John 8:34-36
1 John 1:5-8

Contents

1

Prologue

In 2010, it was announced that one of the biggest record labels in the world, Ex-S Records was hosting auditions to create a new co-ed act. Anyone aged 8 to 16 who could sing and dance was eligible to be selected.

In short, 25 people of different backgrounds were chosen to be part of a group called BFF. We were considered a failed investment until 2012.

Our name was changed to Switch and ten more members were added while one particular member got kicked out.

The group skyrocketed in popularity but were no stranger to controversy. Cheating scandals, teen pregnancy, and fights internally and externally happen for the world to see. However the group was very good at hiding the real deep issues that happen behind closed doors.

The now CEO of Ex-S Record, Mr.Smith lied to us. He stripped us away from our families and isolated us all in a house deep in the woods of New York. We didn't know what a 360 deal was. We sold millions of copies but each made pennies for six years.

It wasn't till one day in 2016, we broke free from Ex-S Records and went independent. We continued to reign on charts for another six years as the music industry slowly grew a hatred for Switch. But the members didn't pay any attention to the hate. There were bigger problems that we had to deal with.

Four members took the role to help manage the group, though it would be nice if we had a staff of on-site therapists.

Now we open the first volume of Les Archives de BFF or translated to English, The Archives of BFF. I, Valen Valentina, will be your archivist in this journey. This is our testimony. The testimony of how God saved Switch.

"So where should we start," asked the interviewer.

2

Switch's Roster (as of 06/01/22)

*Credits to the Kenyan Flames Chapter for the fan art.

VARSITY GIRLS

VARSITY GUYS

JV LINE

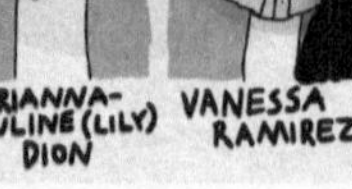

DUO LINE
TERRANCE (TORAN) SMITH
DOMINIQUE (DICE) HERNANDEZ

UNIT LEAD
HIATUS
RAP LINE
JEAN GONZALES
LEO SANCHEZ JUNIT
SIMON FISCHER
KENDRICK FAYE
NAM LEESUNG

Inactive Unit: British Trio Line
Included Brionna Russ-Hawkins, Saige Queen, and Jackie Sean.

* * *

The Discography

Albums (As of Oct. 2022)

(* Blacklist songs are songs that have been banned by another member or themselves. Unless requested, the song may not be performed, played on the radio, or be available for commercial use.)

2010: Introducing BFF

- 22 Songs. No blacklist song included.

Jan. 2012: Hand N'Hand

- 24 Songs. One blacklist song included.
- *Apologize – Romeo*

June 2012: Kiss N' Tell

- 19 Songs. One blacklist song included.
- *Like You – British Trio Line*

Feb. 2013: Around The World

- 34 Songs. One blacklist song included.
- *Reasons – Saige and Theo*

May 2013: Precipitation [Brittany Solo]

- 8 Songs. No blacklist songs included.

May 2013: The Golden Hour [Carlos Solo]

- 9 Songs. Three blacklist songs included.
- *Make Her Smile.*
- *Love*
- *Mirrors (Feat. Kendrick)*

Aug. 2014: Around the World Part II

- 41 Songs. Fourteen blacklist songs included.
- *Smile – Cameron, Courtney, Mia*
- *Soon We'll Be Found – All Girls*

- *Your Song - British Trio Line*
- *Explosions - British Trio Line*
- *Littlest Things - Cameron*
- *National Anthem - All Girls*
- *Love - Mia*
- *The Way That I Love You - Mia*
- *If I knew - Carlos*
- *Te Busque - Group*
- *Because I was - Carlos*
- *The Heart Wants - Mia*
- *When I Was - Carlos*
- *It Will Rain - Carlos*

July 2015: Under the Impressions, Thoughts at the Party

- 33 Songs. Three blacklist songs included.
- *Somebody That I know - Romeo and Brionna*
- *Dead In The Water - Lily, Vanessa, Jackie, Maknae Girls*
- *Beware - Jean and Cameron*

Oct. 2016: For Mines Only. Its My Loyalty. [LeeSung Solo]

- Off the market. No information available.

June 2016: Summer Love

- 36 Songs. No blacklist songs included.

Aug. 2016: The Good, Ugly, and The Bad [Cameron and Jean Duet]

- 12 Songs. No blacklist songs included.

Nov. 2018: Cold Weather, Life without Fame or Money

- 37 Songs. Three blacklist songs included.
- *War and Love – Cameron*
- *Complicated – Cameron, Brionna, and Saige*
- *All The Way Home – Cameron*

Nov. 2019: Dreams and Nightmares

- 38 Songs. No blacklist songs included.

Sept. 2020: Sex, Money, Feelings, All Have Die

- 38 Songs. Two blacklist songs included.
- *I Get Lonely – Cameron*
- *Climax – Varsity Guys*

June 2021: In The Name of Love

- 39 Songs. One blacklist song included.
- *I Remember – Sammatha*

July 2021: Solo About It [Dice Solo]

- 10 Songs. One blacklist songs included.
- *I Never Was There*

Feb. 2022: Tainted Hearts [Simon Solo]

- 12 Songs. Two blacklist songs included.
- *Be Quiet*
- *Endlessly*

July 2022: Simpler Days (Mini Album)

- 8 Songs. No blacklist songs included.

July 2022: Tes Yeux [Simon Solo]

- 6 Songs. No blacklist songs included.

Aug. 2022: Behind the Door [Romeo and Brionna Duet]

- 8 Songs. No blacklist songs included.

Blacklist Artist (As of June 2022)

1. xxxxxxxxxxxx
2. Grace C.
3. Nathaniel W.
4. Alec W.
5. xxxxxxxxxxx
6. xxxxxxxxxxx
7. xxxxxxxxxxx
8. xxxxxxxxxxxx
9. Scott ST.
10. xxxxxxxxxxx
11. xxxxxxxxxxx

12. XXXXXXXXXXXX

13. XXXXXXXXXXXX

14. XXXXXXXXXXXX

15. XXXXXXXXXXXX

16. XXXXXXXXXXXX

17. XXXXXXXXXXXX

18. XXXXXXXXXXXX

19. XXXXXXXXXXX

20. XXXXXXXXXXXX

21. XXXXXXXXXXXX

22. XXXXXXXXXXXX

23. XXXXXXXXXXXX

Pending....

· Kylie Torres upon request.

3

06/11/22: BFF World indicated a change in pace.

Today was the last day of BFF World and simultaneously the last day of the Asian American Pacific Islander (AAPI) Festival. To have the different sub-units having to run around three to four various venues was rather tiring, but finally, at the bell's strike, it was 11pm, and we were done.

Congregated backstage at our home base arena, The BFF Stadium, I was chatting with some of the girls from the JV line when I noticed Sammatha was isolated off to the side, looking visually uncomfortable and upset. Mixed with Moroccan and Sicilian, I promise you I've seen her cry more than smile lately as her thick brown bangs hung above her eyes. Which is unfortunate for someone who is a Varsity lead singer.

Though how could I forget what had happened just a few weeks ago? Kylie, an ex-member of the group, went on the airwaves and live television to ultimately pick and pull apart Sammatha to the point of no return. All because Kylie is jealous that Sammatha is dating Leo.

"Do you think she will be alright," Rebecca said as we glanced at Sammatha. "I hope so...Though she has been pretty closed off lately. She barely wanted to perform today," Saige said.

Rebecca is nonetheless the wild card of the group. Puerto Rican and Dominican while Saige, on the other hand, claims she is of South African descent. However, she looks more Northern Irish with her naturally long orange/reddish hair.

"I think she will be fine," I said.
   "Maybe we should at least check up on her," Rebecca suggested.

Taking another look behind us, we saw Leo approaching Sammatha. Without hesitation, she fell into his arms as he held her close. Leo is a tall, muscular, Brazilian American, and ever since he has been with Sammatha, he refuses to cut his hair to a buzz. Shoulder length just like Sammatha.

"Is she crying," Rebecca questioned.

What a way to end the night. We just had our biggest concert that every fan wishes they were at, and instead of celebrating, Sammatha could care less.

Without much further thought, Rebecca, Saige, and I went to Leo and Sammatha to see what was happening.

"Hey, is everything okay?" I said, concerned.

Sammatha quickly turned away from us and used Leo as a shield to cover her tears. Leo looked at us, somewhat worried.

"We will be okay. I think Sammatha and I are going to leave," he said.

"To the house?" I questioned.

"To our apartment, actually."

"Well, Sammatha, if you ever need someone to talk to, we are always here," Rebecca said.

We left the two alone and headed to the dressing room to grab our belongings. It wasn't long before we found Alanna, Maknae Line's youngest member, knocked out on a couple of chairs put together to form a bed.

"Alanna," Saige said, poking at her arm with her brush. Though she did not budge.

"Alanna??? Get up, girl. You can sleep on the bus unless you want to stay here overnight in the suites."

Alanna pouted as she slowly sat up. Her golden hair was very frizzy, and the girl looked so drained out. Rebecca and I watched her sit there with one eye open as she observed the room. Then suddenly, she fell back into the chair to go back to sleep.

"Alanna! Just get on the bus. We are not about to pick you up and take you there," I said.

I watched her get up and walk out of the room, all grumpy, as the three of us followed behind her with our belongings.

Eventually, we made it onto the bus, where everyone seemed to have commuted to when I noticed Maxwell in his little corner reading his book as his long silky hair hung down to his chest.

"Hey Valen, have you seen my sister?" he asked. I looked at Rebecca and Saige in conviction. Was I really interested in telling him that Sammatha was crying again or that she was running off with the guy that Maxwell hates?

"Don't worry about it. She just needs some space right now," I said.
　　"Is she with Leo right now?"
　　"Maybe." I hesitated to say.

Maxwell turned to his side in disapproval and went back to reading his book.
　　I shrugged and went to my seat further in the back. Not too far, though, because Maknae Line always has the very back reserve.

"Today was draining. I just want to take a nice bath and go to bed," Saige said as she sat beside me.

"Same and..."
　　Saige and I suddenly got a little quiet once Dice came and sat beside Rebecca. He is the current Latino heartthrob from Duo line with his goldilocks fro, though he can sometimes be very loud.

"XAN, CAN YOU TELL TORAN THAT I AM NOT GETTING ON

THAT STAGE WITHOUT HIM NEXT TIME!" Dice said as he yelled to the front of the bus.

"Bro shut up!" Alanna said, trying to sleep in the back.
Xan, who was upfront, shook his head.

I looked over and saw Toran coming down the aisle. He was Dice twin with a much darker complexion and tighter curls. Even though they are the only two in Duos, they certainly can be quite the opposite in personalities.

"You did it once; you can do it again," Toran joked as he sat beside him.
"Right, I guess I have to wait till Vanessa gets back from her little vacation before you can do a full set list with me again," Dice sighed.
Rebecca nudges Dice.

"What? Do you even know when she will be back?" he asked.
"Vanessa will come back when she feels like it. I don't know where she ran off to, but she'll be back. It's only been a few weeks." Rebecca said.

Finally, everyone arrived on the bus so that we could leave. The house is northeast of the metropolitan, in the middle of nowhere. Usually, it's about an hour's drive without traffic. The bus ride from downtown Brooklyn was quiet, with small talks and conversations scattered here and there.

4

06/12/22: Moonlight.

Time passed, and finally, around 1:45 in the morning, we safely arrived at our massive mansion tucked away in the deep backwoods of Hidden Estate, New York.

It was once abandoned by some gilded-age millionaire until our old record label, Ex-S Records, remodeled the place for us all to live in. The exterior is covered in white marble and shaped like an awkward L. It had a right-wing and a left wing.

The upstairs was dedicated to living arrangements, and the downstairs was reserved for everything else, like our three at-home recording studios, two practice rooms, home movie theater, etc. Then off to the side of the house, we have a black box production room where we film/stream our Switch Experience show for our fandom, which we refer them as Flames (like a candlelight vigil).

Parked in the driveway, right in front of the fountain, everyone hopped out of the bus.

In the back of the bus, there was the Maknae Line. Alongside Alanna, there is Kyan, Mazen, and Asia. Kyan is Chinese with baggy black hair. Mazen can be a mini Dice in personality sometimes. Even though he could pass as Egyptian at times, he is part Colombian and Chamorros. Last but not least, there is Asia who prefers to wear her hair in different protective hairstyles like box braids .

"Alanna... We are here," Asia said as she lightly shook her.

"And this is why you don't pull an all-nighter before a concert," Mazen said as he got up.

With Asia's help, the two aid Alanna to her feet.
  "Please tell me we are at the house," Alanna begged.
  "Yea, we are, but you still need to make it to your bed," Mazen said.

Kyan followed the three off the bus, hesitant to be near Asia.

"Hey Mazen, can you take Alanna inside, please. I need to take all this stuff upstairs to my room," Asia said. Mazen agreed and helped Alanna up the steps.

Kyan paused in conviction, wondering if he should help Asia or go inside. Once he saw her struggling to pull out a large container from under the bus, he went to help her.

"Let me help you with that," Kyan said as he picked up the container. "Thanks. I had got a message from the Leaders that I needed to condense the amount of stuff I had stored at the stadium. Apparently, I can't use that place as a second closet."
    Asia grabs a stack of hanging clothes and the two walk inside the house.

Coming through the front door, Kyan immediately paused when he saw the stairs waiting for him in front of his eyes.

"Music to my ears..." Kyan sighed.
    "I can get someone else to bring it up, Kyan."
    "No, no, I can take it up." He didn't want to come off as weak in front of Asia. Trip after trip, he carried her things upstairs to her room.

Dropping off the last two bags in her walk-in closet, Kyan debated making a move to her. Unlike the two's closest friends in the group, Mazen, and Alanna, who are both friends who cuddle too much, Kyan and Asia just keep things casual.

Interracial dating is very prevalent in the group. I would argue that 80% of the group's relationships are interracial. So it is not far-fetched or out of the norm to see Kyan and Asia holding hands. But they never consider dating since their debut, minus the mini infatuations here and there.

"Thanks, Kyan. I didn't realize I had this much stuff piling up there," Asia said.

"No problem, glad I could help," Kyan said as he exited the closet.

The room's lights were dim, to a lovely shade of pink and red. It was late, with everyone at the main house making their way to bed after a long weekend of performing. Kyan knew this was his chance to spend some alone time with Asia without anyone witnessing or questioning where the two were.

He glanced up at Asia, sitting on her bed, trying to find something to watch on TV. Slowly he shyly walked over and sat next to her.

"Are you not tired?" Kyan asked.
   "Not really. Are you?" She asked.
   Kyan shook his head. "I'm still standing, unlike Alanna."

Asia laughed a bit as she looked into Kyan's eyes. "
   "Want to watch this new movie that came out?" Asia asked shyly. Though he was intrigued that Asia was interested in watching a movie at this time of the hour, Kyan nodded in agreement.

Once she put on the show, the two moved to the bed's headboard and watched the movie.

I doubt they even recalled what happened or knew the main character's name since they were too busy being cuddled up. Asia didn't question Kyan for wrapping his arm around her, and Kyan didn't question Asia for laying her head on his chest. In their minds, they see the situation as two friends just watching a movie. Nothing more of that.

They were so tense about someone walking in on them. Even though most members paid no mind or attention to Maknae Line, the two would get anxious whenever they heard a door shut or someone walked pass Asia's door.

Because of this, Kyan had been having difficulty making things official with Asia, for the timing always seemed off.

5

06/14/22: News for Me. Part I

"Oi, do you want the camera here or there?" Leo asked in Portuguese .

With his thick black frames, Xan pointed to the middle of the practice room.

"You can place it here. Do you know where Rebecca and Dice are?" Xan questioned.

Leo looked around the room and noticed they weren't there.

"Maybe in their room or hiding in the production room. I couldn't give you an honest answer," Leo sighed.

Today was a live stream for our online show, *The Switch Experience.* So the members in the house, aka the BFF members, all gather in Practice Room A downstairs.

One thing to note is that only some members live in the main house. Essentially it comes down to if you have a kid, then you don't live here. That is about five members, with an additional three solo, off doing their own thing.

After helping Xan set up the camera, Leo noticed LeeSung entering the room where everyone else resides. With a smile, he walked over and dabbed him up.

"Hey man, sorry, but this is an exclusive BFF event," Leo joked.

LeeSung is our oldest member in the group at the age of 29. As part of Rap Line, he is what some people consider a tall darker-skin Korean.

"I am just here for the food," LeeSung said.
   "The food isn't that good to commute all the way from Manhattan. Which, by the way, where's Haru?" Leo questioned.

"She is in the movie room watching TV. Now that school's out, my father's duties have shot up," he said.
   "Well, there's always Kyan to babysit," Leo suggested.

LeeSung laughed a bit. Taking a look around, he noticed Kyan chatting with Maknae Line by the snacks table.

"See, I may have been his legal guardian for a while, but I am not interested in forcing him to be a big brother for Haru. What about you? Sammatha looked pretty upset after the concert. Is everything okay?"

Leo let out a wide smile and patted LeeSung back.
   "Oh she was just tired. Nothing to worry about."

LeeSung looked off to the side and saw Sammatha chatting with Varsity Girls.

Leo then stepped into LeeSung's view to stop him from further observing her.

"There is nothing to worry about. Trust me," Leo reassured.

LeeSung gave up as he saw no point in trying to get any answers out of the one and only Secret Keeper.

It wasn't long before Jean and Simon came walking over to LeeSung and Leo. Jean surely made sure his waves and line up was crisp for today's show while Simon didn't even try to brush his hair. No wonder why he had a beanie on to cover his long dirty blonde hair.

"I thought this was a BFF-exclusive event," Simon joked. LeeSung shook his head and dabbed up on Simon and Jean.

"All we are missing is Kendrick now," Jean said.

"I actually got off the phone with him not too long ago. He is doing pretty good. He just got back from Nigeria," LeeSung said.

Jean was shocked, "Wait, he's back in New York?"

"Back in the UK. It's going to be a while...you know, before he comes back," LeeSung said.

"Why so?" Jean asked.

LeeSung shrugged because he didn't want to let Kendrick private matters. Only he truly knows where Kendrick is compared to the rest of Rap Line or even Leaders Line.

Leo noticed that Simon was looking off to the side of the room where JV line was chatting. In complete admiration, Simon was checking out Saige.

"Don't sit next to her during the stream," Leo said.

Simon looked at him confused, "I wasn't going to...Or maybe I was thinking of doing it, but why not?"

"She may be single right now, but every fan in the world still thinks she is dating Theo," Leo said.

"So? They broke up back during New Year's Eve. I think she is free game now," Simon said. Though Leo, Jean, and LeeSung shook their heads in disagreement.

"Have you ever taken a chance to wonder why they never came out to the public that they broke up?" Jean asked.

"Because of all the headlines. A breakup is bad for the press."

"They could have come out to the public back in February and March if we were to go off on that scenario, but they didn't," LeeSung said.

Simon wasn't really keen on that information.

"We let you drop your secret love letter album for Saige earlier this year, but the love triangle act does not need to be reborn again. I mean, what about Lily? She's nice." Leo suggested.

"Not everyone has a Sammatha or, for you, a Cameron," Simon said, pointing at Jean, "My options are limited in this group, and I see nothing wrong in taking up the opportunity to get closer to Saige," Simon said.

Coming up behind the four was Lisa, the other Switch leader. She is of Indian descent with rich caramel brown skin.

"Hey, I need you all over the camera for your interview," she said.

"Great time to act like our lives are full of sunshine and bubble gum for our fans to drool over," Simon said.

"Yeah, yeah. Show off those pearly whites so your fans can stop blowing up our P.O. Box with care cards," Lisa said.

Over half a million Flames were on the stream call today, spamming comments in different languages. Jean got distracted when he noticed Xan entered the room, followed by Dice and Rebecca, as if they got caught red-handed. They didn't look like they wanted to be there.

"AHHHHHHHH!!!!"

Suddenly, Jean was in utter jumpscare when a fan got on an exclusive call with a Rap Line. The young lady looked like she was 18 or 19 years old though you could see she put a ton of makeup on to win over one of the guys' hearts.

"I love you so much! Leo, I've seen all your movies and bought all your merch. I've even started learning Portuguese."

Out of nowhere, the lady started speaking in broken Portuguese. Leo just smiled and nodded, trying to not make things awkward.

"Wow, you're pretty good," he said.

Simon waves a bit to get the fellow fan's attention.

"Did you enjoy BFF World?"

"Oh yes, which by the way, thank you so much for the free ticket. Leo when you performed your funk set list and–".

LeeSung tried to hide his chuckle as the fan neglected the rest of the line just to talk to Leo.

On the other hand, Jean looked off to the side again and was intrigued. He saw Dice all hugged up around Rebecca as the two started making out before taking a moment to leave the studio.

Jean tapped LeeSung's back three times to signal that he needed to step away from the stream.

Walking away, he approached Rebecca and Dice to see why they were leaving so prematurely.

"Hey, why are you two leaving?" Jean asked suspiciously.

Dice immediately dropped his arm to Rebecca's waist.

"Jean! Oh, um, we– I was just going to get my phone from my room," she said hesitantly.

"Yeah, I didn't want her to go alone," Dice said.

Jean was not buying it. How often does he have to hear from other members about what his sister is doing at five in the morning with the guy he performs with. Or how often does he have to witness the random PDA performance they are doing on stage.

"Can I talk to my sister? Alone," Jean requested.

Rebecca rolled her eyes as she followed Jean to the hallway. "Funny that you want to talk to me. What's the change of heart?" Rebecca said with an attitude.

"What's up with you and Dice? I mean, did you really think I wasn't going to find out?" Jean said, disappointed.

"It got all cleared up, okay," she said.

"And where were you about to go with Dice?"

"We were just going to my room to grab my phone," Rebecca said, frustrated.

"You must think I am dumb, don't you. You two can't keep your hands off each other for more than 30 minutes," Jean said.

"Oh right, I can't spend time with my man, but you can go off on your little excursions with Cameron whenever you feel like it? Oh, okay," Rebecca said.

"At least Cameron and I have some class," Jean said meanly. Rebecca wanted to slap Jean for his comment, but Dice came out into the hallway before she could.

"Is everything okay?" Dice asked, concerned.

"Yea, Jean was just doing his bi-weekly checkups on his little sister, that's all. Jean, can you tell Xan and Lisa that Dice and I will be leaving? Thank you," Rebecca sassily said. Dice was confused but followed along with Rebecca as she walked away.

"I'll just let them figure it out," Jean said under his breath.

Suddenly he looked up and saw Rebecca and Dice turning around with Xan directly behind the two. That is when Jean remembers the unplugged performance that is supposed to begin in 10 minutes.

"Geez, make my life easy for once. That's all I beg of you," Xan said, walking back into the studio.

Time went by as each of the six subunits did their little interviews before it was time to do our group sit-down performance. We had three rows elevated so that everyone's face could be seen.

Rap Line made their way to the back row when suddenly they noticed Simon didn't come and sit by them.

"He can't be serious..." Jean said in shock. The three watched Simon adjust his beanie before he sat down next to Saige.

Saige was a bit taken aback when she saw Simon.

"Shouldn't you be with your unit?" Saige questioned.
   "Maybe, but I figure I could use some more screen time on the show," Simon said, trying to play it cool.

"Pshh, Saige. Pull your hair back," Lily said behind her.
   "I think she will be fine," Jackie said.
   Lily and Jackie are the final other two members of the JV line. Lily has a more doll face with naturally dirty blonde hair While there, Jackie, who is mixed and can't stay away from a

DIY blonde hair dye kit., .

Saige turned around briefly to them. "It doesn't look good down?" she questions.

Lily shrugged, "If you're going to sit in the center, you should at least let your ears show."Lily took notice that I had a scrunchy on my arm. "Valen? Can I borrow this?" She asked.

In agreement, I let her take my scrunchy, but I had to stop her mid-way as she started to style Saige's thick red hair. "Half up, half down. Or a crown braid. Maybe a low-side ponytail, but not everything pulled back," I suggested.

"Half up, half down," Saige requested. Taking this into consideration, Lily went through with the hairdo. In a smooth transition, Lily started talking in French. "Simon, what do you think of her hair?"

Saige gave Simon a smile as she modeled her new hairstyle on him. In French, he said, "I like it, but what will you do with your hair?"

Every member of the group knows at least two languages for many reasons. The top reason is to commune with fans and among each other. Sometimes it can be playful or an opportunity to practice. In contrast, in others, it is used to have private, coded conversations. Usually, it's English and ______________. That could be a Spanish, French, Italian, Portuguese, Japanese, Mandarin, Korean,

Tagalog, Thai, Arabic, or American Sign Language. Though most members would have a third language under their belt.

Lily lightly nudged Simon in shock as Jackie, and I laughed a bit under our breath. Switching back to English, Lily was about to say something when suddenly, Varsity Guys sat beside them.

Jackie was indeed intrigued when she saw Theo sitting next to Saige. She wasn't the only one when LeeSung, Jean, and Leo were shocked to see the secret love triangle be front and center for the world to witness.

Xan and Lisa went to stand behind the primary camera when they noticed Simon sitting next to Saige.

"What should we do?" Lisa question.
    "Nothing. This is an opportunity for great content," Xan said. Lisa sighed as she pulled open her folder to pull out the group's setlist.

"Shoot, someone made a last-minute change again," Lisa said.
    "Who was it?"
    Lisa took a look but then paused. "Nevermind, that was me. I forgot that I decided to cut the show a bit shorter. I figure some people aren't in the spirit to sing for over an hour," Lisa said. Xan looked at Lisa for a moment as he watched her flip through the pages of notes.

"We have a quota to meet Lisa. Shorter shows are bad for business," Xan said irritate.
    "Burnout, depress members is bad for business. You should know this for being Mr.Smith's right hand."

Xan rolled his eyes as he impatiently wanted to get the show over and done with.

"Are we ready to go," Xan asked.

"I think so," Lisa said.

Xan walked over to his computer and went to play the b-roll intermission.

Then he returned to the center of the room to dail down the conversations.

Xan said, "Okay, I think everyone is here. No need to be a show off for this performance. It's supposed to be a casual show I guess. I do not want to see any fours being thrown up. You are not taking anyone's lines but rather sticking to the ones assigned to you only. If you are a lead singer, you are not special. Which means Cameron, Sammatha, Romeo, and Jermany of Varsity Line. You are most definitely not allowed to steal someone's line. Not for this show, at least."

Taking another quick look at her notes, Lisa said, "The show will be 30 minutes -"

"30 minutes???" Xan whispered over to her.

"Yes, 30 minutes. Started off with Hot-Line, with Maxwell singing lead as usual, then leading into a more ballad vocal base performance. For Maknae Line, Xan and I had to cut your songs from the setlist due to our time conflicts, though you four are probably not complaining at its minimum."

"Correct," Mazen said, giving Lisa a thumbs up of approval.

"Don't get too excited, Mazen; you're still on vocal support for Varsity Guys," Xan said.

"Yeah, until Zachary returns from his 1000-year hiatus.

Got it," Mazen sighed.

Lisa nudged Xan to be quiet so that she could talk. Reading off her script, she said, "In final, please understand that The Switch Experience is a live stream. It's okay to mess up, but there is a consequence for creating tension and drama as the current stream total at the moment is 560,231 Flames tuned in for today's show."

"Will you be joining us for the show?" LeeSung questions Xan and Lisa.
   "No," Lisa said quickly, "Not remotely interested as usual."

In the group's run of being together, Xan and Lisa were never really the ones to go on stage and perform. Once exclusive, prodigy producers and sound engineers, they turned into the group's management as Leaders once the Xan got Ex-S Records to sign the dotted line. Free from a 360 deal contract but unknowingly signed up for the world's most stressful job.

Eventually, the intermission was over, and the show began...

6

06/14/22: News for Me. Part II

Simon and Theo couldn't keep their eyes off Saige as the show progressed. A Rap-Line member and a Varsity Guys member trying to win the heart of a JV Girl is indeed an exciting princess story to witness. Though it wasn't long before the performance was over. In harmonization, every unit came together like one great choir as we finished our last song. If only we had our band and orchestra to help us drive in all the emotion that came out of our voices.

Since Saige was in the front row and center, it was decided that she would close out the show for us. In a smooth voice, she said, "Thank you everyone for tuning in for The Switch Experience. We are all grateful for your love and support. We are blessed and breathing, and we wish you the same on behalf of the entire group. As usual, if you need help or assistance, whether from food and living insecurities to mental health resources, please check out the description, as we have a fund to help our fans going through troubling times. Thank you once again. Good morning, good day, and good night to our Flames around the world."

Then the stream ended.

"AHHHH!" JV Line patted Saige's back and showed her some love.

"Goosebumps," Lily said.

"Good morning, good day, and good night to the Flames around the world. You said that too smoothly. Might actually steal Jermany's job," Rebecca said.

Getting up from our seats, Simon and Theo were about to move simultaneously regarding who would say something first. Though Rap Line came and retrieved Simon, and Varsity Guys went to pull Theo aside.

"What's wrong?" Theo questioned.

Varsity Guys host some of the most legendary singers to ever exist in our generation. Carlos, who is more Korean than Mexican, is one of the most successful singers in the group. In addition, there is Maxwell, who you met earlier in the entries, and Jermany. He is Carlos's right hand for vocal support and tends to be quoted as the lead singer of Switch, but that title is given loosely in his eyes. He is a brown-skinned Filipino American who actively wears glasses.

And finally, there is Romeo. The right hand to Theo and a lead singer of Varsity Guys. He once had a solid British accent though it faded away the longer he stayed in the group. With white skin and bush brown hair, a certain demographic of fans is convinced he is their spouse.

"Nothing. I just wanted to say that Carlos and I will be heading back to our homes in a bit. Taking a break from commuting back and forth," Romeo said.

"To be married with kids. Couldn't be me," Jermany said as he drank his water.

Romeo rolled his eyes. "Brionna insisted that I spend more time with Junior before our mini album drops," Romeo said.

Carlos was intrigued, "Funny how I never heard any of the songs yet."

"Don't worry 'cause as Romeo's best man, even I haven't even heard of it," Theo said.

Theo looked off to the side and saw Saige and Simon talking. He began to tune out his conversation with the other guys as he watched Simon flirt with Saige unapologetically.

"Theo?" Jermany said, waving his attention.

"Yes," he said, trying to shift his focus.

"Since these two will be out for like.... two days max before they come crawling back here, we will still have vocal practice tomorrow, okay?"

Maxwell sighed.

"I do not want to have practice tomorrow. Plus, where is Zachary? It's been months since he showed his face around here."

The guys genuinely didn't know.

"I talked to Lily about it last week, and she said she hasn't heard from her brother since Christmas," Romeo said.

"Well, I vote for David to be back in Varsity Line," Maxwell suggests.

Carlos laughed a bit, "He is an external leader now, and he never looked back when he took that role. I highly doubt he will ever even pick up a microphone again. Though I know what you mean. He was your vocal support, and Zachary never liked sharing lines with you, but that is his loss."

"I agree with Carlos," Theo said, "He wants to be solo, then let him be solo with Jordyn. Not like JV Line is missing her anyways."

With another look over at Saige, he froze in conviction. She was gone. Theo quickly surveyed the room and noticed Simon was gone too. Without thinking it through, Theo dismissed himself and left the studio.

Walking down the dark hallway, as it is uncommon for a ceiling light to be turned on, he looked around to see where she was. He went to check the kitchen and the dining room though there was no sign. Walking out of the kitchen room, he checked the main living room by the front door. Though she wasn't there either.

Quickly he returned to the studio and saw Jackie on her phone as she was resting against the wall. He walked over to her and asked, "Have you seen Saige."

Jackie laughed, "Now I told you to not sit by her, didn't I."
   "Jackie, come on, help me out. Please." Theo begged.
   Jackie sighed and then pointed to the ceiling, off to the side.

Without a thought, Theo abruptly left the room and headed towards the stairs, looking to see where Saige was. Coming up the stairs slowly, he paused. He heard the noises of footsteps. Peeping his head out the corner wall from the stairs, he saw Saige making out with Simon before the two entered Simon's room, locking behind.

Theo's heart sunk to the bottom of his stomach. Trying not to be heartbroken since he was the one who broke Saige's heart, he couldn't help but feel upset and betrayed. Hopeless, walking back down to the practice room, Theo went to talk to Jackie. With just one look at her, Jackie already knew what Theo wanted to do. Taking a quick sip of her drink, the two casually walked out of the room, trying to not draw any suspicion.

"You know it is gonna cost you," Jackie said.
   "What do you want then?" Theo said.
   "Your credit card."

Theo paused in his steps. He was shocked by Jackie's request because last time, she asked for a ten-dollar gift card. Theo gave in, though. He didn't want to think about Saige at the moment. Especially knowing Simon is making out with her upstairs.

In Simon's room, the two made out as if they were the only people in the world to exist. No words in exchange. No need to say anything but to face the brutal reality that they are just friends. Just friends. The two stopped after they made out in the dim room for some time.

"Um, I should go. The girls are probably wondering where I am," Saige said as she hopped off Simon.

"Oh, you're good. I guess I'll see you around," Simon said, blushing. Saige kissed Simon one last time on the cheek and left him to be. Simon lay down on his bed, smiling hard like he won a million dollars.

Suddenly he heard his door open. Sitting up, he saw that it was Lily.

"So so so... Que faisais-tu avec Saige?" Lily asked, very curious, wanting all the tea. Simon was speechless as he pretended nothing had happened a few minutes ago.

"Save your breath. I am not TMSZ here to expose you", Lily joked.

Closing the door, she skipped to Simon's bed and lay down, getting extra comfortable.

"This room is a mess, Simon. It's not dirty, just messy. It

still could definitely be clean," Lily suggested.

"What are you talking about? It looks fine in here," Simon chuckled.

"Your room is a mess. Made out with Saige in a messy room? Speaks a lot about your character, huh?" Lily questioned.

"Does it really matter?"

"Uh, oui! I think it matters a lot. My friend is hooking up with my friend in a messy room," Lily joked.

"Okay, and? How will your friend react when she finds out you are hooking up with me?" Simon said.

Lily smirked a bit as she sat up. "I was here first actually. But oh right, 'cause that would be MY problem to deal with anyways. Right. Definitely, my problem that I should be worried about. Okay."

Simon brushes his hand through Lily's hair and pushes it to the side. Though Lily pushes his hand away.

"Gross. I'm not hooking up with you with Saige's lip gloss all over your lips. I will pass for today. Thank you."

"What? Thousands of people would pay for this moment with me," Simon said in shock.

Lily made a pouty face. "Awe, honey. It goes the other way around, but I love the confidence. Try that move on Saige next time."

"What if I write you a song?" Simon suggests.

"You wrote an entire album for Saige and all she offers you is a five-minute kiss once every couple of weeks, which probably means nothing. I don't need a song from the great Simon Fischer. It's already bad enough that you are my sworn-in dance partner for life," Lily laughed.

"You're lost then," Simon said.

"Whatever," Lily said, going into Simon's bathroom. Taking a search around the sink, she discreetly searches through his top drawer. Hidden in the very back, Lily found his stash of pills. Though she froze when she saw a needle. In panic, she quickly put it in her pocket before grabbing Simon's pills.

"Hey Simon, we should hit up the trail sometime. The blossom trees would be pretty to look at during sunrise," Lily shouted.

"Yeah, and hurry up with your search warrant, officer," Simon said as he came up behind Lily.

She jumped as she saw Simon looking at her through the mirror.

"I..."

"You got the pills, right?" Simon questioned.

"Yes... yes. See," Lily said as she pulled out the bag.

"Let me have five at least..." Simon requested.

Lily froze, not knowing what to do. "I can't... you promised me that you would stop with the drugs, okay. That is the only reason I help make your album, and don't interfere in your little crush with Saige, but when she doesn't, hit you up. Taking one of these is not the solution. And this???" Lily pulled out the needle.

Simon took a step back. "I'm done with them. They are only there for emergencies."

"Emergencies, Simon? Really? Where are you even getting this from?" Lily questioned.

Simon paused before he could continue.

"Who?" Lily demanded.

"I remember Dice was telling me about a place and–"

Lily slammed the glass needle onto the countertop.

"You're kidding me, Simon! Really! Dice used to be addicted to this stuff. You have too many drugs in your system already. This could kill you!" Lily said.

"I know, but –"

"Does the guys know? Leo, Jean? Any of them? DO THEY KNOW!" Lily questioned.

"No! They don't, and they don't need to know. I haven't tried it, so there's nothing to be hooked on," Simon said.

"You just told me that you already experimented with it!" Lily yelled.

"It was just once or twice, okay!"

Lily looked down at her hand and noticed that her hand was bleeding a bit from the glass.

"Help me clean this glass up," Lily said, disappointed.

"I'm sorry," Simon said softly.

"Yea... but I am really not interested in finding you over-dosed in the shower again."

7

06/18/22: Hide!

Kyan and Mazen were organizing the new shipment of outfits for some upcoming photoshoots and performances in the storage room. Kyan's mind was going 1000 miles per hour as he couldn't stop thinking of Asia. For a while, Kyan and Asia's chemistry has been growing closer as the week passes by. Varsity Guys, in particular, have been taking note, saying in the quote, "He must be in love because his singing has dramatically improved."

Kyan has never officially been in a relationship with anyone. Not to mention the need for examples to look up to. Kyan is very aware that most of the relationships in Switch are beyond perfect and somewhat complicated.

"Hey, check this out," Mazen said as he handed over his phone to Kyan.

It was a headline about another celebrity upset about not being invited to perform as an opening act at BFF World. They were more frustrated that Lisa and Xan allowed smaller acts to perform for free but declined bigger-name artists even though some were willing to pay over a million dollars for a 5-minute spot.

"They realize that if they got to be on the lineup, they would have to sing live, right? No mp3 track in the background to lip sync to", Mazen laughed.

Mazen looked up from his phone and noticed Kyan was zoning out. "Aye, what's wrong? Is it Asia again?" Mazen questioned.

"No it's nothing,"Kyan said.

Mazen sucked his teeth a bit because he knew Kyan was lying.

"Ask her out, man. Romantic dinner, then you know, take her to -" Kyan stopped Mazen.

"No way. We can't be seen out in public alone. I already get tense when we are together. I'm not ashamed to be seen with her. I just don't want to add more attention to the group. Plus, I think Asia wants ultra private things if we were to get into a relationship", Kyan said.

Wanting to help his best friend out, Mazen sent a text message to Alanna, requesting she bring Asia to the storage room.

About 15 minutes later went by, and in came Alanna and Asia.

"Geez, how many shipments came in?" Alanna gasped.
   Kyan locked eyes with Asia briefly as her eyes glistened back to him. His heart fluttered as he couldn't resist looking away from her.

"Yeah, there are a ton of things we still need to go through. Asia. Kyan. Could you two grab the last box of clothes from the tour bus? Tour bus A, to be specific," Mazen requested.

He hinted to Kyan, saying this was his chance to make a move. The two agree and set off to the garage.

"So you send them to the tour bus?" Alanna smirked. "Yea, and we have the room for ourselves until they get back," Mazen said as he pulled Alanna in for a kiss.

Asia and Kyan's hearts beat fast like a drum and hard like an 808. Inside the bus, they started looking around for the box. Searching high and low, they quickly realize there was no box in there to begin with. With a final look, they went to the back of the bus .

"Do you see it," Asia asked.

"All I could find was my jacket from the concert. Didn't realize I left it in here," Kyan said.

Taking a seat on the sofa, the silence in the air grew as the two sat next to each other. Building up the courage, Kyan glimpse into Asia's eyes as they lock in place. Slowly, leaning in, two were about to kiss when suddenly they heard someone come out into the garage.

The two started freaking out, not knowing what to do. Kyan quickly went into one of the bed bunks.Asia helped close the curtains when she was jumped scared by Mia.

She is on the Varsity Girls' line, though some would say she is the least active in the unit. Mixed with Colombian and Mexican, she was once lead singer of the group.

"Hey, Mia. What are you doing here." Asia said awkwardly.

"I think I left my charger in the back. What are you doing here?" Mia asked. Asia noticed that the curtain was not closed all the way and quickly pulled it.

"Nothing," Asia said nervously.

Mia shrugged off Asia's weird acting and proceeded to move down to the back of the bus when Asia stopped Mia from moving forward and quickly went to find her charger.

Looking in the back of the bus, Asia looked through the drawers and the cushion seats when she found the charger.

"Here. Not sure if it's yours, but it's a USB-C plug. It should work for your phone," she said, handing over the charger.

Mia was about to question Asia's urgency and why she was on the tour bus but her alarm went off before she could say anything.

"Thanks. Now I was going to say something 'cause you are acting funny, but I will let this slide. Maxwell and I have a reservation to catch."

"What's for dinner," Asia asked.

"Moroccan. Maxwell wanted some that reminded him of his mother's cooking. Sammatha and Leo were supposed to join us, but you know how Maxwell is. Want to spend time with his sister but doesn't want Leo to tag along," Mia sighed.

Asia sighed as well, "And Leo goes wherever Sammatha goes. Why can't Maxwell just get along with him? The past is the past."

"You tell me. The day Maxwell acknowledges that Leo exists is when penguins learn how to fly," Mia sighed.

"Sounds like it will never happen at this rate."

Mia thanked Asia and dismissed herself from the bus.

Once the bus door closed, Asia went to Kyan's hiding spot.

"Coast is clear," Asia said.

She helped Kyan out of his spot, laughing at how silly they

reacted to having their little secret exposed. "Let's take things slow, okay," Kyan said softly. Asia agrees wholeheartedly.

Later in the evening was practice for the guys in the dance studio. More specifically it was a midnight practice.Very common to practice often and stay proactively ready for any last-minute show.

"Okay, everyone, we can take a five," Romeo said tiredly.

It was a taxing practice that required 100% energy and memory. Not only do you have to practice new choreography, but you have to remember the different variations for just one song. Today practice was required for all the guys except LeeSung because his daughter Haru was not feeling too well. So he couldn't make the drive over to the house.

As everyone took their water break, Kyan pulled Leo aside to speak privately.
    Leo is the best person to go to if you have a secret. He will hold your word without a choice because if he spills any of the beans, everyone in the group knows about a hundred ways to get him canceled by the public eye.

"I need some advice, Leo. Asia and I...want to start dating," Kyan whispered.

Leo was not shocked to hear this piece of information.

"It's about time. Maybe four years overdue, but man, parabéns" Leo said, cheerful as he daps Kyan up.

"You are aware of what happened last month with Kylie right?"

April - May was a horrible month for Switch. We were in LA for the first time since pre-pandemic doing some press work. Whether it was a commercial, movie shooting, photoshoots, etc., it was a work trip that turned into a nightmare and a reason why everyone hates Hollywood.

Ex-member Kylie was doing her usual trolling, but she took it a step too far when she realized we were out of hiding. Every other day was a new headline of false rumors about everyone in Switch. However, she went to town with Sammatha.

She said Sammatha doesn't deserve to be with Leo on the social media and radio waves and that they should break up. All the anti-fans took sides with Kylie and started cyberbullying her, ending with Sammatha locking herself in the guest house for a week.

She refused to come out for a week, severely affecting her mental health for the worst. Kylie called her every name under the sun, neglecting the fact that they used to be best friends. It took a fat check to get her to shut up. But honestly, once the money runs out, she is right back to it.

Kylie is one of the reasons why the bubble in Switch is so tight-knit. Kylie got kicked out of the group for causing chaos left and right. After her cheating scandal with Leo (who was with Mia at the time), she went A-WILD. Fighting with other members, selling our unreleased, and associating with celebrities who had beef with another group member. I think she is just frustrated and mad that she is not married to Leo. That is my guess.

"Because of what happened last month, there is a limit on what news comes out to the public. Relatively best to avoid drawing any more attention to the group's personal lives. You should only let the world know if it is about music. Especially if the relationship ends up being short-lived.

I think it best you two keep your relationship a secret from everyone, including the ones in the house. The last thing you want is Mazen to be on an Instagrand live and fans see you two holding hands in the background. Once the coast is clear, the headlines go ghost. Then the two of you can make your way to the public," Leo suggested.

"To keep a secret in a house full of secrets. How hard could that be," Kyan thought.

How hard could that really be?

Just before Leo could say anything more, he looked up and noticed Sammatha by the door looking visually upset.

"Hey, can you tell Lisa that I have to leave," Leo asked worriedly.

Kyan was confused about what was going on. Turning

around he saw Sammatha as she looked like she was about to break down crying once again.

8

06/19/22: Learn to love thy neighbors.

Today most of the group went to church. The place we attend is a small/medium-ish, nondenominational place in the town next door. Lovely place that we've been going to since our debut. For always being isolated at the house when we were younger, church was the only place not business related that management allowed us to go to.

The majority of the people at the church are out of touch with current media, so we don't get stares and "Can I get your autograph" when we go. Though there is slightly suspicious to see a large group of very handsome and beautiful individuals, multi-racial, not a day over 30 years old, all color coordinated in black and white take up three rows of seats in the back. Maybe to the new people to the church.

As the choir sang, Maxwell saw his sister Sammatha and Leo coming in. 25 minutes late, to be exact. As the usher showed them to their seat, Leo noticed there needed to be more room for him to sit by Sammatha in the middle row. Brittany and Carlos's daughter Kimberly and Romeo and Brionna's son Ashton (though everyone calls him Junior) were in the pews alongside Haru, who was much taller and older than them.

"Uncle Leo, you can sit here," Kimberly said, pointing to the open spot next to Maxwell.

"You know they don't get along," Haru whispered. Leo looked over and saw that there was a spot open next to Maxwell. Sammatha looked at Leo, wondering what his move would be.

"Shouldn't you two be in the kids' church," Leo asked.

"You must have forgotten, but today is Father's Day. The same day that we were going to have our choir performance," Haru said. Sammatha and Leo looked at each other, feeling bad that they missed their niece's performance. Not to worry, because LeeSung got the whole thing on tape. I was extremely touched to hear his daughter's voice; it was her first solo performance

.

"We are so sorry, Haru and Kimberly. We got stuck in traffic," Sammatha said.

Haru and her nosy self was confused by the comment 'traffic'.

"Traffic? Were you guys coming from Manhattan, too?" Haru asked. Leo laughed a bit, "You know what? I'm just going to go sit by Maxwell."

Leo walked over and sat down by Maxwell as the music wrapped up. Looking over, he noticed that Maxwell was wearing a turtleneck with his suit. It was pulled high up to his chin to cover up his vitiligo.

Even though he is more confident in showing his vitiligo to the world, there are more times than anyone can count when his insecurities kick in. The only part clear from the vitiligo is his face, but it can be seen everywhere else, including his hands.

"Good morning," Leo said, trying not to be awkward.

Such a ground-breaking moment for the two to even be sitting close together. Taking one more glance at Maxwell, he saw that the scar by his right eye wasn't covered up with foundation. Feeling ashamed to see the cut, he looked up at the altar and watched the praise dance perform. Maxwell was not interested in talking to Leo, but during the announcement sections of the church, he could not help to wonder why the two had shown up late to service.

"You know we go to the 11 o'clock service, right," Maxwell said under his breath. Leo was shocked that Maxwell was even communicating with him.

"Sorry, we were coming from Manhattan. Traffic had us a

little backup," Leo said in honesty. Not the wisest to lie in the Lord's house and say they were coming from the main house.

Maxwell rubbed his forehead and combed his hair back in disappointment. .

"What's up with you two going to that apartment? After practice yesterday, I overheard your conversation with Sammatha. She seemed upset, and you mentioned going to some 'escape spot.' What is that supposed to be about," Maxwell said.

Leo looked over at Maxwell. He did not appreciate Maxwell always investigating and policing him on his relationship with Sammatha.

Save by the "Dear heavenly father" prayer, Leo was relieved to find a chance to not explain himself to Maxwell. Sammatha was upset, still trying to cope with the hate comments Kylie had posted on social media. All that was indeed targeting her, making the poor girl more and more insecure, especially in her relationship with Leo.

Today's message of the day was to learn to love your neighbors. That included your fellow group mates Maxwell and you, Kylie as well. Being mean to God's children is not a good look to have on your list of sins. Though luckily, God is very forgiving. I tweeted that today, leaving out the names, of course. Though they know who they are.

9

06/20/22: Welcome back home.

Today was interesting.

It was group stage practice for "The Switch Experience." I can't believe the show's been running for this long since it started back in 2020 when Covid was taking the world by storm. The show is free to watch, but if you were part of a registrar fan club, you got a whole bunch of extra content like leaked songs, exclusive music videos, and fan meetings.

Today was a nonstop practice.

This meant Xan would select a random song from any of the eleven albums we may have and treat practice like it was a K-pop random dance challenge.

"Five six seven eight," he yelled as playing the next song.

Xan philosophy is that we should be prepared to perform any of our pieces in a heartbeat.

After multiple formation changes, signs of frustration, and

finally remembering the moves, rehearsal was over. Though excitement came rushing when someone came through the door.

"Welcome back!" Lisa shouted.

Everyone turned in shock. It was Guam's favorite eight cow princess. Miss Vanessa Ramirez. Her hair grew some inches as it was now to her waistline, and her skin had tan more brown like mine. As the best dress member in the JV Line, she did not want any of us to catch her lacking.

"Hey! I hoped to get back before practice started, but my plane flight got delayed," Vanessa said as she hugged Lisa. "What! I could have sent the jet to pick you up," Lisa said.

As everyone welcomed Vanessa back from her month hiatus, she noticed Toran off to the distance, grabbing his belongings. Dice, who was beside him, tried to get Toran's attention.

"Toran, just say hi to her," he said, but Toran refused to listen before rushing out. Looking over, Dice saw Vanesssa's facial expressions drop as the fake smile could only last so long when she suddenly glanced at him.

"I'll talk to him," Dice signed her over. Vanessa thanked him from a distance.

Dice ran out of the practice room and set off to find Toran. He was somewhere in the house. Going door to door, he ran into Theo and Jermany.

"What are you looking for," Theo asked.

"More like who. With Vanessa being back in town, Toran is not taking in the information well, so I thought of taking him on a walk to get some fresh air. You too can come if you want," Dice offered.

"Vanessa is back?" Theo questioned.

"We literally walked past her. Sure, we can join you," Jermany said. Theo looked over Dice's shoulder, squinting his eyes. "Found him," he said.

Dice turned around in relief. He went to Toran and wrapped his arm around his shoulders. "Let's go on a walk," Dice offered.

The four went to the kitchen and out to the backyard, which was massive, full of greenery. Off they went to the private trail where Cameron's request for Japanese blossom trees to be planted to help brighten the pathways as the clouds covered the skies.

After soft singing of the song "Yesterday" (an unreleased acapella), they made it to a small waterfall stream. The four sat in deep retrospection.

The ASMR of the water trickling down and the wind blowing the trees created a zen environment.

"Is it bad to say that I hate myself," Theo asked abruptly as he looked into the distance. The three turned in question.

What a random comment to say. Theo's face was full of regret and sorrow.

"You know, it's all my fault for why Saige broke up with me. I'd lied and abused her trust multiple times. I can't even look myself in the mirror without seeing the guy who lost his chance to be with her. Doesn't help that every single day someone is tagging me in an edit of us together. It frustrates me that the world is caught up in a lie that we are still together..." Theo said.

The wind blew as the creek water ran in silence. Jermany cleared his throat and hesitated to open his mouth.

"I would be lying if I said I was a good fit for Courtney. I had been trying to spend some time with her, but something was always coming up. Valen or David would shoot me a text message saying I need to be in Brooklyn or in Long Island for this meeting or that meeting to do some composing work. All of it is pulling me away from her. I like doing the work. Just like every member likes to work. Working keeps our minds numb. Numb from the past. Numb from the hurt... Sometimes... I wish I didn't take up the role of lead singer. Though it is the same thing I prayed for, I don't know how to feel about it right now." Jermany said softly.

Theo reached into his pocket and pulled out a pair of keys.

"Here," Theo said. Jermany accepted the offer.

"Where do these go to?"

"It's spare to my rental out in Monroe. I took it off the market last week, so it is free. Have a retreat there," Theo said.

"Thanks, man, I really appreciate it. It's no five-star rental or three, but it's a place away from here," Jermany said.

"Just let me know when you are going to be there. So I can turn off the alarm."

Going down the row, Dice realized it was his turn. "Um... Rebecca and I are thinking about becoming celibate. Sometimes I feel like it's my fault that it got so out of control... I didn't realize our midnight dances from when we first started dating would turn into having it three times a day, 7 days a week. I ignored all the signs and the statistics this whole time. It wasn't... until last week when Rebecca posted that picture of us together, and a whole bunch of anti stan flooded the comment section, calling us both a whole bunch of ugly names... That's when I found out a part of our tape leaked..." Dice said.

The three were shocked, especially Toran. Eyes wide open for what they just witnessed. "Why didn't any of us hear about this?" Theo said, concerned.

"The legal and pr team was able to clear up any trace about the situation before anything went viral. I don't know how the video got out to the public. I don't know the logistics of the situation, but I know it cost me half of my bank account to get the video down. Luckily, the Internet thinks it is a rumor. Still, it didn't stop anti-fans from commenting about the situation on Rebecca's post. According to Xan, the two of us are on lockdown and can't be seen out in public for a while now, which is fine. The public doesn't give a [redacted] about us unless it's something sexual we do anyways. My biggest concern right is Jean right now. He hates me, and now I got to work 10x harder to get on his good side again. I can now see how Leo feels about Maxwell. Not a pretty conversation to have when you have a losing argument. It's my fault for suggesting to do a tape using a freakin laptop", Dice said.

Toran chuckled a bit, followed by Theo and Jermany. "I'm sorry," Toran said, trying to hold back his laugh.
　Dice was taken aback, "What so funny." The guys started cracking up.

"Why a laptop?!?. Someone's gonna see that" Toran laughed.
　Dice shrugged it off, "Alright, alright. My bad for opening up. I thought this was a safe place to talk."

"Aye, we are joking, man," Jermany said as he patted Dice back.

Toran less his laugh when he realized it was his turn.
　"Well, I don't know how to feel about Vanessa being here. Back in LA, our relationship was rocky already and one day, she just left. Only Lisa knew where she was, but neither of us knew why she left. I have thought that maybe we should take a break from dating," said Toran.

"I mean there is no harm in taking breaks. If you want to do that, then you should discuss that with her," Jermany suggested.

Toran knew why he didn't want to talk to Vanessa. To the guys, he said he would speak to her about it. When, in all reality, he wasn't going to talk to her but instead, give her a surface-level conversation until he knew more about the situation.

Toran was given a tip from a mysterious account on social media saying that she was cheating on him with another guy. Even though it is advised to not read request messages, he couldn't help to over-analyzing this message.

Toran looked off into the distance and watched the waterfall endlessly down the waterfall. He knew Vanessa was not the one for him, but why did he entertain the idea of dating her. Our old manger, Mr. Smith prohibited dating outside of the group. However it wasn't like Vanessa wasn't his only option.

Suddenly there was a bell that rang.

DING DING DING.

It was the single that dinner was ready. "What's for dinner today?", Jermany asked.

"Probably paella. I overheard Valen talking to the chef today," said Theo.

It is challenging to feed all or most of the members. So three times a week, we have a catering team who cooks dinner for everyone.

"Let's head back then," Dice suggested. The four started walking back to the house when suddenly they stopped in their steps.

"Oh, right," Theo sighed.

The four chanted together out of order,
    "Everything I have heard will not be repeated or said outside the house but rather respect the privacy of our friend's words."

"In the name of traditional gentlemen," Jermany said.
    "Does anyone even still say it?" Dice said, irradiated.

"Now, with what you said, you would want us to swear," Toran laughed.
    "Whatever. Geez, let's go eat or something. We are losing daylight out here anyways," Dice said as he walked off.

10

07/04/22: "Someone else is here."

So many things have been happening lately. Double the scheduling and double practice times. Even though Simon released his rock album earlier this year, he decided to drop a short EP predominantly in French today. He claims he wants to hold back on his French ghostwriting songs and release them under his name for once. In addition, Switch released a new mini album after popular demands from fans. It was a mixture of early 2000s pop and R&B as we were going for a nostalgic sound.

On July 4th, we had a notable performance at the Empire Building. Performing some old hits, Leo and Jean performed a new song from Jean's new Nexflic Brazil show, "Mind of Heart Soul." The same show that Jean was not supposed to take the leading role in because he needed to be fluent em Português.

The part was originally for Leo, but he didn't want to leave Sammatha's side for the show's filming since it was filmed in Salvador and São Paulo, Brazil. Dice, Rebecca, Xan, and I are on the series alongside Jean, and we all struggled to get the language down. I come from a French background, and the others have Spanish knowledge. Xan was the only person who could speak Portuguese comfortably since he was from Brazil.

"Awesome work, everyone. You guys get home safe," said the stage manager.

"Finally, we can go home. I am so tired. I will lose my last brain cells if I perform "Hot-Line" again." Mazen said, heading towards the changing room.

Courtney laughed at Mazen's comment when suddenly she felt a tap on her shoulder.

"Hey, do you wanna go somewhere?" Jermany teased. With

long golden hair, bangs covering her forehead, and big bright eyes, Courtney turned around and batted her gaze at him.

"And where do you want to go?" Courtney teased back. "Let's go to Theo's place and have a nice glass of champagne and maybe relax for the night," Jermany whispered. Courtney blushed a bit as she looked up into his eyes.

"Let's go then. But wait, is Theo cool with us going to his rental?"

"I was going to ask, but I can't find him. I think he went back to the main house. We should be fine." Jermany reassured.

After an hour-and-a-half drive in the night, they arrive at Theo's house. A decent size, middle-class home, probably made in the 60s or 70s. Theo's place stood out from the neighborhood. His lawn was overgrown with grass and weeds, and his porch was in terrible condition. His house is responsible for lowering the property value in the area.

Jermany grabbed Courtney by the waist, and the two walked up to the front door.

"Oh shoot. Do you think the alarm is set?", Jermany asked.

"It wasn't set the last two times," Courtney said.

Jermany slid the key in and slowly turned the knob to open the door.

No alarm went off.

Walking in, Jermany and Courtney did not waste any time to

start making out. Courtney pulled back a bit suddenly. "Let's go upstairs. Not in the living room", she requested. The two headed upstairs, but Courtney noticed a purse on the kitchen counter while walking over. Moving closer to the stairs, Jermany stopped in his place.

"What's that sound," Jermany whispered.

"I don't know."

The two waited to hear something again, but it was silent. "Maybe it was just a wind," Jermany said.

The two proceed to the bedroom. Closing the door, Jermany was about to take his jacket off when he heard another sound. His ears could not comprehend what was happening. It sounded like two people were talking.

"I didn't see anyone's car in the driveway," Courtney said.

"It sounds like someone didn't want to ask Xan for the keys to the second house," Jermany suggests.

Courtney walked over and stuck her head out the door. "It's coming from the primary room," Courtney whispered.

"Let me see," Jermany said.

Peeking out, suddenly, the door opened. Courtney closed the door immediately. Leaning against the door, they waited to hear who it was.

"Theo have you seen my purse," said the unknown voice.

"No way it can't be," Courtney whispered in Thai.

"I think you left it downstairs in the kitchen, Saige," Theo said.

"We need to leave," Jermany whispered.

Once Saige returned to the primary room, Jermany and Courtney quickly snuck out of the room and out of the house, fetching their bags from the living room.

"Quickly," Courtney said impatiently, waiting for Jermany to unlock the door. Rushing in, they decided to head back to the main house for the night.

"Does anyone know about them being together? I thought they broke up," Courtney questioned.

"Theo still having some form of feelings towards Saige is not surprising, but they are hooking up out here? In Monroe? We are in the middle of nowhere. Now I know why he took the property off the market," Jermany said.

"The secret life of the members of Switch. I thought Saige had feelings for Simon for a second, but this is news to me. Honestly, I have no idea what's happening outside of the Varsity Girls Line right now. Funny how we all live together but still live in two different worlds." Courtney said, looking out the window.

"Just another secret we have to hold onto. We might as well delete the information from our mind", Jermany suggested.

"You know what. Theo and Saige were getting too comfortable with the dancing during the 4th performance. I get they have to pretend they are together on stage, but today or yesterday, I guess, since it is 1 a.m. They were selling the narrative like their life depended on it," Courtney said.

11

07/18/22: Cameron and Jean's Problem. Part I

Today is the day!!! The Mind of Heart Soul premiering on Nexflic.

After our Switch Experience live stream, Rebecca decided to host a watch party in the movie room downstairs.

"Make sure you all repost the trailer on your Instagrand pages. I want this to pop off so we can get a season two, okay" Rebecca shouted as she left the black box room.

Later in the evening, everyone congregated in the movie room, filling all the seats. Rebecca hit play, and the show began.

The Mind of Heart Soul is about the favela life in Salvador. Talks about themes of hardship, gangs, and faith. In the back corner, Cameron was cuddling with Jean. Cameron Minski is the love of Jean's life. She ranks five in the world for most beautiful women and has been considered as Japan's favorite sweetheart.

She was excited to watch the show as she lay against Jean as the show ran. Things were going well until MULTIPLE scenes of Jean making out with another woman popped up in episode two. Her eyes opened wide as her heart started beeping fast. Jean initially didn't see a problem with the scene during filming since it was all acting. But when he saw Cameron's facial expression turn for the worst, he started to regret his decision.

After the showing of the first two episodes, we called it a wrap for the night since each part was an hour long.

"Valen, your Portuguese was horrible, " Simon laughed.
   "Whatever, you can't even speak a lick of Portuguese," I said, throwing my pillow at him.

"I thought the show was pretty good. Everyone did a good job", Asia said.

"Thank you, the filming was fun. Minus the amount of homework we had to do. Jean couldn't get the conjugations down to save his life." Rebecca laughed.

LeeSung raised his hand. "I just got a message from Kendrick. He said, 'He likes the show and hopes y'all get a season two,'' LeeSung said.

"Did he mention anything about coming out of hiding?" Mazen joked.

Over in the back, Jean noticed that Cameron was acting distant.

"Cameron...I", Jean lightly said, but Cameron got up and left the room before he could finish. Leo and Sammatha, sitting right next to Jean, glimpsed what had just happened. "That lady and I did not actually do it. It's just acting," Jean tried to justify.

"I mean, yes, it was just acting, but there were a lot of scenes, Jean. I can see why she would be upset," Sammatha said.

"You should probably go talk to her," Leo suggested.

Taking their word, Jean went to his room to talk to Cameron.

Cameron and Jean's relationship is beyond pure, true love. However, I would be lying if I said their relationship is perfect but rather full of insecurities.

Being one of the group's first couples to be formed, they are the definition of enemies to lovers after the iconic slapback at the 3rd BFF World concert.

12

07/31/15: All because of a water bottle.

Varsity Girls were performing Can't Remember on stage in front of a packed stadium. The crowd was singing word for word to a song that just came out two weeks ago.

"Wow, that you guys can sing, can't you," Brittany said once the song ended.

"The people in the back. I heard you guys loud and clear", Mia chimed in. Cameron looked by the stage's corner and realized her water bottle was missing. Looking around, she looked off into the crowd, and side stage, needing clarification about where it was.

"Our lovely fans surely know how to sing. But with all this singing and performing, I think we all deserve a water break, no?" Brionna suggested.

"Yes, we all do. So take some time to buy exclusive merch and stretch your legs. The show will continue in a bit," Courtney said to the crowd.

The five walk backstage, hi-fiving the staff.
   "Cameron, what's wrong?" Brittany asked.

"I can't find my water bottle or my towel," Cameron said, confused.
   "Think a fan stole it," Brittany questioned.

Cameron hoped it was not the case because she is really picky about her water choice. Walking out to the hallway, her eyes open wide.

Jean was drinking her water bottle.
   "JEAN!!! Why are you drinking my water??? Don't you have anything better to do in your life," Cameron said, furious.

Jean started mocking her, repeating what she was saying. "You're an idiot," Cameron said angrily.

"You're an idiot. Next time put your name on the bottle, but no, you're an idiot 'cause only idiots think like you," Jean mocked.

"Only an idiot would be named after a piece of clothes," Cameron said, trying to snatch her water bottle from Jean's grip.

"Well, Camera, Cameron. Tomato, tomato. Stop acting so tough, Cameron, like your some hot shot. Varsity Girls singer who thinks she is the princess of the land. How are you not embarrassed to be on stage thinking you are actually doing something," Jean said with an attitude.

Creeping from the corner, the rest of the 32 members notice the two arguing.

"Oh, you think being on Rap Line all of a sudden makes you superior. You can't sing to save your life, and geez, don't let Jean do actual choreography. Let's have him do the two-step and call it a day," Cameron said as her words dug deep into his skin.

"Hey, we should probably get ready for our next set. You don't want Mr.Smith to see you two arguing," Jordyn suggested as she tried to intervene.

"Jordyn is right; we should get ready for the next set. Where you will be in the back of the formation with the rest of the "talentless" Rap Line expect, you just the ugly duckling virgin who can't drive," Jean said harshly.

Quickly he realized he had taken it a little too far. Looking up, he saw Cameron's eyes turn red as a tear poured out.

Cameron walked away, trying not to cry, but suddenly, she felt a pull from her hand.

"Cameron, I..." Jean said when suddenly Cameron turned around and slapped Jean's face, though the two trembled.

Half a second later, Cameron was lying on top of Jean.

For a moment that felt like a century, the two stared into each other's eyes as if there weren't 50,000 fans screaming impatiently for the intermission to be over. Both of them were shocked at what the two just did.

"Did we just kiss..." Cameron said softly.

Jean's heart was fluttering, for he was in shock.

13

07/18/22: Cameron and Jean's Problem. Part II

Fast forward to today, the two are deeply in love, but the love is deeply rooted in high insecurities. Sometimes I blame the fans. Jean's die-hearts who love to bully Cameron about her appearance and make racist remarks (rooted in jealousy). Meanwhile, a ton of wannabe alphas like to threaten Jean that they will do whatever it takes to marry Cameron. Some would outright claim that they want to SA her, leading to Jean becoming overly protected whenever they are at a festival or simply out in public.

This is a perfect example of why they prefer to stay in the BFF bubble. A controlled environment where no one can ideally come in and try to shake the table and cost drama. But something always slips into the cracks of the front door.

KNOCK KNOCK.

Jean slowly opened his bedroom door and saw Cameron lying on the bed.
   Hesitant, he walked over to Cameron's side and lay next to her.

"Are you okay," Jean asked as he caressed her back. Cameron turned around and looked into Jean's dazed eyes.

"I'm fine, Jean," she said softly. She tried to avoid making eye contact with him, not wanting to show signs that she felt insecure.

"Who was that girl? Does he love her?" she thought internally.

"Nothing happened with me and that actress. Ask my sister. Or Valen," Jean said sincerely.
   "Jean. It's fine. Really. I don't want to talk about it," Cameron said softly. Leaning in, she kissed Jean on the lips before turning back around.

Jean was puzzled and didn't know what to do. Jean pulled her in close and kissed her neck softly. Cameron tried to fall asleep, but the tears kept slowly falling down.

Jean dragged his arm over her body as he searched for her hand. Taking notice, she grabbed it and held it close to her heart. As the clock ticked by, 12am, 1am, 2am, the two eventually stopped pretending to sleep. They gently shut their eyes as their heartbeats synced in sintonia.

14

07/18/22: Meanwhile. Part I

After the showing of the first two episodes, we called it a wrap for the night since each part was an hour long.

"Valen, your Portuguese was horrible," Simon laughed. "Whatever, you can't even speak a lick of Portuguese," I said, throwing my pillow at him.

"I thought the show was pretty good. Everyone did a good job", Asia said.

"Thank you, the filming was fun to do. Minus the amount of homework we had to do. Jean couldn't get the conjugations down to save his life. ," said Rebecca laughing.

"I just got a message from Kendrick. He said, 'He likes the show and hopes y'all get a season two," LeeSung said.

"Did he mention anything about coming out of hiding?" Mazen jokes.

"No, he did not. But I know I need to head out to pick up Haru from her grandma's place," LeeSung said, getting up from his spot.

Looking behind briefly, Saige saw Theo on his phone.

"Should I go talk to him... No, he might be busy. But who is at this hour? He doesn't want to come join the conversation?" she said under her breath.

Reshifting her focus back to the conversation, she kept thinking about Theo and what happened at his house on the 4th of July.

"Was it a one-night stand? A one-night fling?" she questioned.
   Looking to her side, Simon sat down next to her.

"What did you think of the movie," Simon asked. Saige let out a little chuckle, hoping to get Theo's attention. "You mean show. I enjoyed it a lot. Aren't you working on a show as well," she asked.

"Yea, I got a couple of scenes left to do. Instead of Portuguese, I got to speak français. No pressure on me," Simon said, flirting with her.

Walking in front of the two was Lily. She lightly tapped on

Simon's leg.

""Danse avec moi, danse avec toi,Lily laughed, quoting their new song on Simon's new EP.

"Whatever," Simon smirked.
   Saige was confused about the inside joke as Lily walked off to grab a drink from the snack bar.

"Sorry about her. Are you ready for your show to come out?" Simon asked.

"You tell me. Love Maxwell, but us having to "kiss for the fans." It doesn't come out till... I don't know. Mid-September? Enough about me. Your album is doing really well right now," Saige said.

Looking back, she looked at Theo to see if he was off his phone, but he wasn't.

"Thanks. I figure dropping some of my ghostwriting projects would be nice. Change in pace from Tainted Hearts. Did you want to listen..." Simon hesitates to ask.

"Yeah, sure, we can go now," Saige said, refocusing on Simon. As the two got up, she noticed Theo was looking at her.

After they left, Theo got up to follow behind them discreetly. That's when he was stopped by Romeo.

"Where are you going?" Romeo asked.

"Nowhere. Just my room," Theo said, trying to keep his cool.

"Well, all the guys... well, except Jean, I guess, and LeeSung, are going to hang out in the secret lounge to play pool. Do you want to stay up for another hour to play," Romeo asked.

"I think I am going to go to bed. Got to rest up, right?" Theo said, leaving the room.

"So what inspired you to make Tes Yeux," Saige asked as she stood by Simon in the recording studio.
Before Simon could say anything, and as the EP played in the background, flashbacks started to hit each other from when it all started.

15

01/10/22: Meanwhile. Part II

"Theo, I can't even with you! We had plans to go out tonight to work on a song together, but no, this is more important," Saige said on the phone.

"We can do it another time, okay," Theo said on the other side of the line. "See, and this is why I broke up with you. Never have the time to be around with me", she said, hanging up.

Simon entered the studio, unaware that Saige was in there. "Oh, sorry, did you have this room reserved?" Simon asked.
   "No, not anymore, at least," Saige said, trying not to get emotional. She sat down on the couch in frustration.

"I am assuming you're in here because Xan is on your back for your album release," she said.

"Yeah, he is. I thought I could have it done last week, but-" Simon paused when he turned around. What he thought was love at first sight, he looked into Saige's eyes as if they were a pot of diamonds.

"I probably just- need une égérie to help me produce this album..." he said.

"A muse?" she questioned. Simon turned around, realizing what he had just said out loud.

"No, no, not a muse. I just need to go outside, and yeah," he said as he tried to cover up his steps.

Simon setup everything so he could start recording the song he had been working on. Saige decided to help him arrange everything since her plans with her former boyfriend were again canceled.

"Okay, ready to go in," she asked. Simon nodded, walking inside the booth. He signaled that he was ready to go. As the intro for the song "New Year" started to ease in, he found himself gazing into Saige's eyes once again.

Admiring her beauty. All his feelings began to rush back from when he first met her in 2010. Trying to snap back from his nostalgic feelings for her from debut and the ones from now, he started to sing out the lyrics.

Giving the lyrics a new meaning, he performed his heart out to avoid messing up in front of Saige. A one-take that would blow her away. Little did he know that the song he was singing would be the staple of his album.

"That was amazing. Your vocals were really up there," Saige said into the mic. Simon smiled and left the booth.

"Thank you, Xan said I needed a vocal session. Thank Maxwell and Carlos," he said. As the two relistened to the song, Simon moved closer to Saige.

The flashback started to get glitchy, jumping from the past to the present and back to the past.

Saige was aware of Simon's presence, moving closer to her till they were skin to skin. "New Year" kept playing in the background when in a blink of an eye, they were making out. The flashback became more glitchy again, flash-forwarding to the present.

16

07/18/22: Meanwhile. Part III

Simon held Saige in his embrace and made out to her. Saige felt like she was in wonderland as Simon made sweet love to her. While Simon kissed her neck, Saige noticed someone by the door... Unaware that they forgot to lock the door, Theo had opened it, peeking through.

Simon, oblivious to Theo being in the room or the fact that he is kissing his friend's ex-girlfriend, continues to kiss Saige's neck.

Theo was upset and heartbroken as Saige was in shock to him there. She wanted to pull away but simultaneously wanted to make Theo jealous for all the headaches he put her through. Quietly, Theo stepped away and closes the door, gently.

Saige couldn't take it any more and pulled away from Simon.

"Sorry, but I have to take a rain check." Saige then quickly grabbed her belongings and rushed out of the room.

"Theo!" She said, though he ignored her as he went upstairs to his room.

Quickly she rushed up the stairs, but it wasn't long before she heard a loud slam from his door.

17

07/19/22: 1000 words of regret.

"Morning," Jean said, walking into the lounge room where Romeo and Jermany were hanging out by the piano.

"You're up early. I saw you and Cameron rushing out of the screening yesterday. Is everything okay?" Romeo asked.

Jean shook his head a bit. "You guys saw the scene. It was just acting. I don't really have feelings for the lady. I don't even remember her name," he said.

"She probably wondering why you agreed to do the scene in the first place," Jermany suggested.

"I didn't write the script though. It's not even my original role. Leo was supposed to do it," Jean said, confused.

"Do you think Leo would agree to do the scene?" Romeo questioned.

Jean took some time to think even though he knew the answer beforehand.

"I'm just saying. Cameron reacting negatively to you making out with another girl shouldn't surprise you. Even if it's just acting, pretending, or they use a stuntman for it. The thought of you with someone else that isn't her? Think about it," Romeo expressed.

Jean began to feel guilty for his actions. Not considering that he could have potentially given Cameron an unnecessary headache. All for a quick check.

"What Romeo is trying to say is, we are siding with Cameron with this one. The fans may like the scene, but Cameron is your girlfriend," said Jermany.

"So, what do you suggest?" Jean questioned.

"Talk to her. Make amends with her. Apologize?" Jermany suggested.

"I did last night. But I think it will take more than an apology,"

Jean said. "Maybe a song?", Jermany said, hitting a note on the piano.

Jean sighed. He thought about making a song, but it's gonna take more than a song to make up for three intimate scenes that were put up for millions to watch from the comfort of their homes.

Romeo looked off to the side and saw Mazen and Alanna passing by in the hallway. "Hey, I will be right back," he said, leaving the lounge.

"Mazen, Alanna..." Romeo stopped them before he could continue. Blinking his eyes twice, he could have sworn he saw Mazen and Alanna holding hands.

"Oh hey... uh, what's up," Mazen said, trying to play it cool.

"Were you two interested in making a song together?" Romeo questioned.

Mazen and Alanna looked at each other, seemingly not inter-ested.
   "No? Sorry Romeo, but the Maknae line has been pretty busy lately," Alanna said.

Romeo was displeased by their response. "What, come on. I saw the choreography for Spinnin'. It took y'all 30 minutes to learn the whole routine. How busy can you possibly be?" Romeo questioned.

"You caught us. Spinnin' is embarrassingly easy to perform. But breakfast is calling our name, and afterward, umm...." Mazen paused in his words. Romeo waited for Mazen to finish his excuse hoping he would agree.

"Yeah, no... I know you want to get a head start on the group's next album, but... we are more in a procrastinating mood," Mazen said as he and Alanna slowly backed away from Romeo.

"Fine, but... when you are ready. You know where to find me", Romeo said as the two walked away.

Walking past him was Theo. "Hey man, what's up with Mazen and Alanna?" he asked.
    Theo, half awake, "I... Bro, I have no idea. But they are like gum under the table. Best to leave it alone."

Romeo was taken aback by the smell of alcohol coming from Theo.

"Oh man," Romeo said, returning Theo to his room. Walking inside, Romeo looked around the room and saw alcohol bottles on the ground.

"Theo, what happened last night," Romeo asked, concerned. Theo was feeling nauseous as he sat down on his bed. Suddenly he rushed up and ran to his ensuite bathroom to throw up in the toilet.

Still waiting for a response, Romeo decided to pick up all the bottles and place them in a bag. "You know alcohol is banned in the main house. I'm surprised no one came in and busted you for this.", he said.

Theo stumbled out of the bathroom and sat back down on his bed. Clearing his throat, he said, "They can take the fine out of my check for all I care. After the screening, I saw Saige talking to Simon or whatever his name is. She was over there giggling to all his jokes."

"Theo, she can talk to Simon," Romeo said, laughing a bit.
   "Yeah, she can talk to him, but does she have to wander her hands around his shoulder," Theo said upset. Romeo needed clarification.

"I walk in on them making out," Theo said, slightly heartbro-ken.
   Romeo sat beside Theo, trying not to take in the smell of liquor and vomit. "I thought you two were seeing each other again at your house," Romeo said.

"Yea, we are seeing each other as friends," Theo said, reaching over to his night table for a beer. Though Romeo quickly took it off his hands.

"No drinking. You can't be depressed if Saige sees Simon when you see Jackie. Yeah, I still remember that conversation where you slipped up about it. I suggest you take a break from crushing on anyone. You are not ready to be in a committed relationship ."

"I am too ready...." Theo responded.

"Sure you are. But when you two were dating, you spent more time on that phone than with her unless it was performance time. Be like me. A father and a husband", Romeo said, standing up.

"I guess. I guess," Theo said, looking off into the distance.

"Take a shower, and clean up this room. You don't want Saige walking in here and seeing this mess. Make her wanna run over to Simon's room." Romeo joked.

Theo threw his pillow at Romeo.

"I don't even know why you did that. Just another thing to pick up in here. I will throw away some of the bottles I could grab, but the rest is on you," Romeo said, leaving the room.

Meanwhile, Cameron was relaxing on the couch in Jean's room, hanging out on social media.

Scrolling mindlessly, her feed was filled with people talking about the new mini album and Jean's scene. Video after video of fans and even non-fans lusting over the scenes. More and more continued to fill her feed, making her feel insecure.

Entering the room, Jean came in. She quickly closed the app and pretended she was playing a crossword puzzle on her phone.

"Hey babe," Jean said as he leaned in to kiss her on the lips. Very hesitant, he sat down next to her. Cameron leaned into

Jean and rested her head on his chest. Jean hugged her to pull her closer to him. Leaning back, he lay down as she laid on top of him.

"Did you sleep well last night?" he asked softly.

"Jean, I'm fine," she said.

In Japanese, she said under her breath, "Why did you have to kiss her," she said under her breath.

"I assume you said something in Japanese, so I must be in trouble," Jean said. "I'm fine. You are not in trouble, okay," she voiced.

The room became dark as the storm came and poured down. Listening to the thunder and rain pour. Jean continued to hold Cameron in his arms for the next couple of hours, missing practice in the process.

Causally they talked, not about the show or music. Just talked. Meanwhile, in his head, Jean was trying to plan his big apology ceremony. Usually, they would argue about things like what happened on the show, and Cameron would go make some diss track song that Jean would later ban her from performing. Trying to handle the conflict without war, he carefully pinned out a plan to make up for his actions.

Flowers and a song were indeed not enough. But a night to never forget, maybe.

18

07/20/22: Actions have consequences. Part I

"That's not fair! Switch has a monopoly on the Pillboard Hot 200 Charts."

  Executive of RCCA Records

Today everyone woke up to the news that our songs were dominating the charts. More specifically, we were taking up the top 20 with our hit song 'Hot-Line' dominating #1 for the last 55 weeks. With some of the title tracks from our previous albums, In the Name of Love, Simple Days, and Simon's French EP, I can see the frustration, but at the same time, it's not our fault that they are performing well.

Multiple labels, including our former label Ex-S Records, were pressed about the situation because many of their artists' music was not charting. In contrast, others constantly pushed back their artist release date until we dropped from the #1 spot. Sure, I could apologize to the industry for dropping so many projects close together. However, it was because of popular demand. Plus, we are independent, so who can stop us?

Thankfully the grand public was not complaining. The hash-tag 'Make better music' is trending under Switch defense. Of course, some netizens are siding with the labels, but most are on our side. Not everyone wants to listen to a twerk song this summer.

This is nothing new to us. Since we went independent, labels have been complaining every day about something. They try to send out "spies" or "instigators" to start some mess with the group, spread rumors, etc. However, it is hard to even come close to a success story because, in the last two years since the Covid outbreak, we barely socialize with anyone outside the group (with the exception of close family).

DING

A notification came from the BFF group chat.

Lily drops a screenshot of an article about Ex-S Records being mad about the music charts.

"We should drop another album just to piss them off again."
  Dice

"Make BEtTeR MUSiC"
  Mazen

"Ngl, how is the hotline still on the chart?"
  Vanessa

"I like hotline tho."
  Valen

"Same. I don't see a problem with it being number 1."
  Maxwell

"Easy for you to say when you sing lead, lol."
  Carlos

"Aye, I think Ex-S is weird to be complaining. Biggest label in the country, and no one on their roster can beat Hot-Line?"
  Simon

"Can you stop blowing up the chat? I am trying to sleep."
  LeeSung

"No"

Mazen

"Practice today at 3 pm at the main house."
  Xan

"NOOOOOOOOOOOOO!"
  Mazen

"Dang, today…"
  Toran

"I broke my leg."
  Dice

"That boy is fine, TT."
  Rebecca

"Hope you all learned the choreography for today. Guys: Your Perfect Man Ladies: So Real."
  Lisa

"Version 2 and 3 for both"
  Lisa

"Wait, there is a version three to 'So Real."
  Asia

"Right?????"

Lily

"The choreography tutorial should be further up in the chat."
  Lisa

"Does anyone want to practice with me at 1"
  Jackie

"Yes, Alanna and I will be there 'cause we haven't version 3 or…. Two… And I forgot one…."
  Asia

"Please stop spamming the chat."
  LeeSung

"No"
  Mazen

The guys went to practice, and the girls went to practice as usual at 3 pm, as Xan said.

The practice was pretty good. Of course, the hardest part was the formations and remembering which version we had to perform. Getting stuck with Xan as the supervisor can have its pros and cons. Crisp performance but little room for errors, so lots of "stop, again."

Rebecca and I were looking at each other in confusion as we

both noticed Cameron's lack of luster performance on her lines.

"Water break!" Xan said.

"Valen, Is she okay," Rebecca said as we walked off to the corner of the dance studio.

"Uh, I have no idea. I thought she liked performing So Real. Plus, she is third lead," I said.

"You don't think it's because of the show. We were both at the filming so that we can both testify that my brother didn't do anything," Rebecca said. "Yea, he barely talks to the girl once the cameras stop rolling," I said.

We both glimpse over at Cameron, concerned.

"He should have given her a disclaimer or something before he had her watch the show, at least," Rebecca said. We walked over to Cameron, hoping to clarify the air about the filming.

"Hey Valen, Rebecca. What's up," Cameron said, trying to keep her spirits high.

"Hey, how are you? We didn't see you yesterday for practice," I said.

"Oh, I decided to take the day off...I didn't feel good, that's all," she replied. Rebecca looked at me briefly, questioning whether she should discuss the scene.

"Ah- Cameron. Valen and I just want to testify and say that

nothing happened with Jean and that actress. The filming was shot quickly, and he didn't even want to film the scenes," Rebecca reassured.

"Yes, it was like in and out," I chimed in. It might not have been the best choice of words, mas não sei. Isn't Cameron an actress herself? She should understand. Yet, I can see why she is upset with the May drama incident between Kylie and Sammatha. An outside threat trying to break up her relationship with Jean. But it's not a threat. It is all in her head.

"1 minute left," Xan yelled. "It's fine. I'm not mad about the scene or the show or anything. Really, I'm not. I'm just a little tired," she said, clearly lying.

"Formations," Xan yelled.
   "What version," Jackie asked.
   "Formation 4," Xan joked, "Kidding, formation 2, and I want it clean."

Rebecca could not help but feel bad for Cameron and disappointed at Jean for not controlling this situation. "Where are you going," Xan yelled over the music. "Bathroom," Rebecca yelled back, leaving the studio.

She walked down the hallway over to where the guys were practicing. She peaked her head through the door to see if she could spot Jean.

Jean noticed her signaling him down and met with her outside in the hallway.

"I should slap you," Rebecca said, disappointed.
"Why slap me?" Jean questioned.

"Your girl is a mess in there and still upset about your little stunt. Why didn't you tell her you were going to film that scene? Whether you guys really did anything is not important," Rebecca said, frustrated.

"I'm trying. She told me she was fine," Jean said.
"But you know she is not, right?" she replied.
Jean's mood tanked. He knew she was not okay.

Rebecca stepped closer to Jean. "Fix it, Jean. TO-NIGHT. And not a day later," she said in a very serious tone.

She knew her brother very well. If he doesn't fix this situation as soon as possible, he will turn into a depressed Jean. That, my friend, is not a pretty sight you would want to see. Trust me on that. She left him alone in the hallway and went back to practice.

Jean lay his back against the wall, not knowing what to do. He turned and looked at the door where the girls were practicing. He thought about going inside and taking Cameron out of practice for a moment. Till, suddenly he felt a tap on his shoulder.

"Hi. Is everything okay," Lisa asked.

"Yes, everything is okay," he responded quickly. He took one last look at the door before walking back into practice.

19

07/20/22: Actions have consequences. Part II

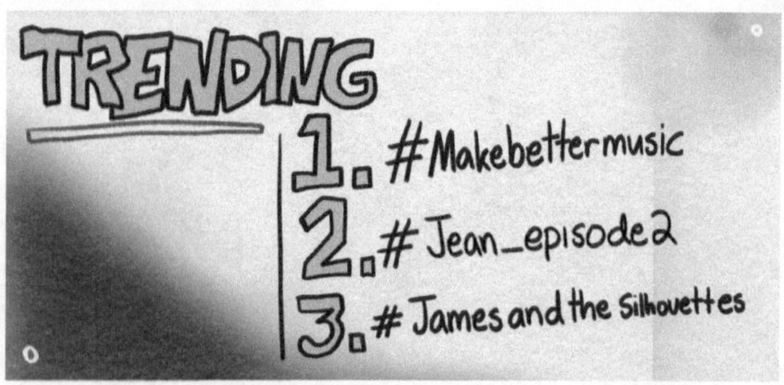

After a long day of practice, Cameron returned to her or Jean's room. (They share a room together.) Tossing her bag by the door, she fell to the floor. Resting in a squatting position, she stayed down for a bit before getting up and taking a shower.

After a rather long steamy shower, she walked out of the bathroom, shocked that Jean was still not back from practice.

"Practice must have gone overtime again," she said.

Walking over to the bed, she laid down under the covers. Looking up, she noticed her phone charging at the bedside.

At first, she thought about grabbing it but decided not. But then, randomly, she grabbed it. Opening the Nexflic app, she couldn't help but play episode two from 'Mind of Heart Soul".

[FROM THE EPISODE]

It was dark and late at night in the favelas of Salvador. After a long day of partying, Jean departed from his friend group. He stumbled to his flat when he noticed a lady with dark brown skin (probably Guyanese) standing by his front door. Her name was Dafine.

In Portuguese, Jean questioned why the lady was waiting for him.

"You keep saying you are in a relationship, but I don't see your girlfriend anywhere," Dafine said as she stepped closer and closer to Jean.

"She left to go to university in the States," he said, trying to not give in to Dafine.

"And you think she is coming back to see you next week. Let's go inside and talk. It is getting late, and I can't walk back home by myself," she said flirtatiously.

Taking one more puff of weed, he gave in to the temptation and took her inside.

Cameron's heart sank as she watched her man make love to this actress. (Even though it's all acting, and nothing really happen. Just the power of camera angles and effects...)

It didn't help that in the show, Jean was cheating and being unfaithful when he promised his in-show girlfriend that he wouldn't cheat on her in episode one. Forhe said, "I will not see anyone while you're gone."

She replayed the scene over again in disbelief and anger. Then a wave of sadness came over her. Going to her photo gallery, she looked back at all her intimate moments she had with Jean. From the flowers he gave her on Valentine's Day to the sunset drives they would take. Laying in bed, scrolling through the memories all the emotions came rushing in.

About 30 minutes went by when Jean came into the room. Reacting very quickly, she pretended she was asleep.

Jean's happy meter was non-existent. Not wanting to wake up Cameron, he quietly put his stuff down and took a shower. After washing up and getting dressed, his heart began to hurt when he heard Cameron crying. Quickly he rushed out of the bathroom to Cameron's side.

Cameron was sitting on the side of the bed, crying. Tears drop to the floor. Jean dropped to his knees and tried to wipe the tears away.

"Leave me alone!" Cameron cried. She pushed Jean's hand away as tears continued to fall down.

"I will take down the show. I'll call the whole thing off. I only love you, Cameron. You only, not anyone else. I'm guilty. I should have never agreed to be on the show. I should have let someone else do it. I only love you," Jean confessed.

He slowly got up from his knees and tried to get her to stand up, but Cameron refused as she planted her face in her hands.

"Leave me alone," she cried. Jean, trying not to cry, sat down and tried to hug her.

"I fell in love with you day one, back when this group wasn't even debuted. Your beauty makes my world have so much life. From the way you sing to the way you laugh. I love you so much that it hurts me to see you cry," he said, trying to hold back his tears.

Cameron looked up at him. Eyes, bloodshot red. Jean looked into her eyes and knew what he needed to do.

Getting up, he walked into the closet. Cameron was con-fused as she wiped her tears away.

Walking out, he was holding their BFF's signature outfits. A black and dark green blazer combo (long black pants for the guys, black and green pleated skirt for the girls).

The signature outfits are inspired from the first world tour. The outfit was initially shelved after the last show but slowly became a symbolized outfit within the group.

It got named as a symbol of "true love" and "eternal love" It also illustrates the remembrance of how the love for each other started. Usually, we wear the signature outfit at the end of a tour season. Though, since we don't tour very often, it sits in everyone's closet. However, some members find an occasion to wear the outfit.

Without a word, Cameron watches Jean pack her belongings into a duffle bag. Then she watched him pack his bag.
   "Jean... what's going on," Cameron said softly.

"Follow me," Jean said as he stared into her eyes.

Quickly the two left, not caring that they weren't fully dressed. Without anyone noticing them leaving, they made it to Jean's car. (I forgot the name of it, but it's a costly blue sports car. Most people would say a 90k car isn't expensive, but it is. God forbid you wanted to sit in the back seat cause it doesn't really exist.)

20

07/20/22: Actions have consequences. Part III

After a 45-minute drive of smooth 90s r&b music, the two arrive at a fancy, small, two-star hotel in a random town that no one has probably ever heard of. Jean put on a mask and a hat to "hide his identity" and went inside.

"I need a room. A couple, actually," Jean asked the front desk concierge. Looking up, he noticed the concierge was an elderly black gentleman who looked a day over 85.

"A couple of rooms? Well, we only have about three people booked here for tonight. If you want to, you can book the three top floors," the concierge joked.

"I'll take it."

The concierge was startled by Jean's comment. The two look at each other in question.
"I... I am a manager for a traveling orchestra. We have a

show coming up in New York City and need a place to crash. They will be here in the morning; I just got in a bit earlier than them," Jean said.

"How fun. Would you like to pay now or later," the gentlemen asked.

"Now would be best," Jean said.

"That would be 9000 dollars."

As Jean pulled out his wallet and couldn't help feeling bad for the concierge. Working third shifts at his age when he should be sleeping at home. After paying the bill, the man handed him 60 key cards.

"I hope everything is okay with you and your lady," the gentlemen said.

Jean was startled by his comment.

"Oh, come on, you've been coming to this hotel for the last couple of years. At the same time too. 1:30 am."

Coming to the realization, Jean realized the concierge was the same guy who had been checking him in since 2016 (when he started dating Cameron).

"Oh yes, I remember now. How are you doing," Jean said pulling down his mask.

"Better now since I got you to spend 9k for one room. I will get a nice bonus in my next check," the man laughed.

"Here is an additional 500 then. You never saw us," Jean said, handing over some cash.

"Legally blind in BOTH eyes," he said excitedly, accepting the money.

Leaving the concierge to himself, the man started counting the cash happily.

"Wait, this isn't 500 dollars!"

Jean ignored the man and walked out of the lobby. He didn't give the man 500 dollars, more like 2000. He would have given more, but that was all the cash he had on him.

Walking back outside, he helped Cameron out of the car and got his car cover to hide his 90k asset that was sitting in a parking lot where only 2 other vehicles were at.

Taking her inside (through the side entrance) and to the room of their many choices, the two didn't say anything. With not a single word exchanged, the two change into their signature outfit. The two sat down on the couch and created a therapy session.

Cameron looked into Jean's eyes, scared to talk.

"I...was jealous. I knew it was just acting, but I couldn't stand seeing you in another girl's arms. Watching the scene made me uncomfortable. I thought I would get over it, but... I couldn't stop thinking about it," she said.

"I promise you, the kiss meant nothing. I'm yours only,' Jean said as he got on his knees.

Cameron started tearing up as she begged Jean to get up. But that just put Jean into his "depressed stage." Which is really a cover-up phrase that Jean actually meant became a hardcore simp to Cameron.

He poured his heart out to her in the most vulnerable way possible. Leaning in, he kissed her in between his love poems as tears fell down his cheek. He tried to do everything in his power to get Cameron to forgive him.

After a long night of love-sharing, the two rested in each other's arms as the two tried to heal from the situation.

21

07/21/22: "I'm sorry."

The two were doing better the following day. Instead of returning to the main house, they hung out at the BFF stadium and spent the day in the Switch lounge. There they made love again in the lounge. As the final stamp, Jean spam his story with old pictures of him and Cameron from when they first got together.

"Where are Cameron and Jean!?! The stream starts in one hour," Xan yelled.

Today was our live-stream concert though instead of filming at the house, we decided to do it at a film studio for a change of scenery.

Rebecca was a little worried about her brother's whereabouts as her eyes wandered the room.

"Are you okay?" Dice asked as he wrapped his arms around Rebecca's waist.

"Yea, I just want to knock out this show and move on with the day. But, no. Jean is nowhere to be -". Rebecca stopped in her words when she saw Jean and Cameron come into the production room.

Rebecca looked at the two in question.

"He must have talked to her," she said.

"Where have you two been? I have been trying to call you guys, and I got nothing, "Xan asked in concern.

Cameron looked at Jean, wondering if they should have said where they had been hiding.

"We are here now," Jean said.

"Right, I guess. Well, the dress attire is all black. Please hurry and change so I can run the set list with everyone," Xan said before walking off.

"Jean, you think he's gonna find out where we were," Cameron pouted. He laughed a bit and assured her everything was fine. "If he finds out, then he finds out. It's worth it all to be with you," Jean said.

While those two went over to the wardrobe, Lily and Simon sat by the wall, waiting for everything to kick off.

"Simon, don't even start with the lies, okay," Lily laughed.

"What? We do not "see each other". We kissed a couple of times in the studio and then she called for a rain check. Strictly friends we are," Simon said.

Lily blushed a bit. "So what are we? Strictly friends?"

Simon tried to comprehend Lily's question. Trying to find the words, he couldn't let them fall out.

Trying to play off like her feelings weren't hurt, she punched Simon's shoulder playfully. "I am just kidding. Geez. Um, your friend Jean is here. You should probably go check up on him and make sure he's okay," she said.

Simon felt terrible for not giving Lily a response to her question. To be honest, I don't think he knew the answer to it. Does he like her, or is she no different from Saige?

As Simon got up, Jackie came and sat down next to her.

"Boys," Lily sighed.

"Tell me about it," Jackie said as she watched Theo secretly pour some liquor into his drink.

In the dressing room, while Vanessa finishes her makeup, Cameron couldn't help but ask about her relationship status with Toran.

"Oh, we are doing fine. We tried to play boyfriend and girlfriend. Though earlier this week, we decided to take a break from the relationship, but we didn't break up, if that makes sense. We are just taking a break," Vanessa said, trying to not feel fazed by the situation.

"Enough about me; how is Queen Cameron? You seem different from yesterday's practice."

Cameron started laughing a bit.

"What! I am the same person. Nothing happened," she said, smiling ear to ear.

"Cameron, no. Now you have to tell me. What happened?" Vanessa said, rushing by her side.

"Okay, well, Jean took me to a hotel. Not going into the details, but it was so romantic, and then we went to the stadium, and you know... Then he drove me off to the sunset. Up all night," Cameron said, trying to keep her cool.

"And for clarification?" Vanessa asked.

"Oh, the show. It's just acting. I know where Jean's heart is," she said happily.

Suddenly they heard a knock. Lisa pops her head through the door. "Showtime, let's get moving on," she said.

Lights, Camera, Action!

The show began, and it went really well. Until the first fan request came in.

DING DING DING DING DING!

"It seems like we have our first request," Jermany said. One of the production assistants handed the envelope to Jermany.

"I can't open it. Not the first one, at least."

Jermany gave it to Maxwell.

"No, I will pass," Maxwell laughed.

"Come on, someone opens it," Alanna said impatiently.

"I'll open it," Jean said, grabbing the letter.

Everyone got rally up waiting to hear what the note said. "Okay, it's –" Jean's heart sank to the floor, deep.

Struggling to find his words, he said, "Please have Cameron perform I Remember, solo."

Quick context, from last year's album, there is a song by Sammatha called, I Remember. It's a blacklist song, and this fan wants Cameron to perform it... With everything that happened in the last couple of days, things just got better with her relationship, and now you want her to perform I Remember.

Xan and Lisa don't have control over what requests get picked for today's show. First, come, serve bases...

"Oh, okay, um. Cue the song," Cameron hesitated.

Giving her the floor, Cameron sang her heart out that song. A little too passionate (shedding a tear). Too passionate to the point, Jean became upset but also moved. Once she finished her song, suddenly, the music changed to Trip (From Under the Impression, Thoughts at The Party Album).

While Dice and Toran sang the chorus, Jean held Cameron close,performing her favorite song,made especially for her only. Shout to Toran and Dice, by the way. They hit the notes perfectly.

Then the light went out, and a spotlight shined on Cameron and Jean. Someone must have got a hold of the set list (cough cough, Jean probably did). I Know started to play. Though once it got to Cameron's part, Jean began to get emotional as he tried to keep his eyes on Cameron.

Making it through the song in one piece, Xan must have gotten a hold of the setlist and put down his request cause Take Care (from The Good, Ugly, and The Bad) played next. Strategic and classic Xan to play that song cause it sure got a reaction out of Jean.

While Cameron tried to keep her composure, Jean started to tear up a bit. Everyone was questioning what was going to happen to see Jean shed a tear, which is very much unheard of on a stage performance that is live. Social media caught on quickly because the live stream numbers doubled, with one million people watching.

Xan pushing the buttons to the limit and had All The Way Home from Cold Weather, Life with Fame, or Money play, and wow. Jean hates this song because it's about their fights in their relationship behind closed doors. Though Cameron did not waste no time performing.

On the stage together, Cameron sang out every word as tears fell down her eyes.

Varsity girls try to sing to backup for her, but Cameron is in her own world at that point.

"Xan, I think this is enough. We – "Lisa whispered, but Xan interrupted her.

"Just one last song. The numbers we are pulling in will make Ex-S shake in their boots," Xan said.

As the song finished, the most blacklist song ever from Cameron's catalog played. War and Love from the same album. I would describe this as the fear of break-up songs.

Everyone in the room was moved as her voice sounded so angelic. I don't know what happened, but I looked over at Jean halfway through the song.

He was crying. They were both crying.

Everyone in the group was in awe. Varsity Girls had to pull out their vocal cords to finish the song because Cameron couldn't finish the last chorus. Center of the stage, Cameron and Jean hugged each other, crying into each other's shoulders as the music played. This broke the internet as many people flocked to the stream to witness the emotional moment.

"Now this is a performance," Xan said excitedly. Lisa on the other hand was not happy to see her friends crying on stage. It didn't help that the cameraman kept zooming in.

"We need to do something," Maxwell whispered to the Varsity Guys line.

"Uh, what do you have in mind," Theo whispered.

"I don't have anything," Maxwell said.

"How confident can everyone hit a high note," Carlos asked.

The Varsity Guys line rushed on stage as the extended version of War and Love fizzled out. On came Love In The Ice from the Cold Weather, Life without Fame or Money album. Cameron and Jean didn't budge from their spots as the five sang around them.

Risky to sing Love In The Ice because it's a challenging song to perform because it takes one person to mess up. Did I mention they perform the Japanese version? Though they were able to do it. Jean and Cameron slowly waltz, not caring that a camera is pointing at them.

We performed songs from that 2018 album, sticking to the slow jams. A 40-minute show turns it into a two hour performance. The group very quickly decided to perform songs with lyrics that were positive and loving.

Forget the fan request; we just want to cheer up Jean and Cameron. I help sing Share My World with Sammatha and Maxwell. My way of contributing to the cost.

The overall show was memorable. Fans immediately took it to SNS, and we knew they would be discussing the incident for days, coming up with theories on why the two, especially Jean, were crying. Cameron has cried on stage many times but Jean???

After the show and once the filming crew left, we all went outside to the parking lot to chat. After a share of hugs and a couple of light laughs, Jean came out to explain why he got emotional.

"I am not perfect. Cameron… and I are not perfect. We aren't the powerhouse couple the world thinks we are. We are just two regular people's problems that run deeper than anything right now," he said as he held Cameron's hand.

Jean and Cameron have lately been under a lot of pressure to upkeep a pitch-perfect lifestyle for the world when everyone BFF member knows they are beyond perfect. I argue they are more imperfect and have a lot of issues on their plate. The two come from a hurt childhood, and there have been too many triggers happening all at once for any of them to handle. The feeling of rejection or losing the love that never was had as a child. Everyone in the group understood Jean clearly as we all had one big group hug.

"We are all here if you need someone to talk to," Mia said.
    Lisa went to Jean's car as everyone returned to the house.

"We got you two back. Xan wanted to apologize for what happened during the stream. He told me to give it to him."

Lisa gave Cameron the keys to the hidden second house. "Stay there as long as you need. If you need anything, just call me,"

Lisa said.

The two thank Lisa.

Sitting in the parking lot alone, the two stared off to the sky as the sunsetted on the horizon.

"We will be okay, right?" Jean asked.

Cameron looked over at Jean and saw he was emotional. His eyes were slightly red still.

"I know we will," she said.

Leaning in, she kisses him. Two tears from each eye fell in sync.

22

07/31/22: A Problem.

"This is so annoying. I think we should have called off this whole performance and made a move on with our life," Simon said, frustrated.

Simon, Leo, Jean, Dice, Rebecca, Cameron, Toran, Vanessa, Lily, and I were sent on a "top secret mission" to do a surprise performance at the Lola Festival in Chicago today.

It would be nice if Jackie and Saige tagged along and completed the JV Line. Saige used the "I'm sick" card to spend time with Theo. While Jackie is in Atlanta for some unknown reason. Couldn't tell you why.

Coming straight from the airport, we were packed into a limo and headed toward Grant Park.

"What's the game plan?" Vanessa asked as she brushed her hair.

Pulling out my phone, I check the Leaders group chat.
   Finding the message I said, "Um… Simon, Leo, Jean, Dice, and Rebecca… you all will be performing that one song… Tubarão and-"

Jean sighed, "I'm not performing that song."
   Cameron lightly hit his thigh for his response.
   "What?" He whispered.

"Why?" I questioned.
   "Because I don't remember the lyrics. If Simon can do his lines in French, then I should be able to do mines in Spanish. No offense Leo but I have no idea what I'm saying half the time when I speak Portuguese," Jean said.

"Say the guy who has a lead role on one of the biggest shows in Brazil right now," Rebecca said as she rolled her eyes.

Dice quickly hopped in to defend Rebecca, "What she meant to say is that she believes that Jean should be able to do his part in Spanish."

"Thanks, Dice, but don't think this doesn't cover up your little scandal with my sister," Jean said.

Cameron, once again, hit Jean's thigh a little harder. "Shut up. You're acting like a child," she said to him in Japanese.

"It's completely wiped off the internet," Dice said defensively.

"Yea, real great boyfriend you are for turning my sister into a slu-"

Before Jean could finish, Cameron slapped him in the face.

All eyes froze at what we just witnessed.

Leaning into his ear, she whispers, "Shut up, or I will dump you right here. Right now." Then Cameron straightened up, pulling out her pocket mirror to finish applying her lip gloss and blush. I looked at Leo, who was quiet the whole time, and even that got his attention.

Classic Cameron using the "I will break up with you" tactic to get Jean to stop talking. I like how Jean is just sitting there, distraught by what she just said. While Cameron is acting like she didn't just say the one set of words that he very much fears.

"Perform the song in Spanish then," I said.

"Will do," Jean said softly.

Continuing on, I said, "Anyways, Cameron... As usual, you're on solo duties plus a small duet with Jean. I don't care what song you choose; just keep it clean. For who is present for JV Line, we are doing 808 and Tell Me. Toran and Dice, you will be performing Guidance. We will have to find a finale song to do together. Though we are missing well over half the group, so we might skip it. Too bad the festival could only afford to rent out a couple of the members for the show..."

Lily raised her hand a bit.

"What's up, Lily?" I asked.

"Um... well, who will be here at this festival?" Lily asked.

I shrugged my arms.

"I can check real quick," Toran said.

As Toran pulled out his phone and searched for the festival poster, I glanced at Leo again. He looked so on edge. Getting him to come on the trip to Chicago was a hard sell for him. He did not want to leave Sammatha "alone" in New York. Even though she is at the main house, probably hanging out with the rest of the Varsity Girls line.

"I don't see anyone on the blacklist, so the coast is clear, I guess," Toran said.

Vanessa and Toran made eye contact briefly as they sat on opposite sides of each other. "That must be a good thing," Vanessa said softly.

"David wouldn't sign us up for something that would put us in harm's way," I said.

Time went by when we officially arrived at the Lola Festival. The limo swung around to a decent size white tent that was parked behind the central stage platform. Coming inside the tent, we were all in great shock.

"Oh great...The members of Switch get an outdoor tent, some wobbly folding chairs, and two fans that blow nothing but hot air. Oh does the industry love us with all their heart," Simon said as he pulled out a pack of weed. Though Lily snatched it away before he got the chance to light it up.

"I think this place is fine. It gets the job done," Vanessa said.

I laughed. The place was an absolute piece of garbage. There was trash on the floor from yesterday's show, and we were given four small water bottles to share. Not to mention the lack of privacy due to the front entrance of the tent being widely exposed.

"What time does our performance start," Cameron questioned.

"We have one hour until we go up," I said as I put my hair bag on the table.

Cameron sighed. Going into her purse, she grabbed a fancy red and orange folding fan before she sat down on Jean's lap.

"It's 100 degrees! How come we don't have a trailer like everyone else," Cameron pouted. Jean ignored Cameron's complaining as he started to massage her other hand out of sight for everyone to see.

"It's because we are the most hated group in the industry," Dice said as he drenched his curls and tried to define them for his fro.

"Not everyone hates us," Rebecca said.

"They couldn't even put our tent over some grass. We are standing on dirt," Toran said, pulling out his clippers.

Toran paused as he held the plug to his clippers. Looking around the space, he was astounded by his predicament.

"What's wrong?" Dice questioned.

"There's no outlet here," Toran said, looking around.

Dice turned in question.

"Oh shoot... your right," Dice said.

Toran walked over to Leo, Simon, Jean, and Cameron as they occupied a corner of the room.

"Hey, do any of you have a portable outlet or clipper I can use?"

Leo and Simon shook their heads while Cameron sat there laughing.

"Oh, come on, Toran. Those two haven't got a proper haircut in years," Cameron said as she tried to remove her hand from Jean's embrace.

"What about you, Jean? You have a dang near-perfect lineup and swimming waves 24/7. You must have something I can use," Toran said.

"I guess I do," Jean said.

Tapping on Cameron's thigh, he signaled for her to get up.

"Here," Jean said as he handed over a portable clipper. "It's just for a lineup, right?" Jean questioned.

"Yea, just that. Thanks," Toran said.

After some time of preparing and getting dressed in the porta potties... We all went over to the stage to do our performance. We had a diverse entrée to give the audience, and the crowd went wild to see us. Being the only act to have funk in our set was pretty cool. Though most of the ladies were more keen to see Leo taking off his shirt as he performed his part of Tubarão.

It was a show to witness, for no one knew we were even on the lineup.

After our thirty-four-minute set, we were all finished for the day. It was about 5pm Central Time, and we were super hot and tired. As we maneuvered backstage, there was a tall black guy heading our way. He had cornrows and black shades, but none of that mattered in the description, for he looked intoxicated.

"That's Ketrean!" Vanessa whispered to me, excited.
   "Who?" I said.
   "He made that one R&B/pop album last year. Attractions of the Poles. How could you not know him," Vanessa said.

In excitement, she walks up to Ketrean to introduce herself.
   "Who is that?" Jean questioned.

"Oh yea, hi, it's a pleasure to meet you," Ketrean said as he held Vanessa's hand.
   "Big fan of your music," Vanessa said as we all approached the two.

Ketrean was in full starstruck as he glanced up at Cameron. He was stunned to be in her presence.

"Your...".

Ketrean walked past Vanessa to Cameron.

Before anyone knew it, Ketrean pulled Cameron close to him and tried to make out with her as he held one hand on her bottom.

In total rage, Jean pulled Ketrean off Cameron as she stood there in shock, appearing very uncomfortable.

Jean swung a punch at Ketrean and started to beat him up. The guys didn't try to interfere for the first 15 seconds as Jean went all in. Cameron began to cry as us, JV Girls comforted her.

Cuss word after cuss word, Jean lost it. Boom, boom, boom as time passes by.

"We can't let him keep going on like this," Simon said in a panic to Leo in French.

"I agree," Toran said.

"15 more seconds," Leo said in full determination.

Leo looked up at Ketrean's entourage. Not a single one of them wanted to help fight for Ketrean or help him out. Some flat out turned a blind eye.

Ketrean face was bloody as Jean kept swinging. Dice couldn't look anymore as he had never seen so much outrage in Jean.

Leo looked up and noticed security coming their way from a distance.

"Now we can get him," Leo said.

Leo, Simon, Toran, and Dice helped Jean stand up.

"I'M GOING TO SUE YOU!!!!" Ketrean yelled as he tried to get up.

"YOU ASSAULTED MY GIRL! [REDACTED] YOU MEAN YOU GOING TO SUE ME!" Jean yelled back.

"YOUR DATING CAMERON MINSKI. WHAT DID YOU EXPECT!" Ketrean yelled.

Oh, the rest of the group stood there, shocked. Cameron was frightened by what Ketrean said.

"Blacklist! CALL XAN AND LISA AND TELL THEM TO PUT HIM ON THE BLACKLIST! I will personally make sure your career is done for!"

Ketrean paused in conviction.

"Hey man, it- it was a joke. It was a joke. You were supposed to laugh, right," Ketrean said as he finally stood up.

Though when he saw the anger on Jean's face, he knew he was serious.

"IT WAS A JOKE! You can't put me on the blacklist. Hey Cameron, it was a joke. I'm sorry –"

"Don't talk to her," Jean said in Spanish.

"What did he say?" Ketrean questioned.

"He said don't talk to her," Rebecca chimed in.

Security came up backstage, where we were all at.

Jean pointed to Ketrean. In a monotone, he said. "He assaulted my girl. I fought in an act of self-defense. You would do the same. May we never be seen in the same room together and mayI personally welcome you to the Blacklist."

Suddenly everyone's phones started to ding. Word travels fast.

[Breaking News: Popular R&B singer Ketrean Williams has been recruited to the infamous Switch Blacklist]

Ketrean's heart sank when he heard the news.

"No, please!" he begged.

But Jean, along with the rest of the group, ignored him. Jean grabbed a hand towel and wiped the blood off his hands. Tossing it to the ground, he walked off, followed by the rest of the group.

I sighed a bit as I walked up to Ketrean. I rolled my eyes a bit and sucked my teeth as I prepared to give my scripted speech.

"What's your name," I questioned.
   "Ketrean Williams."

I stood there, shocked.
   "Oh wait, you are signed to Ex-S Records. I see Mr. Smith is continuing to do his job flawlessly," I said.
   "I never got to meet the guy," he said, upset.

"Yea, you're not missing out on anything. He will screw you over and treat you like a dog. Um, anyways, I got to say this to everyone who gets on the list, so I'll make it quick. Sorry to break the news, but I have to say that you, Ketrean Williams are now officially on the Switch Blacklist. If you decide to sue, you are guaranteed a losing case, for it is a waste of money to follow suit. At spot...23, 24 maybe, your name will be removed from the list on July 31, 2032."

I looked at Ketrean, and he looked like he was about to cry.

I place my hand on his shoulder in shame.
   "Tsk tsk tsk... Jean is one member to not mess with, and you went after Cameron. Tell a friend what you did, as it was the dumbest thing one could ever do. Be happy we didn't call the cops. Bien? Bien."

I walked away in shock at what had just happened. To violate anyone in such a gruesome way, then be shocked that your actions have consequences.

"CURSE YOU SWITCH!" Ketrean yelled.

I turned around in laughter. "Yea, love you too. Tell you mum I said hi."

Walking inside the tent, I saw Cameron trying to get Jean to calm down.

"We are leaving, okay! I'm fine, okay! I'm good!" Cameron said as she placed her hand on his face.

"I'm going to kill him," Jean said, heading to the exit. Though Leo jumped in front of him before he could escape.

"A blacklist label is not enough for what he did, and you know it Leo," Jean said angrily.

"I agree, but at the same time, you already did your part" he said.

Cameron rushed over to Jean's side, "His career is ruined now! Giving him another bloody eye isn't going to solve anything!"

Jean didn't care as he tried to leave the tent.

Dice, Toran, and Simon quickly rush over to pull Jean back inside.

"GEEZ, MAN, CALM DOWN! IT DONE FOR," Simon said.

Jean kept fighting, breaking free from their grasp.

Quickly he looked around to find Ketrean.

To his left, he saw Ketrean leaping as his entourage took him inside his trailer. As they shut the door behind themselves, Jean came marching over, though before he could grab the door handle to go inside, he was pulled down the steps by Dice and Toran.

Leo got a hold of Jean and quickly passed his hand over Jean's mouth so that he wouldn't make a sound. Suddenly the door to Ketrean's trailer opened. In quick timing to react, the four drag Jean over to the side of the trailer to get out of sight.

"Jean, calm down. Toran, show him your anxiety counting thingy. The five sense stuff," Dice said frankly.

"Bruh, I don't remember it off the top of my head," Toran said, freaking out.

Jean broke away from Leo's grip. Before Jean could say anything, he knew something was up when he saw Simon's eyes open wide.

"Are you Jean Gonzales?"

Jean turned around in question. There were two police officers standing in front of him.

"You're not seriously going to arrest me, are you?" Jean questioned.

Before the police officer could say something, someone from Ketrean's camp came over. He was an older black gentleman with trim beard and clean bald cut, dressed in formal attire.

"As a manager of Ketrean Williams, we do not want to press charges," he said.

"But sir, the ambulance-"

"He will be fine. We are not interested in having any more conflicts with the Switch collective. Jean Gonzales, I would like to apologize on behalf of Ketrean for his actions. I... I resigned from being his manager two minutes ago. I hope that will be good enough to ensure that my name isn't tied to his new blacklist label."

Before Jean could say anything, Simon, Leo, Toran, and Dice, knocked on Jean's back three times, signaling for him to not say anything.

"You will be fine," Leo said.

The guy's expressions change for the better.

"Thank you so much. Again I apologize for everything."

The police officers looked so confused.

"So everything alright then?"

"Yes. Everything is fine," Jean sighed.

23

07/31/22: A Problem. Part II

We couldn't stay long at the Lola Festival after everything that went down.

Every artist there feared to cross or look at us in the wrong way.

Packing up our belongings, we set out to the hotel David had booked for us to stay at for the night. Packing into the elevator in our "disguises," Toran hit the button to take us to the sixth floor.

"That's not the top floor," Lily questioned.

Toran looked at the room key, which read 611.

"Maybe they have a penthouse on the sixth floor," Toran said.

Rebecca sighed, "As long as I have my own room. I don't care what floor it's on."

Looking to her side, Rebecca saw that Jean was holding Cameron tightly by her waist as he rested his head on her shoulder. Rebecca looked concerned, for Ketrean's blood was still on Jean's knuckles.

We heard a questionable ding as the elevator reached the sixth floor.

I took a step out of the elevator, carrying my duffle bag, and was immediately disgusted by the odor of the hallway.

"Valen, are you sure this is a five-star hotel?" Simon questioned.

I turned to the rest of the group, pondering what to say.

"I didn't book this place. Maybe there was just a recent accident that happened. I mean, a huge festival is happening a couple of blocks down."

Giving it all the benefit of the doubt, we walked to room 611.

"6.1.1," Dice said, placing his hand on the braille, "Just like June 11th. Switch's anniversary."

Leo laughed a bit under his breath, "That is not our anniversary."

"Then when is it?" Dice questioned.

As they tried to figure out when it was Switch's anniversary (still an unknown date for us all), I was struggling to get the key card to work.

"Do you need help," Vanessa questioned.

Giving up, I handed her the key card. In one try, she got the door to open.

"Uh, I could have done that," I said, frustrated.

Opening the door, all of our mouths drop.

Walking inside, there were two queen size beds, one night table, a TV screen that wasn't mounted, a desk with a flimsy coffee pot on it, and an armchair.

Jean releases himself from Cameron's grip as she grabs his hand.

"Let me get you all cleaned up," she said softly, glaring at Jean's hand.

"Are you okay though," Jean asked.

Cameron nodded before taking him to the bathroom.

With some wings to eat, Dice place them out on the desk.

"You know it would be nice if we had, I don't know, our own rooms????" Dice said.

Toran sat down next to Simon, who appeared to be texting Saige,sighed in agreement.

"There are about ten of us here and two beds for us to work with..." Toran said.

"Well, David did say that most of the hotels were sold out," I said.

Vanessa took a seat on the other bed, sitting directly in front of Toran. Toran watched her get all comfortable as she swayed her long thick hair to her side and took off her heels.

Taking a look up, Vanessa noticed Toran staring at her.

"You want a kiss or something?" Vanessa laughed.

Toran blushed a bit until he remembered the cheating allegations that Vanessa had.

Vanessa noticed Toran started to become distant as he shifted his body to the side.

"Hey, Dice, can you turn on the TV," Toran requested.

As they tried to find something to watch, I questioned what we're going to do with the sleeping arrangements.

"What is the game plan?" Rebecca asked me.

"Should we flip a coin and see who gets the bed and who gets the floor? Or better yet, the guys sleep on the floor, and we get the beds," I voiced.

Dice turned at me in shock. "What??? I don't want to sleep on the floor."

Rebecca side eyed him. "Yes, you are. It's just for one night anyways."

"How about I sleep next to you? I'll become a toothpick. Won't even take up a fraction of space," Dice begged.

Rebecca laughed, "Boy, bye. You are sleeping on the floor, and you can use your fro as a pillow. Simon, Toran, are you two okay with sleeping on the floor tonight?"

"Not a problem for me," Toran said.

Simon raises his hand. "I'll sleep on the floor, but the plane has to be here to pick us up first at dawn."

"It will be here at 6 a.m," I said.

I walked over to the door, where I saw Leo camped out on the floor. He looked pretty concerned, as he was probably on the phone with Sammatha.

"Hey, are you okay with sleeping on the floor tonight?"

Leo shook his head in agreement.

Then I went to knock on the bathroom door where Jean and Cameron were hiding.

"I'm fine, Jean, okay. Now toughen up," Cameron said as she wiped a tear from Jean's cheeks.

Jean pulled Cameron in close as he rested his head on her shoulder.

"I failed you, Cameron. I shouldn't have let him get close to you like that. It's all my fault."

Cameron's heart fell and trembled as she knew how upset Jean was by how hard he was holding her close to him. He started to whisper words of affirmation to her, constantly mentioning how stunning and beautiful she is. Suddenly, they heard a knock on the door. Three knocks, to be exact.

"Hey, Jean, are you okay with sleeping on the floor?" I said from the other side of the door.
  Jean closed his eyes in avoidance of the question.
  "Bae..." Cameron whispered
  Jean sighed, "Not a problem for me, Valen."

Cameron smiled a bit, "I know you want me to sleep with you in the bathtub like in the old days, but I think I deserve to sleep in style."
  "Can we lay there for at least ten minutes..." Jean request.

Cameron pinched Jean's arm to signal him to let go of her.
  "Ten minutes," she whispered.

Jean took Cameron by the hand as he got into the bathtub. Cameron got in after he sat down. He held her close as she rested her head on his chest. To slow down the time, Jean kept checking his watch as he took the ten minutes to calm himself down and clear away the redness in his eyes.

Cameron stayed quiet as she still felt uncomfortable for what Ketrean did to her earlier in the day. Though she was happy that Jean stood up for her, for in the past, there was no one near to hear her cries for help.

Cameron begged for Jean to hold her tightly and tightly again once more. So he did, and her tears started to fall down her eyes.

Meanwhile, on the outside of the bathroom, Leo was starting to panic about Sammatha. "I can't do this anymore, Leo. I can't," Sammatha said as she cried over the phone.

"Everything is going to be okay. I will be back in New York tomorrow morning," Leo said.

Suddenly Leo's heart started to race when he heard Sammatha let out a cry.

"Sammatha...Sammatha, please..."

"It hurts Leo... It hurts so much," Sammatha said, choking up her tears.

"Please wrap yourself up," Leo said, trying to keep his voice down.

Moments went by before Sammatha came back to the phone.

"Let me call your brother-"

"No! I'm fine. I'm fine. I'm fine. It doesn't even hurt... I'll go to LeeSung place for the night," Sammatha said.

"I'll have him pick you up, okay?"

"He stays two blocks over. I- I can walk there," Sammatha

said.

Leo refused and went ahead and sent a message over to LeeSung to have him pick Sammatha up.

Attached to his request, he wired over eight hundred thousand dollars to LeeSung's bank account. That was when in a speedy response, LeeSung called him.

"Sammatha... He will be on his way, okay? Just stay put. I love you."

"Love you too..."

Leo hung up and picked up LeeSung's call.

"LEO!!!! WHAT IS THIS!" LeeSung said in shock.

"Whatever you're doing, I need you to stop and head over to my apartment and pick up Sammatha," Leo said.

"You want to pay me almost a million dollars to go pick up your girlfriend who lives down the street from me? I get it! You have money! However, you don't need to pay me-"

"LeeSung. Please, I need you to go pick her up right now and let her stay at your place."

LeeSung paused for a second as he could hear the panic in Leo's voice.

"She tried to do it again," Leo said.

The silence was in the air as Leo waited for a response.

"Tell her I will be there shortly. If you can... Tell her to wear some long sleeves. I don't want Haru to see it. Plus, I'm wiring the money back to you," LeeSung said.

"Keep the money."

A notification bell then went off on Leo's phone.

"Again, you do not have to pay me to respond to an emergency. I'm heading out right now."

Looking up, Leo saw Jean and Cameron coming out of the bathroom.

"Everything good?" Jean questioned in Spanish.

"Everything good with you two?" Leo questioned back in Portuguese.

Before they could say anything, Dice got all extra loud when he saw Brionna and Romeo on TV.

Quickly Leo put his acting face on and joined the rest of the group.

"What's going on," Leo said, trying to crack open a smile.

"Brionna and Romeo are dropping their EP tonight at midnight," Lily said as she tried to style Simon's hair.

The Varsity Line couple was on the Late Night Talk Show with Peter Manny, aka the heartthrob for any soap opera lovers that are over the age of 55. The man was old and very nosey.

Brionna and Romeo sat on a leather-brown couch next to Peter. They were dressed down in 70s vintage as Brionna looked like the famous singer Cherri with her long straight, yet frizzy brown hair. Shoutout to the hair team for giving her curls heat damage.

Peter raised his hand a bit for the crowd to stop screaming and cheering.

"Thank you for coming onto my show tonight. Brionna, you look stunning as usual, and Romeo, you embody the 70s with your outfit."

The two thank Peter for his compliment.

"Now tell us about your new album, Behind the Door."

"Well, it's an EP and not a complete 50-song album like with Switch," Romeo laughed.

Brionna smoothly transitions in, "Exactly. Romeo lately got into producing and songwriting. It wasn't till maybe early June that he asked me to make a couple of songs with him. At first -"

Peter rudely cut off Brionna to abruptly switch the topic.

"What is it like to be the mother in a world renounce group? Unlike your linemate Brittany who had an unplanned pregnancy at 17, you were trying to get pregnant at 21 during the 2016 Summer Love era."

Romeo glances at Brionna, who is taken aback by Peter's question.

"I have no problem being a mother. Once Romeo and I got married, we thought it would be best to try and have a kid," Brionna said as she held Romeo's hand.

"Really? A rumor has recently circulated online that you, Brionna were actually depressed during this time and felt that having a baby and marriage would bring stability into your life."

Romeo was not a big fan of how the conversation was going. Stepping up for his wife, he said, "I think we came here to talk about our new album, Behind the Door? This kind of conversation can be saved for our therapy session."

Peter laughed a bit. "Hear that everyone. Romeo Hawkins and Brionna Hawkin-Russ are in therapy. We love to see that. My question, though, is whether or not the other members of Switch are? It was said that your bandmate Jean Gonzales assaulted R&B singer Ketrean Williams after he got caught making out with Cameron Minski at the Lola Festival. John!

Please play the video."

Romeo and Brionna look at each other, confused. Turning around to the jumbo screen, they saw a video of Ketrean assaulting Cameron and another video of Jean pounding Ketrean's face from various angles.

Peter cleared his throat and continued,

"Shortly after the video was over, Jean Gonzales uttered the words no musician would ever want to hear, "You're on the blacklist." Switch is no stranger to controversy and scandals. Child stars who gone wrong as they are all indeed in need of therapy. Though one thing they love to do is blackball people in the industry. Those who do them dirty can be on the list for ten years. One singer said in quote, "Being on the Switch Blacklist is like having a dishonorable discharge on your music career. It's over. Opportunities stop coming your way, and no one wants to work or be associated with you. I had no choice but to file for bankruptcy and move back to my hometown, all because a member from Switch couldn't take a joke." What are your thoughts on this?"

Romeo and Brionna sat in silence as the camera zoomed in on them. Romeo turned to the audience as they waited for their response.

"It must have been an offensive joke," Romeo said.

Peter Manny was not buying it. "Though is a joke worth

ruining someone's career? If I said an offensive joke to you right now, would I be put on the blacklist?"

"Can you guys change the channel," Cameron requested as she sat Jean down on the bedside.

Toran took up Cameron's offer and fetched the remote by the lamp.

"It's much deeper than an offensive joke," Brionna said.

"Really? Your superstars. You should expect people to not like you for a multitude of reasons. You live the life that everyone in the world wishes you have. Money, fame, and community. You honestly can't be surprised if someone wants something that you have."

Romeo rubbed his forehead, "That's what Behind the Door is about. It's a tease into the group's un-perfect life."

Romeo and Brionna started to become irritated with Peter Manny as he disregarded Romeo's statement.

"Oh, come on. Your lives are too perfect. You all won the lottery when getting signed to Ex-S Records back in 2010. Millions of people all around the world were fighting for those places, but you were the lucky ones to make the final cut. Does this EP, Behind the Door, talk about the dormcest that happens in the famous Switch estate or -"

"It's about nothing but a sneak peek, and we would prefer you do not use the word dormcest," Romeo said, getting heated.

"I apologize for that. Does this album talk about the other relationships in the group, like Vanessa and Toran or your fella Leo and his girl Sam? Lots of speculations right now with the status of those two relationships and –"

"It's Sammatha," Brionna said, offended.

"Sam, Sammatha, same thing," Peter said with no care in the world.

"It's not the same thing," Brionna said.

"Oh, oh, it seems that I have offended a member of Switch. Does this mean I am going to be on the blacklist?"

Brionna looked at Romeo as both looked uncomfortable being there.

"Any answers?" Peter question.

With the most fake smile ever, the two turned to the camera.

"Hi, my name is Romeo. Current lead singer of Switch's Varsity Guys line. Beside me is my lovely wife, Brionna. Say hello, dear."

"Hi there. It's Brionna from the Varsity Girls line. We are healthy and breathing, as we hope you are too."

Peter Manny was so confused as to what was going on.

"We will be dropping our new EP, Behind the Door, tonight

at 11:59 Eastern Standard. We hope you enjoy the songs and truly, Romeo, and I wish you a blessed rest of your night."

Romeo and Brionna took their mini mics off their chests and transmitter before heading off the set.

"Toran, change the channel," Vanessa said.

Without any thought, Toran changed the channel to some badminton game.

Lily slowly stopped playing with Simon's hair as the room got quiet.

She asked, "Is everyone enjoying their perfect lives as members of Switch?"

All eyes turned to her attention. "Cause I haven't heard from my brother since Christmas last year. Not to mention my parents, who I haven't seen since I debuted," Lily said, a little upset.

Jean took a look over at Leo, who seemed resentful.

"If the media wants to run a narrative that we are perfect, stuck-up rockstars, then so be it. Not my problem. I bet if we did some kind of reality TV show, everyone would be saying otherwise," Rebecca said as she took a bite of her wings.

Lily sighed, "If only the public knew. If we could just archive what had happened through the years or even in these last few months alone, the world would know all the reasons why they shouldn't idolize us."

I was intrigued by Lily's comment, as I, the archivist of BFF, am currently recording all of what's happening to the best of my ability. Once everyone goes to bed, I can document all that has happened today, July 31, 2022. Still keeping it a secret from everyone, for I am still determining when I would break the news.

"Flight leaves at 6 a.m. Let's be out of here by five if possible," I said.

Everyone winds down for the evening. The girls shared the two beds while the guys tried their best to find a spot to sleep on the ground. Leo tried to fall asleep but periodically woke up to check up on Sammatha to see if she was okay.

Meanwhile, Jean stayed up the whole night as he rested near Cameron as he held her hand tight the entire night. He drowned himself in Cameron's unreleased music as he kept guard by her side.

In the dark room, he looked out at the Chicago skylines. Closing his eyes, he prayed that he would never return to this city. He then prayed that he never run into Ketrean ever again.

24

08/06/22: A Special Friend.

I was hanging around Jackie when suddenly she got a phone call. I leaned over to see who it was.

I was taken aback a bit when I saw that the caller ID was Theo.

"Hey, Jackie!" I yelled from the living room. Catching her attention from the kitchen, Jackie came out in question. That was when she saw her phone ringing.

She signed a bit as she already knew what he would ask.

"Yes?" Jackie said with an attitude as she answered the call.

"Hey can you meet me at my place in a little bit," Theo asked over the phone. "Yeah...," Jackie said as she glimpsed over at me.

"What's wrong?" I questioned.
Jackie shook her head, signing that nothing was wrong. "I

just need to go... drop something off, that's all," Jackie said, grabbing her purse and walking out to the garage.

"You owe me dinner money then," Jackie said to Theo as she got in the car. "I can do dinner then," he said.

So Jackie was off to Theo's little suburban cottage. She questioned why Theo would call her over to his place when Saige was out of town doing press work for some show she would be guest-starring in. How convenient.

Theo with Jackie feels like a cheat, but he is technically not dating Saige, so free game?

After a 20-minute drive, she arrives at Theo's house. It could not kill him to cut the grass or trim the bushes as they continue to overgrow.

Jackie banged on the door, smacking a pack of gum, frustrated by the humid, cloudy weather. Suddenly she received a phone call from Theo.

"Um, you gonna come to get this door or?" Jackie said, irritated.
    "The door is unlocked. Just make sure to lock it when you get inside," Theo said over the phone. Surely enough, the front door to a mega star's home was unlocked.

Walking inside, the house was dark and tense. Locking the door behind and moving up the stairs, Jackie made her way to Theo's room.

By the way, even though Theo's house looks slightly run-down, he sure does got a pretty view of the landscape in his room. The one place he invested money into.

Theo was on his phone, sitting on his armrest, playing games on his phone. Honestly, he acted like he didn't want to be there.

"Oh, where is the hospitality? I'm a guest, no?" Jackie asked.

Theo laughed a bit, putting his phone down. "Oh please, not now," he said.
  "What? You called me. I also find it funny how the Varsity singer and soloist of Switch leaves his front door unlocked for anyone to walk in. Free of charge," Jackie said, folding her arms.

"The door loc now, so I'm good. We are good," Theo said.

Jackie put her stuff down, and the two started making out though one person was getting too carried away from the action. Jackie stopped for a moment and pulled away.

"Okay, let's stop for a minute. You kiss me like you mean it. Now I strictly said no strings attached," Jackie said.

Theo looked so confused and taken back a bit. "What are you talking about? I am doing nothing out of the norm," Theo said.

Jackie was baffled by his statement. "Well, we can start with meeting up to three times this week. Are you good?" Jackie questioned.

He didn't want to answer the question. Avoiding eye contact, he replied, "Let's just keep kissing, please." Jackie knew something was up but wanted to maintain the mood and vibe.

After a shower, the two sat down to chat.Theo looked over at Jackie and tried to clear his throat. "Sorry about earlier. I just didn't want to explain myself," Theo said sincerely.

Jackie turns to Theo, briefly taking a moment to admire Theo's slight muscular build. Geez anyways. Jackie shifted her focus to Theo's comment.

"You be like, 'Let's get straight to the business.' I prefer that cause most guys just like to take forever. Delay the whole thing for like an hour or... three," Jackie joked.

Theo rolled his eyes and let out a little smile. "Whatever. Well.. the reason why I keep asking you to come over is that Saige and I... Saige and I hooked up a while back. Things were going well, but it went away. I don't know why. Maybe I did something, or maybe she was actually seeing Simon again. As time passed, my adrenaline started to make me go crazy," Theo expressed.

"So you call me to take the high away. You want me to put on a red wig or, even better, dye it?" Jackie joked.

Theo looked at Jackie as her comment peak his interest.

"It was a joke. Technically, I shouldn't even be seeing you in the first place," Jackie said.

"Sorry, the fan-cam edits just make everything worse and -. " Before Theo could continue, Jackie cut him off, changing to a serious tone.

"Okay, Theo. Be honest with me. Why do you still have feelings for Saige? You've been acting funny since you saw Simon and Saige in the studio making out. Do you still love her?" Jackie asked.

Theo's heart started racing, but he didn't want to fold.

"No, no. How can I love her when we are not together. I, um, think it's just random peaks of lust. That's all. I don't want to date anyone. I don't care about Saige's kiss with Simon. Not at all," Theo said.

Jackie smelt cap from the North Pole and back. Theo being jealous is not a good look. No point in asking more questions.

25

08/07/22: "Tone it down", they asked.

Dice and Rebecca have had a change of lifestyle. Not all lovey dubby on each other, if I may say indeed. It was something that many members started to notice as the days passed by. No longer was anyone fearing walking into a room to be scared of witnessing Dice and Rebecca making out in the most gruesome, explicit way possible.

When practices happen, Dice and Rebecca are not skipping. No more "sick days" rain checks. I had the excellent ole secret keeper, Leo, check up on Dice to see what that was all about.

"Hey Valen, I talked to Dice," Leo said, coming down the stairs.

Oh, do I appreciate him for his service as a secret keeper at times. Makes my life as an internal BFF leader ten times easier. I put my journal down to take a break from writing and followed Leo to Studio A.

"So, according to Dice, Rebecca had received a comment from a random old lady online. It read in quotes, 'Need to tone it down.' It was from that one post Dice and Rebecca took. I guess the comment made her more self-conscious about their sex addiction habits," Leo said.

I knew what post he was talking about too.

"The one where they are being a little too intimate," I questioned. Leo nodded his head.

Dice and Rebecca are known as the dirty dancing couple because of their stage presence. They always make out on stage and in some random room at any request and demand. Though recently, it has gotten out of control since the COVID restrictions have been lifted. They no longer limited the kissing from inside the main house but out to the public eye in a more careless approach.

"Well, I don't want Rebecca to feel judged for her actions," I said.

Leo pulled out his phone and scrolled through her feed. There he noticed that many of her more skin-revealing pictures were taken down. Same for Dice. No more thirst trap selfies and after-the-showers pictures. Leo handed me his phone.

"There has to be over 3/4th of his feed just gone. Millions of likes just missing," Leo said.

He was right. There was so much stuff missing. And...oh, um...

"Hear your phone," I said, handing Leo back his phone.

I saw that Sammatha sent him a text message and immediately had to hand it over before I read something that would give me jump scares. I don't know what those two be talking about, and I prefer it stayed that way.

"So what are you going to do about this? My job as secret keeper is done, which I should not be telling this anyways, but since it's technically a check-up, I will let this one pass," Leo said.

I gave it a thought before coming to my conclusion: "I will let them figure it out. Best to not have anyone point out their lifestyle change. It was rather unhealthy anyway. Though Leo, can you make sure your friend Jean doesn't take too much notice of his sister. The last thing I want to hear is his smart Alex comments and adding more wood to the fire"

Leo agreed, and after our chat, we decided to head out of the studio and part ways. Before leaving, Leo stopped by the doorway.

"With all this talking and conflict I deal with it as a secret keeper. I think I deserve a raise," Leo smirked. I laughed at his comment.

"Uh yea, a raise. What? You want a promotion for your service," I questioned.

"Yes, and the only next promotion that would be fitting for a new and improved job description would be," Leo stopped in his words, hoping I finish the sentence.

"A BFF leader?" "You said it, not me, Valen," Leo said.

I wonder if Leo would really want to be a BFF leader. Yes, it's been a rumor there is a new position being added to the leadership team, specifically to becoming a BFF leader or an internal leader like myself. Is Leo that guy?

"Being a BFF leader is a lot of work. Plus... there are some things you need to work out before you want to run...to be a candidate," I said, trying to not come off in any wrong way. Though Leo knew what I was talking about.

I mean, he is a secret keeper for a reason. He got a lot of internal work that he needs to deal with first. Mentally and emotionally.He has tons of excellent public relations, though. But that to the public eye. Out here in BFF's house, he got a resume. Some good, some bad, and some ugly. Just when you forget the past, Maxwell comes in to remind everyone about all of Leo's sins.

Meanwhile, in Dice and Rebecca's room, the two were lying down watching TV in their room. The show didn't matter; they mainly wanted something that would distract them from thinking about lustful things. One minute they were addicted to sex, and now it's celibacy. As Dice held Rebecca, he could not stop thinking about breaking their terms and agreements.

"Do we have practice tomorrow," Rebecca said softly as she broke the silence.
   Dice trying to not make eye contact with her, said, "I believe so. I will be heading down to the dance room later tonight to practice. Of course, I must work overtime hours to get the

dances down right."

"You will get it down. I'll join you tonight. I need to practice my routines too for JV," Rebecca said.

Dice looks down at her.

"What, Dice? We can practice together without... you know. We will be fine. We need to take the right steps to have a better, more healthy life, right," she said.

26

08/11/22: It might be something called love.

It was a chill day for everyone. No practice but rather a day to do whatever you want. What do the members of Switch typically do during their free time?

Some would try to write yet another song, play around in the studio, or visit the Big Apple. Get nosy and mess around; you might find a member's car at the Switch Stadium.

Everyone is off doing their own thing. Yes, most of the group lives together, but that doesn't mean we spend every minute together.

As the leader of the house, I usually know where everyone is except for the Maknae Line. They are nowhere to be found, and I typically don't search for them.

Suddenly I hear a knock on my bedroom door. I sighed and

rolled my eyes because who DARES ruin my peace and quiet time. Putting down my pen and leaving my bed, I opened my door.

It was the one and only Romeo.

"Were you sleeping," he asked.
    Even though I was still in my pajamas and had a bonnet on, I was wide awake.

"No, no, just...relaxing," I said. Spoiler alert I was not relaxing, mindlessly scrolling on social media but writing in the group journal. (The days before everyone found out. It was much less detailed than the final draft released to the public. Everyone and their significant other wanted all the details added to the archives, hence the version you are reading right now.)

"Have you seen Mazen and Alanna? I know they are some-where in this house, but I can never find them," Romeo said.
    "They are probably in the Maknae lounge," I said.
    "Great, I have to wait for them to get out now. That could be aged. They are probably watching some movie marathon," he said.

Romeo sighed, checking his phone for the time. "I can't stay long; I need to pick up Junior from school. Might as well head back to town," he said, a little upset.

"Is this about the whole song you wanted to produce for them," I asked. Suddenly Romeo's phone rang. Poor soul got excited, thinking it was Mazen calling him, but it was a scammer.

"Great," he sighed.

A door opened down the hallway; it was Dice leaving his room. Romeo and I looked over and waved to him.

"Hey, Dice, make sure you go outside today and get some Vitamin D," I shouted from the other end of the hall.

"No," he yelled back, heading downstairs.

Romeo was thrown back by the quick response, "What's wrong with him."

I re-shifted my focus back to Romeo, "He has been spending all his free time in the dance studio downstairs. Should have seen his reaction when he saw we needed to learn that new routine for the VVMAs performance," I said. Romeo was puzzled. "Wait, but that show is in a month from now. Surely he has enough time to get it down," Romeo said.

"The performance is September 2nd. He will get it down," I said.

Need to mention that there are four versions to remember. It will come down to the wire to see which one actually gets to perform, and when you are someone like Dice, trying to work up to becoming a lead singer, someone gotta put that leg work in.

"Well, if you see Mazen, Alanna, or even Kyan and Asia, tell them to call me. We got to eventually work on the next album, and I would like to get a head start on it," Romeo said.

Will they call? Probably not. Romeo would have better luck waiting till the next practice to pop the question. Mans has to schedule an appointment. I mean, come on. It's the Maknae Line. They are very much a pro at moving around in the shadows. Their lounge is literally behind two hidden doors.

Though, to my surprise or not, Mazen and Alanna were indeed in the Maknae secret lair lounge. There the two were alone watching TV.

The two were sharing a couch as Alanna lay next to Mazen.

"Mazen, stop playing around and watch the show, okay," Alanna laughs as she grabs the remote from him.
   "Of course, you don't want to watch something more entertaining than a rerun of my old shows," Mazen said as he cringed at his acting performance. The glory days when Mazen would get thrown into a random sitcom for an episode or two to help boost the ratings.

"Okay, fine, let's change the channel then," Alanna said,

putting on a movie, whereLeo was co-starring in. "Oh look, I know that guy," Alanna laughed. Mazen shook his head.

DING!

"Who is that," Alanna said as she watched Mazen reach for his phone.

"25 text messages. One from my mother and the rest from Romeo," Mazen jokes. Mazen stomachs up, and he finally decides to call Romeo.

"Aye, man, where are you?" Romeo said over the phone.

"I am at the house. Where are you? By the way, you are on the speaker," Mazen responds.

"Leaving the house now. I mean, it seems like you and Alanna don't want to work on this song I have for you guys. A chance for you to break away from that kiddish pop sound Maknae Line keeps getting trapped into," Romeo said.

Alanna and Mazen sat up, looking at each other. "Hey Romeo, it's not that we don't want to work on the song, just not right now... I mean, there's really no talk about another album in progress, and Maknae line isn't interested in...working right now," Mazen said.

Alanna also grabs the phone to put her two cents in, "I agree with Mazen. Maknae Line doesn't want to spend our free days in the studio. Though once the time comes around for the next album, Mazen and I will be down to work on something. You have my promise."

Mazen looked at Alanna in awareness . Romeo took their words.

"See, wasn't that too hard. Communicate instead of avoiding confrontation," Romeo said before hanging up.

Alanna tried laying back down but noticed Mazen was not following the same action as her. "Uh hey, my neck needs support. I need a pillow to rest," Alanna said as she rubbed her neck.

Mazen laid down and allowed her to rest on him as they continued to watch TV. Mazen is still shocked by Alanna's response. Working on a song together? Why didn't she include Kyan and Asia in the package? Alanna wants to do a duet with him.

The two continue watching TV when suddenly the door opens. Asia and Kyan came into the den with snacks. "You two look comfortable," Kyan said. Jumping from their seats, Mazen and Alanna separated like nothing happened. Alanna was baffled by the comment as she went to the bar for refreshments.

To her surprise, the refrigerator was relatively empty.

"Oh, that's why you have all these bags," Alanna questioned.

"Yes, girl, plus a sale was going on at the grocery store. By one, get one free on the cranberry juice. We got cran-grape, cran-apple, cran-mango, and cran-orange," Asia said as she pulled out the drinks individually.

"I think I'm on grocery shopping duty next month," Mazen sighed, walking over to Kyan.

"Oh, you will be fine. Definitely not hard trying to get enough groceries for 29 people who all want very niche ingredients from different regions in the world," Kyan laughed, patting Mazen's back. Three taps on the back, to be specific.

Mazen mouth over, "What's wrong?"

"Hey, we will be right back. I think I left a bag in the car," Kyan said, signaling Mazen to follow. So the two walk out of the lounge and head toward not the garage but the other hidden door next to the garage. A place we like to call "The Hall of Fame" room. One of the most private places to talk.

It is a decent size narrow hallway room filled with all the member's awards, platinum, diamond plaques, and other prize possessions. Each member has one display full of their individual awards though some members have a lot more than others, like Brittany, who won many awards for her 2013 solo album. At the end of the walkway, there are the group's awards. Mainly filled with an album of the year awards and diamond plaques covering the tall red-painted walls.

Mazen and Kyan sat down on the little steps near the group's table of winnings.

"What was it you wanted to talk about? Are you having relationship problems with Asia?" Mazen asked.
Kyan chuckled a bit under his breath.

"Actually, we are doing really well. Minus the whole keep it a secret from the rest of the world aspect, I have been trying to find different unique ways to have dates without it coming off like we are together to the public eye. However, I wanted to talk about you. Mazen, you seemed really comfortable with Alanna laying on you when I entered the lounge. You over here cheesing when she starts talking," Kyan said.

"What are you saying We are just friends. It's okay to like your friends," Mazen said.
"Oh, but like might not be the word. It might be something called love," Kyan nudged. Mazen refuses to accept that as the answer to his feelings for Alanna.

"Are you feeling the FOMO? Fear of missing out on dating and finding a partner? I know you're against dating anyone, but you might have feelings for Alanna. When you perform any love songs, do you think of her? I know I think of Asia, and the rest of the guys think of their lady," Kyan said.

Mazen shrugged in defeat, "I am not sure, to be honest. I think the more love songs I sing, the more I associate Alanna as the girl I'm singing to. But only because she is my dance partner."

"Well, just in mind when you see her. I don't want you to go down the rabbit hole that some of the members are in right now," Kyan said, getting up. Kyan reached out and helped Mazen up as well.

"Wait, Kyan... what rabbit hole," Mazen questioned.

"It's all alleged, but it sounded like many friends of benefits were going on with some of the older members. Didn't hear it from me, but I think I saw Saige and Simon making out in his car. Saw it in the garage when heading out to the grocery store. But you didn't hear it from me."

27

08/12/22: It's a different kind of feeling. Part I

Toran was coming down the stairs early in the morning to get breakfast. How kind was it that Brionna, Saige, and Jackie decided to help make breakfast for everyone. Because they didn't, though, they cooked some food for themselves.

"Good morning," Jackie said, trying to flip a pancake. Poor Toran was out here rubbing his hands together. Reaching over, he tried to grab a pancake, "Good morning to you all."

Saige, though, blocked his hand before he could catch a piece.

"Absolutely not Toran. We are cooking for ourselves," Saige said, grabbing a plate. Toran grinned in defeat.

"You're up here pretty early," Toran said to Brionna.

"Well, I didn't feel like being all cramped up at my house.

Junior is back in school, and Romeo went out of town today to do an interview. That leaves me with some free time with the girls to spend some time together," Brionna said as she cooked her some eggs.

Toran walked over to the calendar that was placed by the refrigerator. Looking through the dates, he located August 12th.

"Yeah, I guess he is supposed to be in Atlanta for an interview. Didn't want to tag along?" Toran questioned.

Brionna laughed a bit at Toran's irrational comment.

"And who is going to pick up Junior? Especially on a Friday. I do not want to travel to Brittany's place or LeeSung's little brownstone in Manhattan to pick up my kid. Again, especially on a Friday. Plus after that Late Night Show interview, I am not interested in doing anymore press work," she said.

In came Vanessa. "Good morning," she said, walking to the pantry to grab cereal and an orange. Toran felt a little awkward seeing her. He was still hooked up on the idea that she might be cheating on him.

"Hey Toran can you come here," Vanessa said, calling him to the pantry.

In shock, he walked around the island counter, to the large, walk-in pantry that was slightly cluttered... Sounds like someone didn't care to organize the place, Kyan and Asia...

Vanessa turned around and was reasonably happy to see Toran. Especially when they don't talk as much as they used to.

"Have you eaten yet? Want some Crunch-Os Cereal?" she asked, holding the box. Toran smirked a bit, daydreaming about giving Vanessa a big hug in front of everyone. Still, the feeling that someone might be loving her hurt him inside.

Before he could say anything, Dice, full of energy, entered the kitchen. "GOOD MORNING," Dice shouted.

"Looks like someone woke up on the good side of the bed," Vanessa said to Toran. Toran smiled a bit, trying to mask the urge to ask Vanessa about what happened on her hiatus.

"I will eat later. I am not hungry right now," he said. Vanessa was taken back a bit, "Don't want to eat before practice? It's supposed to be a long day today."

Toran reassured her he would be fine. As the two left the pantry, Toran signaled to Dice that he wanted to talk somewhere private.

"Pity you all didn't cook me a piece of bacon. Or save me a biscuit," Dice said to Brionna, Saige, and Jackie. Walking backward, Dice and Toran left the kitchen and headed to the dance practice studio. Passing the three recording studios, the two went into Practice Room One. They proceeded in when they noticed it was preoccupied with Varsity Guys practicing.

"Let's just go to the other one," Dice said. So they went into the smaller practice room across from Studio C, and luckily, no one was there.

Going in, lock-in the door, Dice was curious about why Toran wanted to talk, hitting him with the classic Switch phrase, "What's wrong?"

Dice started practicing some of the VVMAs routines as he waited for Toran to respond, but then he realized that the guy was taking too long to say something. Looking through the tall, floor-to-ceiling mirror, he saw that Toran was upset. Slowly he stopped dancing and sat on the floor.

"Sit," he requested. So Toran followed the lead.
"What is on your mind," Dice asked. Finally building some courage and confidence, Toran spilled.

"I think Vanessa cheated on me," he said.
Dice was in disbelief. "Cheating??? What makes you think that? Why do you even say 'think'?" Dice questioned.

"Well, she one day packed it up and left, going on a month hiatus. And during that time, I got a tip from someone that she was seeing another celebrity," Toran said.
"Who is the guy?" Dice, still not believing the accusation.

Toran pulled out his phone and showed the messages he received from his Instagrand private messages to Dice.

"I don't know who the guy is. Definitely not an A-lister. She probably got the contact from Jackie. Though, why would Vanessa go hook up with another guy? What did I do? Did I do something wrong?" Toran said.

Dice didn't know what to say as he read through the messages. Deep down, he knew that Toran had been a bit closed off since the day the group went independent from Ex-S Records.

Not to mention Toran turning down a duet project he was supposed to do last year with Dice. Though because of that turndown, Dice got his own solo album. 10 tracks that would raise Dice to a new level of popularity with the public.

However, Toran does not care about Dice's recent solo discography because he was one of the lead songwriters for all of Dice's works and didn't want to perform them.

"Toran, I think you should try talking to Vanessa about this. Cheating is a serious accusation, and this random netizen, mentioning this to you on Instagrand, is not worth getting all work up about. I feel like if Vanessa did cheat on you, someone else in the group would know. I mean, I can ask Rebecca if she knows anything about it," Dice suggested.

"No, that won't be necessary. I'll just let time unfold everything," Toran said.

Dice looked up and was amazed at how time works. "Well, I

guess the unfold starts now, then," Dice pointed to the glass door. There it was, Vanessa, and it seemed like she wanted to talk.

Dice got up to unlock the door and allowed Vanessa to come in. "Hey, Dice. Um, Toran could we talk later today after practice," she shyly said.

After a long day of practice, Toran met with Vanessa in the movie room to talk.

"Sorry, I'm late. We went a little overtime," Toran said, closing the door behind him. Vanessa's arms were folded as she rested on the side of one of the lounge chairs.

"Um. Toran. Are we good? I know I took off without a word back in May, but ever since I came back, it has been surface level," she said, a little worried.

Toran looked at her, not fully understanding what to say. Should he pull out his "receipts"? For all he knows, they could be fake or real.

"It must be the stress I have been going through. There's just a lot going on with preparation for the weekend live shows and the hundred other performances we got to do."

Vanessa was not a big fan of the word stress. "But you know you can talk to me about anything, right?" she said, grabbing his hand. Toran looked into Vanessa's starry eyes and was confused by everything. He could tell she was holding back something, too, but what was it?

28

08/12/22: It's a different kind of feeling. Part II

Down the hallway from the movie room was the office where Xan had been camping all day.

"What are you doing?" Lisa said, coming into the room.

Pulling up a chair to Xan's grand, messy bureau, she watched Xan finish some paperwork.

"Well, I finished booking some performances for next year. How was practice," he said, avoiding eye contact with Lisa.

"Well, everything went perfectly. Everyone is on track to being ready for the VVMAs show. Though it is worth mentioning that many of the member's minds are wandering all over the place. I suggested that we might need to schedule fewer practice days and create more mental health days," Lisa said..

"Their minds are wandering because they are probably hiding

something and don't want to be caught and exposed," Xan said, pulling up his notebook.

"The relationship book?" Lisa questioned.

"Yes, the relationship book. See here, Lily likes Simon, but Simon also likes Saige, right. So you have Simon and Saige do a song together like Universe and then have Lily perform solo right afterward. We get a top, highly performative yet emotional show and more market share in the music scene. But practice is where all that tension builds up and –"

Xan paused when he looked up and saw that Lisa was laughing. Tears coming out of her eyes. "Oh, my goodness, Xan. You and your fan-fiction lore. I am sure your system works; rather toxic to pull strings on the members, but geez." Lisa could not stop laughing, which contagious made Xan laugh a bit, putting the journal away.

"Oh Xan, you are taking these notes. Like, why don't you just date someone," Lisa asked, wiping away her tears. Though it was pointless because she couldn't stop laughing. Xan watched her laugh her soul off when he randomly started admiring her. Glazing at her silky black hair and mocha brown skin, he works his way to her smile, destination to her eyes.

"Haha, yeah, who's gonna want to date me, THEE Alexander," Xan said, looking down at his desk. "Someone," Lisa said, getting her laugh under control. Xan smiled, looking up at Lisa as the two locked eyes.

Suddenly, Lisa leans in closer to Xan. That was when Xan started to go into panic mode. "Your glasses are so dirty, Xan," she said, grabbing his big wide-frame lens. She breathed some air into the lens and then used her shirt to clean them up.

"Here," she said, putting them back on for him.
Xan was speechless.

Lisa and Xan work very closely with each other and have been for many years. Though all they do is work, Xan is at a more extreme workaholic level. So busy, on purpose, to the point that has he ever sat down and had a crush on anyone? Anyone? Real or fake? An actual human or even an anime character. He was so hooked on other people's relationships that he forgot he could have one for himself.

29

08/19/22: Can't explain.

"Hey Theo, have you seen Xan," Lisa asked, walking into the living room. He was on his phone as usual, unaware that Lisa was even talking to him.

"Theo!" Lisa sighed, trying to get his attention.

"I haven't seen him at all today. It's his day off anyways," he said, glued to his phone. Lisa observed Theo, noting that he sat on a specific part of the couch where no one could see what he was looking at. She watched him twiddle his fingers as it looked like he was texting someone.

"Who are you talking to?" Lisa asked, curious.
   Theo looked up and quickly turned off his phone.
   "No one," he said nervously as he got up.

"Better not be on your burner account catfishing people," she said as Theo walked her.

186

He ignored her, which showed that he might have been doing just that. Lisa walked over in front of Theo to stop him in his place.

"I'm serious. Your track record is getting too long, and I can't keep covering up your errors, okay," Lisa said, concerned.

"That's why you take more money out of my paycheck. Bigger payday for you," Theo said.
   "Bigger payday for me, but this is part of why Saige dumped you. Spend more time roleplaying with internet personas, then see what is right in front of you."

Theo, in denial, refuses to acknowledge the truth that Lisa spilled to him.
   "If you need me, I will be at my house," Theo said, grabbing his keys from the coffee table.

"Where Xan?" Lisa sighed in frustration.

At the end of the hallway in the right wing, upstairs, to be precise, was Xan's room. His room is in front of LeeSung's and Romeo/Brionna's old room, so he got a little privacy since those rooms can be unoccupied most of the time.

Even though upstairs is usually dark because no one wants to turn on the hallway light, Xan's room is even darker. It is a mundane and gloomy feel with a poor style of smokey gray on his wall.

Xan sat at the edge of his bed, completely zoned out. A week passed, and Xan couldn't stop thinking about Lisa. I mean, during the live stream on Monday, he refuses to stand next to her for longer than 30 seconds. Though at the same time, he was so stressed with the upcoming VVMAs performance.

Xan glanced at his digital clock and noticed it was 2pm. "I should probably get some fresh air. Maybe a drive could clear my head," Xan said to himself.

Getting up, he walked over to his dresser mirror and tried to comb his hair back. Once at satisfaction, he went over to his bedside table where his clock was and grabbed his glasses. Though he paused in admiration about when Lisa cleaned them for him.

Leaving his room, Xan was cautious to not run into anyone, including Lisa, as he walked past her room. He slowly descended the stairs and peeped to see if anyone was in the living room. The coast was clear, so he rushed to the garage and down to his car. Once again, no member really owes a vehicle that would be nearly a hundred thousand dollars. Xan probably gets one of the biggest checks in the group and owes a very average, mid-tier car.

Luckily the garage was empty today. When Xan gets a day off, many of the house's residents run down to Brooklyn or Long Island so that Xan can have peace and quiet. Also, so their presence doesn't remind him of work, which could lead to a last-minute schedule practice.

Leaving Hidden Estates, Xan drove to the small town near

the house. Stopping by a fast food drive-thru he bought him some fries, then pulled up to a random small outlet center parking lot to find some alone time. Parked in the back, Xan ate his fries silently, still trying to clear his head.

The thought of having feelings made him uncomfortable, and it only grew as the heat from the sunbeam into the car.

Looking at his rearview mirror, he noticed a store named Daisy's. Xan looked at it in confusion and anxiousness, as the store's name was familiar to him. It was warned by the group to stay away from Daisy's. Though with the stress of work and his uncomfortable feeling of Lisa getting in the way of his focus, he couldn't resist. His palms began to sweat, and his throat started to itch. He felt a dark spirit of energy cave into him as he looked at the store's name when suddenly, Xan was back in his mundane, gloomy room.

Xan looked around his room in confusion. How did he get back? Did he ever leave? Looking over at the floor, he saw a flimsy bag lying by his dresser.

KNOCK KNOCK KNOCK KNOCK...KNOCK!

Xan looked at his door, then back at the bag, then back at the door. Getting up, he quickly kicks the bag into his closet in panic and slightly opens his door.

"Sorry to bother you. Mazen and I were wondering if we could sing lead for the next stream," Kyan said.
 "Lead for the group, not on a varsity guys' song," Mazen

clarified.

Xan was not interested in rationalizing that the two barely wanted to perform last stream. Now, they want to act like a superstar for the next show.

"Sure, just make sure you know the songs we will be doing. They should be on my desk in the office or in the production room," Xan said.

"Awesome, thanks, man," Kyan chirped. The two walked away, but Xan randomly called out to them. "Wait..."
   Xan, rubbing the side of the head, hesitated on whether or not he should ask.

"Hey, could you guys get Leo. I need to talk to him about music," he continued. Kyan and Mazen agreed to do so and sought to find him.

After searching, they found him in the hidden lounge writing some songs on his tablet. "Hey, Leo. Xan wants to talk to you," Mazen said.

"What does he want," Leo questioned. Kyan shrugged, "I don't know. He said in the quotes,'Hey could you get Leo. I need to talk to him about music."
   Leo didn't understand that request, "Music on his day off?"

A few moments passed, and Xan suddenly heard three knocks on his door.
   He took a double look at his closet before going to his door.

"Come inside," Xan said. Leo proceeded to wonder what Xan wanted to talk about. Shutting the door, Xan kept rubbing his head.

"How were you able to date Sammatha? What is the secret? How do you even get into a relationship," Xan blurted out. Leo folded his arms in disbelief. Xan asking for relationship advice rather than about the current state of the economy.

"Uh, well...it's a very complicated story that I'm sure you know. The story told to the public...and the one real story," Leo said uncomfortably. Xan pauses in his pacing as he indeed knows the real story of what happened in 2018. It was the most controversial thing to happen that year. It wasn't no 'Oh my goodness, you too are dating!!!' excitement. It was an "Oh my goodness, you too can't be dating. What is going on?" Let's just say everyone was in extreme shock.

Leo had a bad reputation within the group, and how we leaders and Maxwell discovered their relationship in Miami was interesting. Started from the bottom now we here, right? They came a long way, but that's beside the point.

"If you want to be in a relationship, try starting by being yourself. Separate the music and work from your personal life. If I had to be honest, you have been drowning yourself heavily since we ended our contracts with Ex-S Records. Because of that, maybe you have been scaring off potential girlfriends?" Leo said.

Xan shook his head. "Be me. I could have searched that up if

I wanted that answer."

Leo saw that Xan kept looking at his closet. "Why do you keep looking in that direction, and why are you so tense up," Leo asked. Xan looked at him, wondering if Leo had caught on to what was in the bag.

In the BFF house, a ban list is not allowed on the premise. This includes liquor, weed, cigarettes, drugs, vape pens, etc. Even caffeine coffee can be a problem from time to time. Did Xan bring in a banned item? I mean, he has been so tensed up for a while.

"It's nothing," Xan lied, showing Leo to the door. "Well, is there someone you like?" he said, walking out. "No, I don't like anyone. But she's in the group if you're curious," Xan spilled out.

Off the corner of his eye, Xan saw Dice leaving the bathroom. "Hey, Dice, I want to show you some new beats I've been working on," he said. Leo laughed a bit and walked away.

"What were you two talking about?" Dice said in a lower voice to Leo as the two passed by. "Just music," Leo said, trying to keep his cool.

In Xan's room, Dice wondered what Xan wanted to talk about when he froze. Xan had handed his mystery bag over, and Dice was shocked to see what was inside. "Um, I didn't know what to do with it," Xan said nervously.

"So you read my files. Amazing. Then you must know I don't

dabble in this stuff anymore," Dice said, handing back the bag. Xan, feeling hopeless, didn't even know why he bought this. I don't understand why he goes to that ghost town anyways, messes around, and gets sucked into another scary path.

"I figure you would be a good consultant about this stuff," Xan said. Dice couldn't believe Xan. "Since you read my file, you must have known where to buy this stuff. My mind is blown; Alexander Davi Oliveira wants to get high on crack. Is this what you told Leo?" Dice said, concerned.

"Hey!!! This... this is not crack," Xan said, trying to not raise his voice. "It's just as addicting. Poking needles into your arm is not fun, is it," Dice clapped back.

Dice looked over at Xan and saw that he was really tense.
   "I just need something to relax me. That's all. With all this work going on and–"
   "Xan, there is no AND. If you stress out, take a walk or hire an external team. But you skipped about seven options and thought injections were the way to go????"

"Just show me how to use it," Xan asked. Dice could see the desperation in Xan's eyes. "Show me. Just show me how," he demanded.
   Dice refused to and took the bag out of the room. Xan followed behind him as he saw Dice approach Simon's room. Without even knocking thrice, Dice went inside his room.

"Woah, wait a minute. What going on," Simon said in shock as he sat in bed.

Xan watches Dice in a rush and hands over the bag of needles to Simon.

"Were you behind this?" Dice questioned.

Simon looked inside the bag and was shocked by the needles in there.

"Are these yours? This must have cost a fortune," Simon said in shock.

"It's not mine. It's Xan's'," Dice said.

Just before Xan could defend himself, Lily came out of the bathroom wrapped in a towel and her hair wet. Looking up, she was in sheer embarrassment.

"What are you doing here?" Xan questioned Lily.

"My shower doesn't work... What's going on?" Lily questions.

"Nothing is going on. Dice, it was a joke. I will throw them in the trash, okay," Xan said.

"I will throw them away. I didn't spend a year in rehab just so another group member could get hooked. LIKE, ARE YOU KIDDING ME, XAN! YOU'RE THE ONE WHO MADE THE BANNED LIST IN THE FIRST PLACE!"

"You act like I'm not able to have errors in my life," Xan said.

Simon got out of his bed in hopes of calming down the situation.

"Hey, Xan. All he is trying to do is prevent this error because it doesn't need to happen. Right, Dice?"

"Right."

"I'm going to go," Lily said as she dismissed herself.

"I'm sorry," Xan said as he leaned against the wall.
   "It's fine. Just promise me you won't-"
   "I won't," Xan said, interrupting Dice.

Xan, in shame, left Simon's room. Leaving the two alone.
   "Knock next time," Simon requested.

Xan didn't leave his room as he was too ashamed to show his face to anyone. The sun was setting, and dinner time had passed. It wasn't until around 9pm when he finally left his room to come downstairs to get some ice water. Passing the main living room, Dice was chilling on the couch when he noticed Xan had come out of hiding. Rushing over to the kitchen, Dice went to check on him.

"Hey...." Dice said.
   Xan didn't seem interested in talking to Dice as he poured a drink but, to some level, couldn't help to thank Dice for helping him out.
   "I just don't want to see you ruin your life and reputation," Dice said.

Leo walked into the kitchen and was intrigued to see Xan and Dice. "Talking about music or someone special," Leo said. Dice didn't know what the second thing Leo was talking about. Xan signals for the two to follow him across the kitchen to the patio.

"Someone special?" Dice questioned. Leo then realizes that

Xan had a completely different conversation with Dice. "Oh nothing, I meant-" Xan cut off Leo as he knew he had to tell someone about his emotions instead of bottling it up all inside.

"I do like someone. And she is in the group," Xan said, glaring at the floor. Dice was just getting hit with back-to-back news updates from Xan's life.

"Wait, she has not taken a right," Leo asked.

"No, No," Xan clarified. Dice started doing the math in his head.

"I doubt you like anyone from Maknae Line, so that means you like someone from JV. Is it Jackie? Lily? I mean, Vanessa might be free in a month or so. There was also Saige and -" Dice was about to continue until he saw that Xan and Leo were looking at him funny.

"What do you mean Vanessa might be free in a month?" Xan asked.

Dice looked at him, realizing he slipped up some information that should have stayed private. "Delete what I just said, okay. You should talk to the rest of the guys about this. It couldn't hurt to open up instead of spending all your time alone. Might mess around and do something that you might regret," Dice said, battering his eye at Xan.

Suddenly there was a loud sound of thunder. "Let's go back inside," Leo said.

"Agree. My fro is getting bigger and bigger with all this

humidity," Dice said, trying to compress his hair.

Inside they went. "Where are all the guys at? Maybe I should spend more time with them," Xan asked.

"Everyone is in the hidden lounge playing video games and cards. Though Varsity Guys are having an insanely long round of poker,," Leo said.

"I guess I could join as well," Dice said.

As they leave the kitchen to the hallway, Xan asks Dice, "What were you doing earlier?"

Dice scratch the back of the head. A little shocked by what he was doing. "I was reading a book I found lying around."

Before Xan could ask what the book was, he paused when he saw Lisa walking in his direction.

"What are y'all doing?" Xan's eye's lit up as he was not ready to see her, especially after what happened earlier that day. Noticing Xan's delayed reaction, Dice chimes in.

"We are going to go hang out in the hidden lounge. Plus, we were talking earlier about maybe proposing the idea to paint some of the rooms for a change in scenery," Dice said.

Xan smiled a bit but then fled to the wall, pushing a spot to reveal the secret hallway leading to the lounge. "He was just excited to play some poker. Good big or go home," Leo said.

30

08/20/22: Truth be told... Part I

It was a rainy day today and very foggy as well. We had some light filming to accomplish in the quiet countryside of New York. B-Roll content for concert transitions.

Dice and Toran were overlooking the field on the top of a hill. Toran seems like he really can't get over Vanessa and that dang cheating allegation. It has been exactly two months since she returned from Virginia, and he still hasn't brought it up.

So she took a hiatus to visit some family. I doubt she was hooking up with anyone.

"Toran, fix your face. We are around outsiders. Can't let anyone draw any suspicion," Dice said as a worker passed by.

Toran was very moody and gave off an energy that he didn't want to be there.
   "Why should I care," he said.

"Dude, we can't even confirm she actually cheated. You got a message from some random anti-fan with some potentially 'too good to be true' tip. Plus, how reliable is Jackie's contact list? Just filled with a whole bunch of gold-digging guys. I mean, there's a reason why Lisa, Xan, or Valen don't even consider anyone from her network to come near the group," Dice said, and he was so over it.

"Dice, there is no point anymore. I don't want to talk about it right now."

The two walk down the hill and over to the filming site. Then came Mazen, ready to troll, "Dice and Toran, it's a pleasure to meet you both. I will be your videographer today, and I already see the vision for how the picture will come out. Shouldn't you two be with your ladies? Where are they?"

"Where yours?" Dice clapped back.

"Funny, real comedic," Mazen said.

"We were actually going to the wardrobe," Dice said as he tugged Toran into the tents. As the two walked away, Dice quickly turned around and began signing to Mazen.

"Don't bring up relationship talk around Toran."

Mazen was confused. "Why?" he signed back.

Dice shrugged his shoulders, "Just don't, okay."

Dice then turned around and headed into the tent. Mazen sighed and proceeded to walk over to the wardrobe.

The outfit of the day was old money, boarding school uni- forms. A classic outfit that we usually wear for big perfor- mances. Because we have worn that style since we were tweens, fans still associate us with this look. Though the colors were Beige, forest green, and black, it was not the same outfit as the signature. Thank goodness, cause we are in public.

"Lisa, sorry that we're late, traffic," Toran said, walking over to Lisa.

"Not a problem," she said, walking toward him. She pulled him to the side as her demeanor changed.

In a low voice, "Toran, did you and Vanessa break up?"

"I don't want to talk about it actually," he said.

"Well, that's fine. But for clarification -".

Toran interrupted Lisa,

"Yes, I want my b-rolls to be solo."

Lisa didn't understand.

"You realize that you texted me last minute saying you don't want to do your b-roll with Vanessa could lead to only one meaning: you two aren't together anymore. I mean, does she even know?" Lisa said, concerned.

Looking over Toran's shoulder, Lisa saw Vanessa. "I'll ask if SHE is okay doing her b-roll alone. Because it looks like there is a lack of communication between you two, and I'm not going to sit here and let it go on any longer," Lisa said.

"Vanessa!"

Toran's heart sank as his anxiety level rose.

"Vanessa... are you solo?" Lisa asked.

Vanessa's face turned red as she was so heartbroken. To hear those words had to be so heart-wrenching. "Is this why you have been avoiding me!?! You're breaking up with me!" Vanessa said, trying to hold back her tears.

All eyes turned as Xan quickly pulled out his walkie-talkie, demanding all the workers to leave immediately to the alternative filming site. I was over at my little makeup stand, confused about what was happening. Clearly, the good ole

BFF leader was not doing her job of handling this situation. I shot up from my seat and looked to see what was happening.

"What the actually F Toran?!? I took a month-long hiatus, and you want to break up!"

"You're the one who cheated," Toran finally says.

Vanessa was baffled by Toran's words.

"I didn't. Ha, I definitely didn't cheat. Why did you think I took that hiatus in the first place!?!"

Silence filled the room. Everyone was looking at each other; honestly, no one knew why Vanessa took that hiatus.

"What happened in Los Angeles Toran?" Vanessa said seriously.

Cameron was sitting on Jean's lap when she noticed his eyes were wide open. All the guys looked at each other, trying to remember what happened in Los Angeles. Though the memory started returning as some of the guys looked at their girl in full shame.

Romeo was sitting down at his station, trying to piece together everything. "Miami? Like last May, Miami?" Romeo whispered over to Theo. "We didn't go to Miami in May. We were in Los Angeles, man. Keep up. Which, by the way, what happened in LA that I missed?" Theo said, confused.

That was when Romeo's memory hit him like a tidal wave.

Immediately he rushed over to Toran's side. "Vanessa, whatever you hear or saw about the Diaomond Club, it's probably a misunderstanding," Romeo said.

Brittany was even more confused by the situation and hit Carlos's arm. "So that night when you came back late, it was apparently the strip club?"
Kyan and Mazen were in awe on the other side of the tent. "They went to the strip club without us," Kyan whispered to Mazen.

Toran was the most speechless as his memory returned to him.

31

05/10/22: Truth be told... Part II

"Okay, where are we going, boys," Theo said, drunk. "Where real men go, especially when you rent out the entire place," Simon said messy.

Out late in the city of problems, Los Angeles, the guys were what they claimed as "slightly drunk" after a long day of practice. It seems that while they were at the studio, they got drunk on some liquor, and someone had the bright idea to go to the strip club.

Everyone except Maxwell, Kyan, and Mazen (they were out doing international press) packed into the van and headed to the club. What a disgrace, as these guys were getting absolutely wasted as the music was bumping, which is wildly uncommon.

Carlos, Jermany, Romeo, and LeeSung watch Theo drink

another shot of liquor at one of the booths. Then he pulled out his wallet, which was loaded with cash THAT HE WASN'T SUPPOSED TO SPEND!!! That cash was supposed to be donated to the homeless crisis downtown.

"Don't, don't tell anyone about what happened today, okay,' Theo said, very sloppy. Looking like he was about to fall, he left the booth and walked over to the stage. Then he started throwing 100s of dollar bills at the ladies.

As the four watches Theo make poor financial decisions, some girls try to come to the booth. But Jermany kept shutting them away. "We are in committed relationships! Except LeeSung; he is free. Have him," Jermany said, wrapping his arm around LeeSung.

LeeSung, though, stopped Jermany from proceeding. "Woah, man. Hi ladies, it is not going to work with me either", LeeSung said as he showed his ring.
   "Oh, come on, lock in bro. It's okay to love again," Carlos said.

LeeSung took another shot, "Even if I wanted to, not here."
   Romeo asked when he would be interested in dating again.

"You keep waving that ring as if you got married. I think the engagement is called off when your fiancé dies," Romeo laughed. Jermany immediately threw some fries at Romeo. "Seriously, Romeo? Why would you say that," Carlos said.

However, Romeo was too drunk to care and kept laughing.

"So you propose to a girl you met on a Korean reality show after a few months of dating. You adopt a kid, and she forgets to tell you, "Oh, I have cancer." Stage four, and she dies a month later. That was what was in 2015 or 2016…and it's now 2022. It would be best if you got back into the dating pool," Romeo said as he ate some of the fries Jermany threw at him.

LeeSung got up from his seat and grabbed the whole bottle of liquor. "Oh, don't go! He was kidding! "Carlos yelled.

Dice was wandering around, tripping over his steps. Falling, Leo picked him up. "Woah, man, how many did you have," Simon asked as he rushed over to help Dice up. Dice looked so dizzy as the loud music was making his head explode.

"Trash can!" Dice said, running over to throw up. Here came Xan looking like a tourist. Patting Dice's back, he said, "Simon, how did you get this place!"

"I didn't get it! David did," Simon said, pointing over to the stage. Turning around, he saw David throwing countless money at the ladies on stage. Then he tried picking it up and doing the cycle all over again.

Xan sighed and pulled out his phone. "Everyone here on an NDA, right!" he yelled. "100 percent!" Simon said, dancing.

Xan proceeded to call Lisa through video chat. He waited and fixed his hair as he looked at the reflection. That is when he saw Dice still throwing up in the trash can, so he moved away.

"Most beautiful girl, my partner in crime, please pick up," Xan said in Portuguese, very intoxicated.

Over at the house rental in Calabasas, Lisa was hanging out with Vanessa. The two were listening to lo-fi music and painting on a small canvas. "Oh, Xan is calling me. I wonder what he wants," Lisa said. Answering the video call, Lisa was in shock.

"Lisa! I, um, forgot what I was calling you for. Oh, Diaomond Club. We are here right, right now. Could you double-check that all the workers here had signed an NDA," Xan struggled to say. Lisa and Vanessa were shocked to hear that the guys had gone to that club. Yes, it was the talk of the town, but it wasn't an elite strip club. It was most definitely on the more budget side of things.

"Oh my gosh, Xan, now you know better! Vanessa, could you stay on the call with Xan while I go do a quick call in the office," Lisa asked. Vanessa agreed as Lisa handed over her phone.

"Yea, what's up...Xan," Vanessa said as she wasn't used to seeing Xan drunk. "Hey Vanessa, check out his place," Xan said. He gave her a 360 tour of the club like a show-tell presentation.

Meanwhile, Dice rejoined Simon, Leo, and Jean after throwing up everything he had eaten in the last 24 hours.

"Where Toran," Dice asked.

Leo, Simon, and Jean didn't know. Coming off the stage was Theo, looking slightly more than just drunk and potentially high. "Where is Toran," Leo yelled to Theo.

"I just saw him; he over there," Theo said, pointing to the other side of the second stage. "Oh no," Jean said, concerned.

"No, um, we should be okay. This is nothing but a fever dream," Simon said.

"And this is the stage," Xan said as he panned the camera around. On the other end, Vanessa could not believe her eyes as Xan walked closer to Toran, who was slightly off to the side. He was making out with one of the exotic dancers.

"YEAH, TORAN, GET ON THE ACTION!" Dice shouted.

"Where is she taking him," Simon questioned. Toran got up as the lady dragged him down the stairs.

"Ah, we need to stop her," Leo said. Dice and his lack of self-awareness didn't understand why they needed to intervene. "She's gonna try to collect child support," Leo said.

Leo and Jean rushed to the other side before the two went upstairs.

Lisa came back into the room after taking care of some business. "Thank you so much, girl. Sending the van over to pick them up," she said. Pausing, she notices the frown on Vanessa's face. "Everything okay?" Lisa asked.

Vanessa wiped a quick tear before dismissing herself. "Oh yeah, I'm just exhausted."

"Hi, sorry he is not available like that," Leo said. As he tried to distract the lady, Jean took Toran to Romeo's booth. But the lady refuses to let go of Toran's hand. "Well, he looks pretty available to me. You know I got a friend over there who has been eyeing you all night," she said. Leo sighed in frustration as she thought Leo was drunk like the others, but nope. He was beyond the definition of sober in oath to Sammatha.

"Oh, I don't even want to deal with this. How much," he asked.

"50k," the girl demanded.

"How bout a lawsuit for thinking a drunk guy's "yes" was consent."

The lady folded in and quickly walked away. "It's criminally dumb if you think I'm going to give you 50k!!!" Leo yelled.

Jean and Leo help Toran over to the booth to sit down.

"What's up with him," Carlos asked.

"Whatever happened here, forget that it ever happened," Jean said concerningly.

32

08/20/22: Truth be told... Part III

"Tell me what happened," Vanessa yelled.

"I don't know," Toran said, confused. Jean requested for Cameron to get off his lap so that he could stand up.

"Um, Vanessa... we were just hanging out, and things got a little out of hand," Jean said as he slowly walked over to her.

Maxwell was looking around like a lost puppy. Leaning in towards Jermany, "Why didn't I get the invite."

"We figure you and the other two were too tired from your press tour. Plus, I thought you didn't like clubs," Jermany whispered back.

"Fair enough ," he said.

"Stay out of this, Jean! Toran here doesn't seem to remember making out with that stripper and... You know what? It doesn't matter anymore 'cause we are done," Vanessa cried. She then proceeded to rush out of the tent, as tears flowed down. I quickly left my station and followed suit to go comfort her.

The tent was quiet.

Slowly all the girls headed out of the tent, not saying a word. They just wanted to give the guys some space as this information was news to everyone. Meanwhile, Toran was frozen like a mannequin.

I did come back in the tent briefly, as I forgot there was a message I had to pass over. While I was talking to David on the phone before everything went down. I found out about that cheating allegation. Apparently, the same person sent it over to David.

"Oh, Toran, by the way. That guy you saw her with was her cousin. She was out on the pier with some family members to grab lunch," I said before leaving the room.

Dice slowly got up and sat Toran down. Patting on his back, Toran fell to his hands.

Sounds of sorrow and pain filled the air. All the guys didn't move and went into self-reflection as Toran cried his heart out. The video shoot was canceled. Though us leaders made sure, everyone got paid handsomely for their time and to not spread the breakup news to the internet.

I had a talk with Lisa later in the day, though. There is a reason why she is a Switch leader and not a BFF leader. Yes, the conversation needed to happen between Toran and Vanessa but not while at work in front of the entire group. I deal with the group problems and I prefer she sticks to the music side.

33

08/22/22: La La La. Winner to the heart. Part I

"Hey, the show is about to start if anyone wants to watch," David texted in the group chat.

Apparently, David secured Jean and Cameron a spot to be on a famous celebrity's couple cooking competition that was a live taping. Interesting choice for a PR stunt. Cameron and Jean cooking??? Should have asked Brittany and Carlos or even Mia and Maxwell. They do not practice prior because I rarely see them cook anything unless another member is in the room.

LeeSung and Lisa tag along to make sure everything went well as for moral support and to mainly keep an eye on them.

In the dressing room, Lisa pulled out her agenda from her bag.

"Okay, so some people still remember the whole situation that happened back on the 21st of last month and just can't stop bringing it up. So, hopefully, this TV appearance will help change the conversation. All the fan clubs have been notified, and you know they will be on the lookout for any moment worth going viral. So please, for the love of God, Cameron, Jean, I do not want any funny business happening."

Jean glanced at Cameron with a little smirk. "You have nothing to worry about," he said.

LeeSung was by the wall, keeping a steady eye on the two. He knew something was up but didn't know what it was.

"Here."

Lisa handed three fancy brochures to Cameron. "You guys will be making California roll sushi with some miso soup. If you, for some odd reason, make it to the final round, then you can make taco salad. It's the easiest recipe you can possibly make," Lisa said.

Looking up, she saw that Jean wasn't paying attention and was cheesing hard. "Jean, what did I say," Lisa said, folding her arms.

"Uh, something about sushi. We will be okay. Honestly."
Cameron lets out a little giggle as she brushes her hair back.

Lisa walked over to LeeSung as the two looked through the recipes.
"Why are they acting like they are high or something," Lisa whispered.
"I have no idea, but judging by their body language, you can tell they are more than just friends. However, we may be reading a little too hard into the two. Last month, they were having trust issues, and many tears were shed in front of thousands of fans. It was the talk of the town for days. Then you have the incident that happened in Chicago during that festival... Maybe they are simply at a stage of recovering, getting back to a more healthy relationship," LeeSung whispered.

Suddenly they heard a knock on the door, and in came the floor manager. "Filming will start at 5, "she said before closing the door.

"Okay... Well, let's get out of here. Remember, this is a LIVE show," Lisa said. She and LeeSung left the room as Jean and Cameron followed behind.

Jean tried wrapping his arms around Cameron's waist. Though, Cameron kept teasing him as she tried to stop his action from following through.

"Stop, Jean. Not now," she whispered.

It was a nice set. Four kitchens for four couples to compete. As the workers showed the two to their spot, LeeSung and Lisa went off to the side where all the other couples' managers were standing.

"Do you want me to get you a chair or something," LeeSung asked.

"No. Well, maybe, actually. Well no. I don't think the filming will be long," she said. Suddenly she heard someone calling her name.

"Well, well, it's Lisa Devi. How have you been?"

Lisa and LeeSung turned around to see what it was. He was a tall white man with a black, clean-shaved beard. He was probably in his late 30s or mid-40s.

"Oh, Jarred. What brings you here?" Lisa said, a little suspicious.

"No, hello? I may not been your group's manager at Ex-S Records, but-"

"You are Kylie's manager," Lisa said.

"Former manager. She fired me recently, but I am TKtimes's guy now."

The man pointed over to the set. New famous Somali/Trinidad

rapper in the New York drill scene.

"No way! I have been hearing him a lot on the radio lately," LeeSung said in shock.

"You're absolutely right. I think I will strike gold with this one. Especially since he has only been in the industry for a year. Which may I ask…" Jarred glanced around before leaning in.

"Rumor has it that a third wave of members will join the group. Can we work up a contract to get my client a spot in Rap Line?"

LeeSung and Lisa looked at each other crazily. "Who told you that there was a 3rd wave happening. Yea, back in 2016, there was supposed to be one, but that all got scraped when we went independent. Plus if you haven't noticed, there are already too many of us anyways."

Walking to a different spot, LeeSung whispers, "Another third-wave rumor. I mean, the second wave, when the other half of the group came around wasn't even like a big fuss cause. To my understanding, we were already in the group, just not the official roster until 2012."

"Exactly, but Ex-S is still running that "It could be you too" narrative. Doesn't shock me why Jarred brought this TKtimes guy to the same cooking show episode we would be at. Typical Jarred thinking I wouldn't fall for his stunt just because I'm 25 and not some old white dude like him."

Arriving at their new spot, Lisa and LeeSung waved to Jean and Cameron when they noticed TKtimes walking over to him with his dark skin girlfriend. By the way, her skincare was flawless. She must have been some high-profile model.

"Hi, my name is TKtimes, but I prefer if people call me TK," he said, reaching for a shake. Jean was caught very off guard by TK's presence.

Noticing the multiple cameras and people in the room, he didn't want to be rude and deny the handshake. "Jean. Nice to meet you," he said, shaking his hands. Jean was feeling very hostile as he held Cameron behind him. He already threw someone on the blacklist in the last 30 days and didn't want to double it.

"You must have heard my song. Calabasas Rock? It has to ring a bell," TK said. Jean pauses for a minute to think about the song. Again I didn't know what to be rude during first impressions. "Oh yes, I heard the song online. You had put some serious numbers on the chart this summer for a debut artist," Jean said, friendly.

"Yeah, and soon, I will work on my first album that should be released next year. I know Switch is very open to working with smaller acts and -" Jean intervened. "I don't have control over collaboration talks. But... If you want, I can give you my e-mail address, and maybe we can work something out."

TK was excited as Jean tore a piece out of a notebook and wrote down his burner email for him. He probably gave it out so willingly so that he could have the guy stop talking to him and keep him 100 meters away from Cameron.

As Jean turned around to hand TK the note, he noticed TK flirtatiously looking at Cameron.

"Here."
   "Thank you so much. I'll have my team contact you."

"Yeah, whatever," Jean said under his breath as he walked Cameron over to their station.

Jean wrapped his arms around Cameron from behind as the two waited for the tapping to start.

"That was nice of you to give him your email. You probably made his day," Cameron smiled.
   "I am wondering if that was a good idea."
   Jean held Cameron closer as the two swayed side to side.

"Why?"
   "I saw him looking at you Cameron," he said, worried.
   "I'm sure that is not true, and if it is, I can assure you have absolutely nothing to worry about."

Jean was about to lean in to kiss Cameron's neck when he heard a loud snapping sound. The two looked over and saw Lisa and LeeSung shaking their heads disapprovingly. Jean started laughing a bit. In Spanish, he said, "They act like we are going to do it here in front of all these people. I can't have one kiss."

Cameron looks up at him. "What did you say? You were speaking too fast," she said. Jean smiled.

Suddenly the theme music started playing as the taping was about to begin. Jean releases his hug lock and moves over to his side of Cameron as the host introduces each couple. Four in total, all rappers and or singers. Minus TK's model girlfriend.

So the cooking started. All the ingredients were in the bottom cabinet, and surprisingly, the rice Cameron needed was already cooked. She just had to pretend that she made it.

"What is she doing," Lisa questioned.

Cameron was pouring the rice out into the trash can.

The host came by with the cameraman and noticed the rice. "So it's Music's favorite couple! Cameron Minski and Jean Gonzales! How have you two love birds been?"

"We are doing great, and we want to personally thank our fans for all the love and support," Jean said flawlessly because we leaders got stuck writing a script for them to go off of.

"Amazing. And Cameron, do you realize that the rice you threw in the trash was your special all-ready-to-cook ingredient for your California roll sushi." Cameron opened her eyes wide in panic.

She rushed over to the trash, "Oops… I- I- My bad, but we will have the rice cooked on time."

The host went on to the other contestants leaving the two to low-key struggle in making the sushi. But with 5 minutes to spare and the miso soup already accomplished by Jean, the rice was finished cooking in the rice cooker.

As the two prepare the sushi for the judges, Jean keeps brushing against Cameron as he grabs some plates. "Excuse me," he said in a sweet voice. Cameron eventually caught on to what he was doing and started blushing again as they set the rolls on the plate.

"5, 4, 3, 2, and that is all!" the host yelled.

Hands in the air, the two looked at the dish they had created in under 25 minutes, and it looked pretty good. I was a little impressed as Simon and I watched the show from the house.

As the judges tried each couple's meal. Jean held Cameron's hand and started massaging it under the table, out of sight for the cameras to pick. Finally, it was the two's turn to be judged after the judges liked TK's samosa dish.

The two walked down the steps, and like the superstars, they stood there as the three judges ate their rather rushed sushi and soup.

LeeSung looked around and knew that everyone in the room was beyond the definition of star-struck to be in the presence of a Switch member. LeeSung noticed that some of the workers were drooling over Jean while the others were cheesing hard to see Cameron. Looking around more, he was caught off guard. He saw some people in the back staring right at him and Lisa.

"Oh, my goodness. This is so delicious. Love the flavor and richness of the soup," one of the judges says. Followed by the other two with lots of praise.

"Oh, this game is rigged. They are just saying that so they don't get on Jean's bad side," Simon laughed.

"I think they might have actually done a good job," I said as we sat in the living room.

"Doubt it. I know Jean, and he is not afraid to destroy someone's career."

In came Lily, "Did they win?"

Glue to the screen as the final verdict came in. They scored 90 out of 100. "It's rigged," Simon and I said simultaneously, laughing.

"Uh, poor TK. That food he made looks really good. Should have got a higher score," I said.

Lily tried holding in her laugh but ultimately failed.

"Oh, this is so insane. So you're telling me Jean and Cameron made it to the final round. They are cooking dinner tonight since they can cook so well."

Simon looked behind the couch and noticed that Lily was dressed nicely.

"Where are you going?"

"Coney Island. It was Kyan and Asia's idea. Do you two

want to come," she asked.

"I'm going to stay here. My allergies will be messed up if I go out there," I said. Simon gave it some thought and then agreed to go.

"Let me put on an outfit that doesn't scream, "OH MY GOD, IT'S SIMON!!!". It shouldn't take long."

Commercial break.

LeeSung and Lisa took their eyes off Jean and Cameron for a hot second, and then they were gone.

"Where did they go?" LeeSung questioned as he looked around.

"Uh, the commercial break doesn't mean a 30-minute one," Lisa said as the two rushed around, looking for the two.

DING!

Lisa pulled out her phone and noticed Jean sent her a text message.

[We will be back. I got a headache, and Cameron said she had some medicine.]

"He looked fine to me," LeeSung questioned.

So the two went to the dressing room to go see what was wrong and - "OH MY..." Lisa pulled LeeSung in, shutting the door quickly. Cameron was sitting on the makeup table, making out heavily with Jean. Though it was quickly short-lived when they got exposed.

"Ah, no, no, absolutely not right now. What if I was one of the floor managers. And Jean. 'Oh, I got a headache?'"

Oblivious to what was going on, Jean said, "I do get a headache, and Cameron has the medicine."

"Are you sniffing it or smoking it right now? Tongue kissing and sneaking around like we were in high school. Ah, grow up. Cameron, fix your shirt, and you two get back out here," Lisa said, leaving the room.

"Sounds like someone needs a man," Jean whispered in Cameron's ear before starting to kiss her again.

"I'm still here. Come on. I need to be out of here soon. I have to go pick up my kid. Something you two should already have at the rate you two get down," LeeSung said.

"Come on."

So they went off to finish the competition. And they got 2nd place for their taco salad. Had they gotten 1st, I would have called it 100% rig. But they got 2nd place. After shaking hands with the contestants and taking some pictures for Switch's social media page, the day was over.

In the parking lot, Xan was waiting to pick up Lisa. "How did it go?" Xan asked as she hopped in the car.

"Fine. They won 2nd place. Though I just want to go home. LeeSung going to pick up Haru, and I have no idea where Jean and Cameron are going."

Xan noticed Jean's royal blue sports car and pulled up to it, giving it a light honk for his attention. Jean noticed it was Xan, so he hopped out.

"Where are you going," Xan said in Portuguese. Walking over to the window, Jean responded back in Portuguese, "I don't know yet, but we will be at the house later today." Xan knew that Jean was hiding the truth because he avoided eye contact. He wanted to guess where he was really going. However, judging by Lisa's exhaustion, he decided to keep the conversation short. "Well, drive safe then and parabéns for the win," Xan said.

So where did Jean take Cameron? You guessed it right. They went to the BFF stadium to go "hang out" in the lounge area.

08/22/22: La La La. Winner to the heart. Part II

"Come on, Simon. Can you at least try to get on one ride?" Lily begged.

Simon ignored Lily's request as he relaxed at the picnic table by the water.

"Come on. Get up," Lily said as she tried to pick up Simon from behind.

"Okay, okay. But I am not getting on any rides," Simon said.

"Then let's play some arcade games then."

The two walked into the neon 90s theme game room and looked around the nostalgic games. Coming around the corner, they noticed how much fun Kyan and Asia were having. They were very loud as they tried to shoot as many basketballs into the hoop.

Unfortunately, they missed about 99% of their shots. Absolutely embarrassing if I had to be honest, but you know, physical education wasn't really an elective for them to take during their homeschool days. So I will let them pass on this.

"WAIT, I MADE A SHOT!" Kyan yelled in excitement. "NO, THAT WAS ME WHO DID IT!" Asia laughed.

"Look at them. If I didn't know better, they could be on a date right now, and we wouldn't even know for sure." Lily said.

"So if that were to be true, what are we? The third wheel?" Simon laughed.

"No, it would be more of a double date."

"A double date? I thought we agreed that we wouldn't try that again," Simon said.

"Well, you know I like to pretend, so let's pretend like it's a date. Not like we haven't been on one in over a year," Lily said.

Simon laughed a bit. "You're blind to time, aren't you? We broke up years ago."

"Oh, really. What day did that happen? Or even better, I will give you an easier question. What year?" Lily questioned.

Simon thought about it, but the answer couldn't come to him. "It doesn't matter the time and date because you don't even know the answer," Simon said.

"Right? Okay, well, today is the day we have a fake date."

It was a montage of different activities and fun that they did. From foosball to knocking down milk bottles, the two spent the rest of the day hanging out with each other. Since the pier was relatively low in traffic with back-to-school season in, they could co-exist without the crazy fans stalking them around.

"We should do this," Simon suggested, pointing to a mini photo booth.

Lily peeked inside the booth and noticed the machine didn't take the pier tickets.

"It's cash only," Lily said.

"So? You must have forgotten who I am," Simon smiled.

They settle down inside the booth, wondering how the machine works.

"I haven't done something like this in a hot minute," Lily said as she set up the picture.

"We get four pictures, and each one should be different. Like for the first one, we can do this."

Simon wrapped his arms around Lily as the camera flashed. Then Lily did bunny ears over Simon's head, giving the biggest smile. Then the third picture was a surprise when Lily kissed Simon on the lips.

For some odd reason, Simon was taken aback by it all. Quickly the countdown went for the final picture. "Pose, Simon, pose!" Lily said. At the last second, the two smiled as the flash captured their faces.

"That was short, don't you think?" Lily said casually, hopping out of the booth. Simon followed behind her and felt a bit off.

Lily grabbed the picture and gave it a look.

"Ah, look at that," Lily said, pointing to the fourth picture.

Simon, though, was too busy looking at the third one. "The black and white really did us some justice on the print quality and -"

"Simon! Lily!" Kyan yelled. Lily and Simon looked up as they saw Kyan and Asia looking afraid. "What's wrong?" Lily questioned.

"We just need to go now," Kyan said with urgency.

Suddenly they heard screams as three police guards came passing by. "What's going on?" Simon question. Simon watched Asia bury her face into Kyan's chest as she held him close. "Someone committed suicide in front of us," Kyan said.

Simon took a step back.

"What?" Lily said, concerned. Since they were not too far from the entrance, they could hear the ambulance coming its way as the sirens were at maximum volume.

"Um... Let's go then," Simon said.

As soon as Simon turned around, his face was met with blood covering his face.

Simon started shaking as he heard Lily wail so loudly. Simon looked down at the ground and saw that another person had killed himself. His ears began to ring as he saw the police coming his way.

"EVERYONE, PLEASE EXIT THE BOARDWALK!"

The intercom speaking was loud as the four panicked, not knowing what to do.

"We need to go!" Kyan said to Simon, but Simon couldn't think as his ears continued to ring. Simon fell to the floor as he continued to cover his ear.

As if a grenade went off, his ears began to tune out the chaos as Kyan tried to help him.

"COME ON, SIMON; WE NEED TO GO!" Kyan said as he tried to pull him up. Asia and Lily help Kyan get Simon to his feet.

The weather became cloudy as a storm was about to come in. In urgency and rush, the four quickly made it to the exit. Everyone in the area was running around in panic mode as there was a suicide rage happening. "Where did you park, Simon!" Kyan yelled.

However, Simon was feeling overwhelmed as he could barely stand up. "I think it was over here," Lily expressed.

Suddenly they heard another gunshot, and the four dropped to the floor. Then, their phones began to blow up as every group member started to call them. Weaving through the cars, they made it to Simon's vehicle.

Quickly they all got in and took shelter. Keeping their heads low and out of sight. One by one, they hear a gunshot blow into the air. Kyan tried to confront Asia in the backseat while Lily confronted Simon upfront.

In a panic, Lily started the car and drove away from the area as more and more police cars were passing by.

"My God, we are going to need therapy after this! WHO WOULD DO SUCH A THING? WHY DO WE NEED TO BE THE ONES IN THE AREA!" Lily said in anger.

"Lily, please, just get us back to the house," Kyan cried.

"Yeah, sure, but wait, Simon did you want to get something to eat first," she said. Simon looked at Lily in confusion when suddenly he was back at the pier, and everything was fine. Looking down, he saw that Lily had torn the photo strip in half, giving him the one where she kissed him.

"You okay? Simon to planet Earth," Lily said.
   "Yea, I'm great. Um, let's get some funnel cake and then head back for the day," Simon suggested.
   Lily looked at Simon in concern. "Are you sure you are okay?"
   Simon smiled, "I'm fine, especially now that I got a picture of us to hang on my dresser."

Lily rolled her eyes and took Simon by the arm. "You are paying for my meal by the way," Lily declared.
   As the two walked over to the concession stands, Simon stopped at the trash can. Reaching into his pocket, he grabbed a couple of small pills and threw them away.

35

07/14/13: The Roulette of Neglect.

It was a summer day at the house of BFF. Fans were placed everywhere because the air conditioning was broken for the 100th time. They were blowing at their max speed, but the things were so cheap. They only blew hot air.

In exchange for a better AC unit, we renovated the main house, moving from the nasty gilded age look to a more "modern look." Not to mention the left-wing getting added upstairs.

It all wouldn't be possible if the Around the World album wasn't a smash international hit success. Us, Switch, is off to a whole new level.

Carlos was leaving the practice room when he saw Brittany passing by.

"Hey, Brittany... Can we talk?" Carlos begged.

Though Brittany did not care as she continued onward to the kitchen.

"Brittany..."

Again she ignored him as she opened the fridge. Carlos gazed at Brittany's face as he admired her dimples and soft brown skin that complimented her dirty brown/blonde frizzy hair. Then a wave of guilt overcame him as he couldn't stop thinking about what he said during his Golden Hour solo album that was released back in May.

"Should we go see a doctor?" Carlos question.

Brittany closed the door immediately.

"Why? So they can go leak it out to the whole world? I'm barely 18 in a few days and lead singer of Varsity Girls..."

Brittany started getting emotional as she went to the break-fast table to sit down. "Let me take you to the doctor," Carlos said, concerned.

Brittany put her head down on the table as she tried to ignore Carlos.

"Please, let me take you a clinic or -"

"With what money!" Brittany blurt.

Carlos quickly sat down beside her. "We have money," he said.

Brittany shook her head in disagreement .

"Both of our advancement checks are being used to pay for the mortgage. We don't even have enough money left over to put food in the fridge. There is not enough money for me to go, and my face is too recognizable to be caught seeing a baby doctor... This...This would not have happened if you didn't..."

Brittany started to get frustrated with Carlos. "I shouldn't even be talking to you... I heard your little extended version of Golden Hour. Making a song about me getting pregnant for you and your Varsity Guys friends to laugh off to."

"That was not my intention," Carlos said.

"Really??? My stock in Switch is prime high right now. If Mr.Smith finds out I'm... I can get kicked out of the group. But No, HyunJoong gets to go do whatever he pleases. I'll pass," Brittany said.

"Get an abortion then," Carlos said.

Brittany was in shock at what Carlos said. Standing up from her seat, she was about to say something when she heard Mr.Smith voice on the intercom.

"Everyone, report to Practice Room A."

Carlos noticed how much of a panic Brittany was in.
    "I thought today it was our day off?" Brittany questioned.
    "I think we will be fine. Just stand by me. I'll do the talking," Carlos said.

Congregating in the practice room, there was this tall older white man with a sharp, clean brown beard and thick eyebrows. He was dressed in a suit and tie as he waited impatiently for us to get inside the room.

"HURRY UP AND GET IN HERE!" He yelled.
    Xan and Lisa came into the room last as they stood beside Mr.Smith. They looked timid and tense at his presents.
    Mr. Smith looked around the room as everyone from each line kept their heads down to avoid making eye contact.
    "Where are Sammatha and Maxwell? I know Leo is out for some movie, but where are they at?" Mr. Smith demanded.

Xan look up and notices Courtney wanting to speak, but Xan signals to her to not say anything. Discreetly he tapped his foot three times to get the group's attention before holding up an open hand into a closed fist. It was a code red.

All eyes turned to each other in question.

"One of you knows where those two are," Mr. Smith said, getting angry.

The room stayed quiet as no one made a sound.

"Ah, I get it. Now that your album is doing wonders right now, you think you can just do whatever you want to do. I thought leaving Jesse and Martin as your pretend mom and dad would help keep you all aligned, especially when I was out on my business runs for the last few months. Though instead, you decided to be home builders and color the walls. Because of this, Jesse and Martin will no longer live here. They will come and check up on you once a week, but that's it."

"Are you kidding me? You can't do that," Dice said out loud.

Toran whispered to him to be quiet, but it was too late. Mr. Smith walked over to Dice and started pulling him by his fro to the center of the room.

With all the force, he knocks Dice down to the ground. Little did he know that Dice hit the wood floor so hard that the side of his head started to bleed.

"No double standards around here," Mr. Smith said. All the girls started to go into panic as some took a step back. Carlos slowly had Brittany stand right behind him so that Mr.Smith wouldn't pay her any attention.

"No double standards around here," he said again.

Without much thought, he walked over to Cameron. Grabbing her tightly by the arm, he tried to drag her to the center of the room. Jean was on the other side of the room as he watched Theo and Romeo try to get Mr.Smith to let go of her. Though their strength didn't matter as Mr.Smith pushed them away.

Cameron was crying out loud as Mr.Smith placed her next to Dice.

"Where is Sammatha and Maxwell?" Mr. Smith demanded.

Dice looked at her to not say anything, for Sammatha and Maxwell were never living in the house to begin with. They were the only members to have their own apartment in the city.

"WHERE ARE THEY!!!" Mr. Smith yelled.

Cameron didn't know what to say. Looking up briefly and slowly, she saw Jean looking right at her in fear.

"Hey, Jean! I heard you and Cameron have been fighting a lot lately. Watch this," Mr. Smith said.

Jean froze as he watched Cameron cover her head as Mr.Smith struck her.

Maknae Line stood in their place, scared to make a move.

We all watch Cameron wail in tears, powerless to do anything about it. Dice couldn't take it any more, so he stood up to his feet.

"You're a monster!" Dice shouted.

In attack mode, once again, Mr.Smith knocks him down to

his knees.

"And your mother thinks I'm an angel. I actually was able to visit her while I was in Las Vegas. You never told me that she was deaf. Is that why you know sign language? I also... didn't know that she was addicted. Is that why you are taking heroin in your room?"

Dice looked up at Mr.Smith.
   "Martin found it during room checks," Mr.Smith said.

Xan looked over at David, wondering if he should say something, but David signaled him to not move from his place.

"XAN!"
   Xan quickly straightened his glasses as he stepped forward.
   "Find Dice a rehab center. Not because I care for his health but because I can't afford any bad press on the group or the label. And Lisa, clean up this mess."

Lisa looked down at the floor, where she saw Cameron and Dice's dark red blood scattered around the light-colored wood floors.

No one talked or moved as Mr. Smith dismissed himself.

We waited until we heard a loud slam of the front door before we all rushed over to help Dice and Cameron.

Jean didn't move, though, as he watched Rebecca help Cameron to her feet. Making eye contact with Cameron, she walked over to him as tears fell down her face.
   She slapped him with all her might before leaving the room.

Jean stood there as a tear almost fled down from his eye.

"For everyone who hates Mr.Smith, say 'I,'" Theo said.
   The whole group raised their hands in agreement.
   "Did he have the courtesy to put some food in the fridge," Romeo said in his strong British accent.

"He's going to starve us once again," Simon said.

Dice stumbled over to the dance mirrors to check out his bleeding forehead.
   "Is it true you are taking drugs," Xan questioned.

"Does it matter if I am? I could care less right now," Dice said.

Alanna held her hand up a bit. "What about Jesse and Martin?"
   Lisa looked at Xan in question.
   Without much thought, Lisa said, "We will step up in those roles."

"You're like seventeen," Zachary laughed.

"I don't hear you volunteering," Xan said.

David and I stood forward.

"Valen and I will help out too. In any way we can," David said.

"Yea, we don't need Jesse and Martin. We or…some of us are old enough to drive, so we don't need a chaperone," I said.

"Well, if this is the group's new leadership, as the first line of duty, what are you going to do about the pantry? Are we going on food stamps or something?" Zachary question.

"Leo is gone doing his new movie so that we can have food to eat. David here was able to pull some strings together to get him into his first acting gig. Also, who do you think helped get this house put together?" Xan said.

"Well, the AC is broken," Zachary said smartly.

"And your daddy is rich, and he doesn't want to send money over," David said.

"It's called a trust fund. I can't touch it until I'm 21," Zachary said.

"Well, until then, you can stop complaining," Lisa said.

"I'll stop complaining when Mr.Smith stops asking for Sam-matha and Maxwell," Zachary said.

Lily nudged at her brother Zachary to stop talking.

"They can't move in here! Are you serious? Just a year ago, they were getting assaulted by their stepdad. They literally join the group to get away from him!" Xan yelled.

"Let's just move on from this, okay," Rebecca said.

"How much is our check going to be for this month," Kylie asked.

"Leftover?" Xan questioned.

Kylie shook her head.

Xan sighed, and Brittany and Carlos didn't like the sound of that.

"With the help of Brittany and Carlos' advancements combine with everyone elses' money to split...34 ways..."

Everyone in the room came closer to Xan to hear the number.

"Fifty dollars..."

"Each?" Kyan questioned.

"All together. Everyone will each get about $1.47..."

"You're kidding," Jackie said in shock.

"This is highway robbery! We get a bonus of two cents while our album is at the number one spot of the charts???" Zachary questioned.

"We have bills to pay!," Xan sighed, "This house is expensive to pay for and not like we can move into a smaller space. There are recording sessions, language classes, and traveling expenses to pay for. Not to mention all the radio and tv promotions that we did back in February. Mr.Smith is taking all of that out of our checks. Plus, we all signed a 360 deal, and our parents can't do anything about that. For all they know, we are just at summer camp having the time of our lives. That's why he was gone. He went to tell some lie that everything is fine and handed them some cash as compensation. Oh, and the propaganda about our lives on television. 'The perfect lives in the perfect world of Switch'."

"This place is absolutely corrupted," Rebecca said.
   "Mr.Smith wasn't like this during the first wave," I said.

David said as he rubbed his face, "Valen is right until he found out he out how much money Switch makes for him. Got us in Backwood, New York, with not even an arcade nearby to play at. It's just work work work."

Courtney took a seat on the floor in frustration. Though she almost fell as her hand slid on Dice and Cameron's blood.
   "So we...we are broke?" Courtney asked as she stared at her bloody hand.

We, newly founded leaders, shook our heads.

36

09/01/22: Time after time.

"I'm sick and tired of this, and I need Carlos to hurry up," Brittany sighed.

Over by the front door of the house, Brittany, Courtney, and Brionna were chatting.

Brittany looked exhausted and fatigued from a long day of practice. Didn't help that today was the final preparation for tomorrow's VVMAs performance.

"Why don't you just stay the night? Romeo and I are," Brionna said.

Brittany brushed her long, dirty brown, curly hair back as she impatiently waited for Carlos.

"I can't. I got to pick Kimberly up from Carlos's grand-mother's house," Brittany said.

Courtney was a bit confused. "Pick up? That feels so... pointless. You will be in New Jersey tomorrow; you might as well have her spend the night. Sounds a bit unnecessary when you look exhausted, Brittany."

"I'm not exhausted," she said, "Courtney, you are. You're working double shifts now for Varsity Line."
"More like triple shift, actually," Brionna said.

Courtney laughed a bit, "What? No, I'm not. I - I am just doing my part in the Line."
"Yea, and covering for Mia, Brionna, and I," Brittany said.

"Well, Mia is just taking things slow for a bit, but she is still performing," Courtney said.
"With a small amount of line distribution. Mia is lucky if she can pull through four lines in an entire show," Brittany said.

"Well, you and Brionna have kids to take care of, so I'm not expecting you two to carry any high notes," Courtney said.

Brionna rubbed her neck a bit. "Yea, but that doesn't mean you should be left to be an unofficial lead singer. Once the camera turns off, Sammatha interest level drop immediately, leaving you with Cameron to help co-captain and -"

"Wait, wait, wait, WAIT..."

Courtney did not like what the sound of the conversation was going. She said, "I'm not taking the responsibilities as a lead singer. I already don't like Jermany being the lead singer of Varsity Guys with Romeo."

Brionna and Brittany begged Courtney to think about it.

"I can't. I won't. You two were once lead singers, so you understand the requirements. I would have to pick up an extra three hours of practice to know every dance in the setlist book to the tea. I don't want to be the face of the Varsity Line."

"But it would make sense. You are already putting in so much work in a lead role," Brittany said.

"Yea, and the only way I can get out of a lead position in Varsity Girls is to have a traumatic breakup or get pregnant. I'm not Cameron, who can do a ten-hour dance-a-thon off four hours of sleep. I am also not Sammatha, who can hit high notes and make the entire crowd cry every time."

"But-"

Courtney didn't want to entertain Brionna and Brittany anymore.

"Your kids are not in diapers anymore. If you don't want to show up for Varsity Girls like the old days, that's fine. But don't expect me to go above and beyond to keep the unit name alive. There are seven sub-units, and eventually, we will be knocked off the top of the pyramids."

Brittany and Brionna felt offended by what Courtney said to them.

"This is not fair, Courtney. It's not our fault that we have a kid," Brittany said, irritated.

"Really, because doesn't it take two to tangle? But right, I should be the one to thank you since your pregnancy scare made the group the talk of the town," Courtney said.

"Sounds real entitled now for someone who didn't get hit by Mr.Smith," Brittany said as she stepped a bit closer to Courtney.

Brionna quickly interfered, backing the two away from each other.

"I wish he would put his hands on me," Courtney said, putting her ten toes down.

"Well, yea, I did get pregnant and almost lost Kimberly when Mr.Smith pushed me down the stairs."

Brionna and Courtney looked at Brittany in shock and concern. Then they turned around to see the long brown wooden staircase that led up to the second floor.

"He did what... When did this happen?" Courtney said concerned.

"Forget about it, okay," Brittany said. Unlocking the front door, Brittany went outside, where the moonlight was shining bright.

Courtney and Brionna quickly followed behind.

"When did this happen?" Courtney asked again.

Stopping on the steps, Brittany turned around, getting emotional.

"It happened the day when the news broke out that I was pregnant and had broken up with Carlos. Next thing I know... Mia was announced as lead singer, and I was being yelled at by Mr.Smith."

"Does Carlos know about this?" Brionna asked.

Brittany started to get emotional. "No, and he never will. It would break him if he found out. To keep things quiet, I didn't fight back for my spot as lead ...and I never will at this rate."

Courtney steps forward to Brittany to give her a hug. "You still can. All these free babysitters are here to take care of Kimberly and Junior, Brionna. I don't see why you two can't return to your lead roles."

Brittany smiled a bit as she wiped away a tear. "I doubt Cameron is willing to give up her spot."

Brionna laughed a bit as she walked over to give Brittany a hug.

"So we can all agree that we are waiting for her to have a kid so that her spot can be free to grab, right?," Brionna jokes.

The three started laughing. "Oh yea, Brionna. The day Cameron and Jean have a kid is the day penguins can fly.

Shoot, we are lucky if Jean proposes to Cameron at this rate," Courtney laughed.

Suddenly they saw a blue sports car pull up in front of them.
   "You think he got a wedding ring in there," Brionna smiled.
   "100% doubt there's even a candy ring in there," Brittany said, wiping away her final tear.

Jean came out of the car, followed by Simon, carrying some bags.

"Is my girl out of practice," Jean said excitedly as he came up to the three.
   "Yea, she's probably showering up," Courtney said.
   "What's up with the durag?" Brionna questioned.

Before Jean could say something, he noticed Simon was struggling to pull forward his passenger door seat.
   "Hold on," he said.

Quickly he rushed over to Simon to help him pull the seat forward.
   "Geez, Jean, did you and Cameron have to break this? The mechanics of this are absolutely shattered." Simon said.
   Finally, they got the seat to come forward, and out came Asia and I. Let me say that it was indeed a tight squeeze to get out.

"Jesus, Jean. You better thank God himself that I'm short. It was too cramped for us to be stuck back there," I said.

"Sorry. Though my car is only really meant for two people," he said.

"Yea, well, when you say you're going to the beauty supply store, you shouldn't be shocked and surprised that the black girlies want to tag along. You act like we don't have to do our hair for tomorrow," I said.

"Speaking of hair, Asia, will you have enough time to do your box braids?" Jean questioned.

Asia looked inside her hair bag and then looked at me.

I quickly put my hands up.

"Nope, not me. I already said that I wasn't going to do it."

"Then who is going to help me?" Asia pouted.

"What about Jackie?" Simon suggested.

"Jackie is horrible at braiding," Asia said.

I said, "Well, ask Alanna to help you. She can be a quick learner at times. First, part your hair, and get a braid started. Then have her finish it. How big are the braids supposed to be anyway."

Asia gave us three a demonstration of how thin she wanted her braids to look. In a quick reaction of shock, Simon, Jean, and I started moving up the stairs.

"Wait!" she said.

Coming out the front door was Cameron in nothing but booty shorts and a tank top as her hair hung long down past her waist. Excitedly, she rushed over to Jean, and he picked her up to kiss her.

"Uh, gross," Asia said as she shielded her eyes.

"Psst," Brionna said, signaling Simon, Asia, and I over to her.

"Why does Jean get a durag on?" Brionna questioned.

Simon's eyes wander off a bit.

"I may have had a bit of a shaky hand when cutting Jean's hair," he said.

"Well, that's what happens when you cut someone's hair when you're high," I said.

Courtney glanced at Jean, hoping to see a sneak peek of the haircut. Though she noticed something off between the two.

"Why is Cameron speaking to him in Japanese?" She questioned.

"To deflect. I sent Cameron a message on the way back to act very "animated," so that Jean doesn't be reminded of his haircut," Simon said.

"How bad is it?" Brittany questioned.

Asia gave the three a visualization.

"He wanted a line going to the side to match up with his eyebrow, and Simon gave him a bald spot instead..."

"Jesus, Simon. How did you do that?" Brittany questioned.

"He has a lot of hair, and it's not that easy to cut into waves. Don't worry though, because we got some black tint spray and the powder to cover it up," Simon said.

Taking a quick look behind, I saw Jean and Cameron making out.

"Again. Gross," Asia said before going inside.

"Look like someone is stressed out," I sighed.

Simon shrugged it off. "Give him some grace. He will have 100s of cameras pointed at him tomorrow, surrounded by industry professionals that hate his guts."

The front door opened again, and it was Carlos. For a moment, he was taken aback by Jean and Cameron's love scene.

Walking over to Brittany, he asked if she was ready to go.

Brionna and Courtney looked at Carlos and Brittany in concern.Though, Brittany signals three of them to keep quiet.

"Let's get going," she said softly. Carlos wrapped his arm around her and escorted her to their car.

"Jean, we need to finish this hair," Simon said.

Cameron pulled back as she rubbed her hand on Jean's chest.

"I'm sure it's not that bad," she said with sparkles in her eyes.

Jean blushed a bit as he tried to give his alpha playboy laugh.

"It really isn't, I guess," he said.

"Weaken in the knees," Courtney sighed.

"Stand up, stand up indeed," I said.

We watch the two come up the steps, pretending like they didn't just do what they just did in front of us.

"Ready for surgery," Simon smiled.

Brionna, Courtney, and I started bursting out laughing.

"What?" Simon questioned.

"Why, why did you say it like that? 'Ready for surgery.' Geez," I said, wiping a tear of joy away. Continuing on, I said, "Jean, you will be fine for tomorrow. It's an easy fix."

"Exactly. Right, Cameron?" Simon said, cheesing.

Switching over to French, I said, "Vraiment???"

"What?" Simon shrugged.

"Quit enabling this behavior," I said.

"She calmed him down, didn't she," he said.

"You can't keep using her to 'calm him down'. Uh, you and Rap Line and your ways of coping," I said, cheesing, trying not to blow our decoded conversation's context.

Giving Jean and Cameron a quick smile, I headed inside. Tired and exhausted. It was nine o'clock in the evening, and I still needed to wash and flat iron my hair.

37

09/02/22: The VVMAs. Part I

Finally, after weeks of practice, today is the day we head down to Newark, New Jersey, for the Victorian Vista Music Awards, aka the VVMAs. This is one of the top award shows to be at for anyone who makes music. The prestige you receive from even a nomination is something many talented singers, rappers, musicians, producers, and others dream of having.

Though we, members of Switch, have already won many VVMAs awards. If you took a brief trip to the Hall of Fame room, you would find maybe 25 trophies. That includes some members' individual solo projects. It may not seem like a lot for how famous we are, but we didn't start winning in more than one category until 2016.

We don't care about the Best Performance, Best Music Video, or even Best Group cause it was a clear no-brainer on who the winner is. The real question we only care about is Album of the Year, Favorite Female Soloist, Favorite Male Soloist, Favorite Duo, and of course, the most significant award of the night, Artist of the Year. Winning these awards means we leaders are doing a good job and that we didn't fall off the top of the food chain.

"WE LEAVING IN TEN," Xan yelled up the stairs.

I came into the living room from the kitchen, wondering where everyone was. Though I was abruptly shocked by Xan's outfit.

"Xan! What are we wearing??? Slacks and a T-shirt, all black? Now you know the red carpet colors are going to be rose red, white, AND black, and every guy needs to be in a suit and tie," I said.

Xan scratched the back of his head a bit. "Last minute change... We are doing all black and no suit and tie..."

"When did this happen?" I questioned.

"About five minutes ago."

Oh, so because Xan didn't get the memo, he wants everyone to change right before we leave...

I went over to the intercom button by the stairs to make a speedy announcement.

"Bruh, do not change your outfits. The colors are red, white, and black. Suit and tie for the guys," I said.

Xan raised his hand, "Uh, why did you do that?"

"Ahhhhh, I am the only BFF leader and the creative director. I did not lay out everyone's clothes for you to make a last-minute decision.

Now you can rock the all-black look if you want to cause I already know Dice will ignore my outfit choice for his Edwork Swissorhandz signature look. Plus, Maxwell will slap on a thick black turtleneck that is probably made from a better material than yours and..."

I squinted my eyes at Xan's outfit. Moving closer to Xan, I realize he grabbed the first thing he saw in his closet.

"What a way to represent yourself in front of hundreds of cameras. Sure, we don't necessarily wear name brands all the time, but your shirt looks mad cheap. I mean, look at you. Four different shades of black."

Xan took some offense to my comment, but I could care less at this point.

I checked the clock and pointed out there were now seven minutes till we needed to leave. "Change into a suit and tie and call it a day, pretty please," I begged.

Xan rolled his eyes from Vegas to Richmond before giving in and went upstairs to change.

In Sammatha and Leo's room, the two were admiring each other in the mirror. The room was dimmed as the yellow light gave the room an ambience glow.

"You look amazing," Leo said, moving some of her hair behind her ear. Sammatha started blushing.

The theme we were going for was prom but to a gala. Yea, I didn't put much thought into the red carpet look, to be completely honest. I mainly looked more into the headline performance we will do later in the evening. That will be the classic rhinestone, satin, all-black look. Hence why I wanted a hit of color, at least for the red carpet.

Leo went to grab Sammatha's rose from the bed.

"Save the best for last," he said.

Leo carefully and gently pinned the rose to her chest, right by her heart. Then Sammatha put her rose into Leo's suit pocket by his heart. How cute.

The whole idea was to have the roses symbolize the relationships in the group. For those who are not in a relationship, you don't wear a rose. Sounds depressing, but it really isn't. The roses are mainly there for fan service.

Coming out into the hallway, Theo glimpsed at Saige as she closed her room door. "Hey…" Theo shyly said.

"Suit and tie? Been awhile since you wore one" Saige expressed, walking towards him.

"Uh yea, I guess so. I thought you would wear an all-red dress, not a black jumpsuit," he said as he tried not to make much eye contact. "It was a red dress until Xan said the color would be all black. By the time Valen debunked Xan's comment, I was already changed."

Saige looked down and saw that Theo had two red roses in his hand.

"Right… I totally forgot," she said as she glimpsed back up at Theo. As I said, all couples, more specifically in the group (I don't count because Jackson isn't a member), have to wear a rose for fan service. Yes, Theo and Saige broke up in January, but the fans and rest of the world still think they are together.

"Should have seen Vanessa's reaction when Toran put hers rose on," Theo joked, trying to make the situation feel less awkward.

"Yea, she seems to be taking the break up rather rough. Even though their relationship felt like a pr stunt, I think she really grew to like him, and I think Toran did too. But it is what it is," Saige sighed.

DING!

Saige's little smile turned into a frown when she noticed that Theo had received a notification from his phone.

"Who's that?" she questioned.

"Must have been Xan telling everyone to hurry up in the group chat," Theo said as he pinned the rose onto Saige's top. Then he handed her his rose.

Saige leaned to put the rose in Theo's pocket, but as she tried to stuff it into his pocket, she noticed his heart beating.

"Okay, I think you're good." Saige took a step back to allow Theo to check out the rose.

"Thank you, Saige. Now if you don't mind, we have an award show to attend," Theo said shyly.

On the ride toward the Minute Works Arena, Asia observed some of the member's roses in the back of the van. A wave of sadness overcame her as she looked down at her chest.

Looking to her side, she saw Kyan's hand open, resting on his lap.

Once he noticed that she saw his hand, he tapped on her thigh before putting his hand in between the layers of her glittery poofy dress. While the rest of the members had their own individual conversations, Asia slowly moved her left arm to her side and searched for Kyan's hand. As soon as she found it, the two made eye contact.

"I have a gift for you," he whispered to her. Kyan slowly reached out from his back pocket and placed two rose petals into her palm. "I know it's not the whole flower but –"

"It's perfect," Asia whispered. As the van went under a long tunnel, Kyan quickly put the pedal into Asia's dress pocket. Then Asia proceeded to stuff the other pedal in his suit pocket. Just as the van came out of the tunnel, the two quickly returned to their position, trying to play it cool.

Over in the other van, Simon was very excited to go to the VVMAs.

   "Come on guys, you need to be just as pumped as I am. Tainted Hearts being nominated for Best Alternative Album could mean I can finally win my first solo VVMA award," Simon said to LeeSung, Jean, and Leo.

"Glad to see the album we told you not to make multiple times be nominated," Leo joked.

   "But he did a good job at the end of the day, right? Got our man out of depression. Plus, he slowed down on the substance," LeeSung patting Simon's back.

"Yeah, all it took was for our guy to have a crush on someone," Jean teased. Simon started hushing him as he looked over and saw Lily talking to Saige. Leo took notice, looking over in his direction. "You're still seeing her," Leo said in a low voice.

Simon coming back to his senses, "Who? Lily? We are just

friends…"

Jean glimpse at Leo, then at LeeSung.

The three started laughing, which brought Lily's attention as she briefly looked over at them.

"What? Did I miss something?" Simon said as he took a sip of his water.

"We weren't talking about her. We were talking about…you know… Saige. The same girl you decided to sweep in and be desperately first in line after she broke up with Theo," Jean whispered.

"But what's going on with you and Lily?" Leo questioned.

Before Simon could say anything, the van stopped.

The driver signaled Xan to the front of the van.

"Okay, we are here. Do you want me to pull up to the red carpet, or is this a good spot," the older van driver asked Xan.

Xan looked out the windshield as we were in the V.I.P. parking. There were so many music executives and A&Rs walking over to the arena. "Yes sir, here is fine," Xan said, reaching into his pocket to pay the man.

"Are you sure? Nominated artists can be dropped off at the carpet. If I let you all out here, it will be a lengthy walk."

Xan looked out the windshield again, and indeed the man was right. It was a walk. "We will be fine. I'm not interested in giving the members any type of luxury. Plus, it is a great warm-up exercise for our performance later tonight."

Xan gave the guy a generous paycheck and tip for his service. "Would you like a couple of tickets for the show?"

Xan pulled out four stageside tickets for the man though the old fella didn't seem interested. "Oh, I can't take that. You already paid me over asking," he reassured.

"Well, you can make even more fortune by selling this to a desperate fan in the area. These are useless for me to have anyways. Not like any of the members' families are going to show up."

Xan put the four tickets on the dashboard but noticed he still had about twenty more tickets left in his wallet.

"Hey, just have them all actually. You can throw it all in the trash can for all I care," Xan said before calling Lisa, who was in the other van behind.

"Hey, tell everyone we are walking over to the carpet."

Man, everyone threw a tantrum. We already spent hours doing each other's hair and make-up, then commuting another two hours just to walk another 15~20 minutes to the red carpet is insane. At least we didn't have to carry our belongings for the performance. Some of the members were kind enough to do that yesterday.

As Simon got off the bus, he saw a familiar fancy E Wagon parked in the parking lot. A car that he went and bought for someone a few years ago. Custom-wrapped in a white coat.

"We have to walk!"

Lily walked over to Simon and rested her head on his sleeve. "This is so annoying! I got heels on, and I am not interested in potentially breaking a sweat."

"Simon. Give me the beanie," I said, walking to him.

Grimming, he handed it to me because, yeah, a black cotton beanie definitely works for a formal event.

"Oh, don't mind it. Let me fix your hair."

As Lily fixed his hair, she noticed that something was off about Simon.

"Are you good?" Lily asked. Simon lightly gestured to look at the third car to the right behind her. "They can't be here... I would have known if something was up," Lily whispered.

"Maybe it's a false alarm."

"Should we tell the rest of the group?"

"No. We should be fine. We might not even run into them."

It was about 6pm, and the golden hour was coming through. The sky was pretty pink, blue, and golden orange. Off the group went as we walked toward the loud music coming from the outdoor concert stage.

"Geez. Watch your step. There are a ton of wires running around the ground," I said as I carefully stepped over some cords.

Finally, we stumbled upon the red carpet, and every eye turned to us. Oh, the classic smile and wave face came to all of us like it was copy and paste. No longer were photographers interested in taking pictures of the new Artist of the Year nominees. They desperately wanted about a thousand photos of each member.

"Look who has arrived!!! If it isn't the one and only world, renounce group, Switch!"

Carlos and Brittany went first as respected in line. Have to give your credit to the two for getting our group mainstream. Who knew all it took was a "You got me pregnant right when my career took off" scandal. I argue that the reason why they became the first members of the group to win their own VVMA award.

Group pictures, couple pictures, solo pictures. Vanessa and Toran do put up a show. Cheesing ear to ear like they just got back from their honeymoon.

I kept an eye out on the crowd of celebrities to see if I could spot any familiar faces, but I didn't see anyone in particular. No blacklists and enemies in sight, so all is good. As we pulled away from the carpet into the building, I noticed Jackie was still on the carpet, giving pose after pose.

"Oh, my goodness Jackie come on," I muttered. "One second," she mouthed.

Pose. Pose. Pose. Pose. Pose And Pose. Jackie was giving face and high fashion as if she didn't get her outfit from Rebecca's closet.

Then she dismissed herself to join the rest of the group. "What. I needed a good picture to post on my Instagrand."

The group stayed close as we maneuvered the room. So many eyes looking at us. People who were jealous and envious of our success. But we kept our eyes either straight or down.

38

09/02/22: The VVMAs. Part II

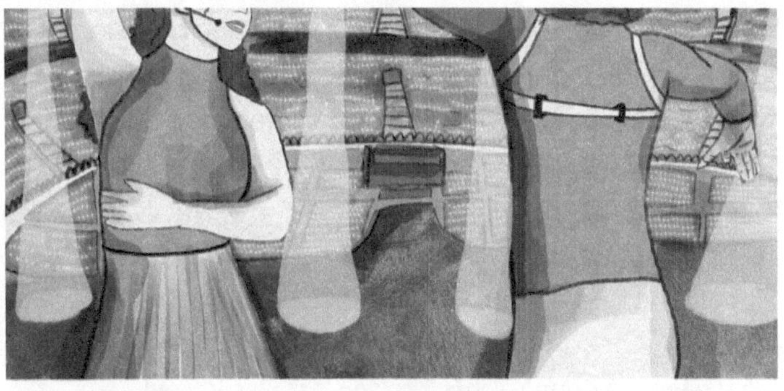

The tension felt unwelcoming while we passed through the packed crowd.

After lots of smiling and waving, we made it to our dressing room.

"Jermany," Carlos called out. Pulling him to the side, Jermany could tell that he appeared rather off.

"I think there might be a problem with tonight's performance," Carlos said.

"What do you mean? Do your vocals hurt? Did you sprain your ankle?" Jermany questioned.

"What? No. I don't think so. Remember the articles about us dominating the charts a while back..."

KNOCK, KNOCK.

Jermany and Carlos shifted their attention to the door, wondering who it could be.

"I'll get it," I said as I made my way over to the door.

With a quick turn of the knob, I slightly open the door to a... journalist. How did a journalist get to this restrictive area? I have no idea, but I gave him the most generic, straight-out the textbook comment about one of the ex-members.

"Despite our differences, we wish them nothing but the best. Now if you don't mind, we must prepare for the show but thank you for stopping by," I said before closing the door. I even gave it a double-check to see if it was locked.

I was starting to feel overwhelmed with being at the VVMAs. I felt like I had been awake for 24 hours and still had to tough out 3 more at its minimum.

"Who was that," Simon asked in French.

"No one. Just someone is trying to meet a quota for their job."

Carlos tapped back at Jermany. "I think they will sabotage the votes so we don't win."

"That's not possible. Where did you hear this information from," Jermany asked.

Carlos rubbed his shoulder as he was holding back his answer. "Well... I saw it trending on social media. The higher-ups are supposedly bending the votes so that their artists have a fighting chance to win. Why do you think there were so many music executives here?"

Jermany was intrigued and thought the allegation wasn't too far-fetched. Yelling across the room, Jermany said, "Xan! Do you think the votes are going to be rigid?"

"If you lose, you lose. Should have done a better job during production, post, and on the stage," Xan signed. He was so busy trying to piece together the final cut that he couldn't care less if the winners were determined by a coin toss or the roll of a dice. Anxious and stressed, he also felt an uncomfortable sense of uncertainty. It was as if a chain reaction was awaiting to erupt.

With nothing to take the feeling away, he decided to drown himself in his paperwork as he mapped out the performance for the 30th time in the last hour.

Looking to his side, he saw Lisa come and sit by him as she fixed her sparkly top.

"Are you going to perform tonight?" She asked.

Xan shook his head in disagreement. "I am going to stay

backstage."

"Boo, you never come out to sing with the group. I mean, the same applies to me, but it is a blue moon today, and I know the routine."

Xan took a double look at Lisa and admired her silk outfit. In a stern tone, Xan cleared his throat.

"You look nice."

Though Lisa wasn't paying attention to him. "Mazen and Kyan! Get dressed and stop playing around," Lisa yelled.

About an hour went by. All dressed up in shiny, black attire; it was time to open up the show, which was contradicting because we usually go last for any award show. It's weird. Putting your grand finale act at the show's beginning is unnecessary. Setting the bar way too high means the rest of the later acts will be mid by default.

Right before we left, we did a harmonizing vocal activity to ensure all our voices were warmed up and ready to go.

Taking action, Mazen went to the back corner to find Alanna as we huddled around.

"Pssssst! Alanna. Wake up; we are about to leave," Mazen whispered loudly. With a big yawn, she rose from her chair, sleepily. "Why didn't you take a nap earlier," Mazen said as he brought her to the huddle.

"Didn't have time. I had to help Asia braid her hair, and now my hands hurt."

Alanna briefly stopped in shock as she checked her hair in

the mirror. Quickly she searched for a brush to fix it.

Searching high and low, she could not find one at her station. In a panic, she notices Sammatha and Leo passing by her.

"Sammatha! Do you have a brush I can use? Please, please, tell you do." she asked.

Sammatha was startled a bit. "Um, yeah. Let me go fetch it for you," she said softly.

"Thank you!"

As Alanna followed Sammatha, Mazen looked at Leo.

"What?" Leo questioned.

Out of nowhere, Mazen started to pretend to style his hair.

"Do you have a hair tie I can borrow?" Mazen asked.

"How many do you need?"

"Two small ones. I have been fancying pigtails lately," Mazen joked.

After spraying in some dry shampoo and brushing her hair, Alanna looked way more presentable. "Okay, we are good now," she said.

Alanna took notice of Sammatha's mood being a little down. "Everything okay?" Alanna questioned.

Sammatha looked up in alarm. In panic she said, "I'm fine. Just want to knock out this performance, that's all."

Taking a quick glance over her shoulder, Sammatha made eye contact with Leo.

"Well... we should probably warm up those vocal cords, right," Alanna said, trying to bring up Sammatha's spirits.

In the huddle, we sang our acapella song Yesterday. The room felt so angelic like a fresh breeze of sea wind blew into the room. It was a combination of sopranos, altos, tenors, and bass. A quick two-minute exercise that would leave anyone with extreme goosebumps as if they transcended to another universe and back.

After our voices collided and birthed a child, everyone in the room grabbed each other's hands. Then we close our eyes for prayer. "Um, who wants to pray?" I asked.

"I will," Mazen offered.

"Dear, our heavenly Father,

We all humbly come forwards toward you today as we give you all the praise and glory. We ask for your love, strength, and protection. I pray that tonight's show goes well. I also pray we don't forget our lines or miss-calculate our steps. God, please forgive us for all our sins that we committed in the past and present and those we may, unfortunately, commit in the future. Lord, please help and lead us to not fall into temptation in this journey we take to be closer to you. Remind us that you are the one and only living God. We accept Jesus Christ as our lord and heavenly savior who died for our sins. And um. Right. In the power of the Father's holy spirit and in the mighty name of Jesus name, we pray to you,

Amen. "

Everyone said "Amen," and a few even wiped a tear away.

"I hope that I did a good job. I just try to piece together what I heard at church."

"You did a great job Mazen," I said.

As everyone got to leave, Rebecca held Dice's hand a bit longer. "Ready to head out?" Rebecca said softly.
"I think so. Or I know so, actually. Toran really helped me prepare last night, and now I feel set to get out there," Dice said.

Leaving the room, the members of Switch headed out to the main stage. Ready to do what we know best. Put on a show.
Coming around the corner, a random woman started walking toward us.
Before we knew it, she "accidentally" splashed red wine all over Xan's tuxedo and glasses.

"You have to be kidding me. You son of a..."
Xan looked up and saw that the woman had a smirk on her face. "And how much money did they pay you to do that, huh," Xan growled.

"I am so sorry. I must have tripped over my steps," the worker sarcastically stated. In came the security guards and roughly dragged the women away, but Xan didn't like how aggressive they were trying to be.

"Chill. The woman knows how to walk."
The security guards relaxed on the woman and showed her out from backstage. "Xan, did you want to change?" Lisa

asked.

Xan turned around and checked out his stained white shirt. "No. If someone wanted to sabotage me, I would let them get all their laughs and giggles out until we win Album of the Year," Xan said.

So watch your step. What's next? A pie in the face? But better yet. How old are we again? I didn't know we were still in high school. Or at least, that is what I think high school is like. Not me getting flashbacks from my homeschooling days. Anyways.

Finally, we made it to the stage. One by one, we grabbed our signature earpieces and walked over to the stage, as the concert hall was dark. A wave of cellphone lights waved around in the arena as the screams got louder and louder.

Romeo was in the front row of three and looked behind him to ensure everyone was in formation. Each member threw up their index finger one by one, signaling they were ready. Then Romeo signaled one, then five, to Xan to ensure everyone was ready.

The stage set was more straightforward than it would tradi-tionally be. All we have is a couple of moving platforms in the back with a 15-minute set time. Which is a long, long time when all the other acts get about three-four minutes, depending on how popular you are as an artist. It is our industry standard for booking at the end of the day.

Bam! The music cue as our traveling orchestra and the band kicked off the show. It was like witnessing history once again. The performance went really well. We did a remix of 5 songs highlighting each subunit with the group. So we had some R&B, some pop, some hip-hop, funk, and a handful of high notes to wow the crowd. It was ultimately great.

Everyone remembered their lines and their formations. Plus, the crowd was fangirling as the couple's dance portion took place. We bought a different change in pace to the VVMAs that night. The other performers barely put much effort into their set and relied heavily on backup dancers for crowd appeal.

After a successful performance and a quick change back to our red carpet outfit, we made our way to the floor to take our seats for the award ceremony.

It was hard to not miss us, as 29 people, minus Kendrick and David, walking down the aisle to the front row.

Some of the nominees were starstruck to see us in person, while others had the biggest disgusted mark on their faces.

"Wow..." Brittany said as she paused in her steps. Carlos, who was escorting her, questioned why she stopped until he saw what was before his eyes. Turning around, he looked at Jermany, and Jermany looked at him, then back at the seats that should be unoccupied, labeled as [Reserved].

Midway through the walk down, Lisa had her arm wrapped and snug into Xan's arm.

"See, I told you Set Eight would work for tonight. Number

one trending online right now," Xan smiled.

"Okay, you win on this one. I guess those sleepless nights paid off. Though I wish you would change your shirt at least..."

Lisa halted when she noticed Dice and Rebecca stopped in front of them.

Lisa and Xan questioned what the hold-up was. Moving up to the front, Xan stress levels began to rise once again. His patience was really being tested. Tested badly.

Moments went by as we all tried to figure out what was going on.

"Why did we stop?" Leo asked Jean at the back of the line. "I think someone is in our seats," Jean said.

"Our seats?"

Coming down, I signal Leo to come up to the front.

In Spanish, Leo told Jean to have Cameron accompany Sammatha while he went up front.

"I'll be right back," Leo whispered into Sammatha's ear. Leaving her to be, Leo joined up with me.

"What's going on, Valen? We got to sit down before the commercial break is over."

"Excuse me, do we have a problem here," the usher asked Xan.

"Yes, these seats are reserved for the members of Switch. We should have at least 30 seats open in the front row."

The people sitting in our seats started to chuckle like a group of entitled nepotism babies. This made Xan's face turn red.

"You think this is funny! Linz, you shouldn't even be here. You really only have one song on your catalog and James and the Silhouettes... Should I bring up your little scandal that happened at that hotel? Or what was found in your car?"

The lead singer of James and the Silhouettes took offense to what Xan said. "Oh, what are you going to do? Put me on the Switch blacklist? I mean, you look like a crackhead by the way your reacting."

"Hey, don't compare me to your mother. I'm just trying to make sure my group is taken care of," Xan said angrily.

"That's not what the streets are saying. 'Switch is a ticking bomb just waiting to explode.' I mean, great performance, but wow. That lack of professionalism from their own "leader" is crazy. Not to mention the whole scandal with Ketrean getting blackballed, but oh, right. You paid the media a handsome check to keep that quiet. Didn't you," James said.

Lisa stepped in for Xan. "What's the point that you are trying to make?"
    James looked at his bandmates and then at her. "You should have let us perform at BFF World '22"

"Well, maybe if you didn't get arrested the week before, we could have worked something out," Xan clapped back.
    "I was bailed out the next day," James said, getting heated.

Carlos and Jermany knocked on Xan's back three times, but he did not care.

"Oh, for real?"

"Yea, actually, and I'm not about to sit here and argue with someone who apparently can't afford a clean white shirt!" James said as he stood up from his seat. Not to mention how tall he towered over Xan.

Making our way up, Leo hopped in to intervene in the exchange.

Switching to Portuguese, "Not here. There is no point in picking a fight with them."

"I don't care if we sit in the back or front row. They are in our spot."

I stepped into the conversation, once I realized they were speaking in Portuguese. "Eh, so what are we going to do then? Fighting is not going to get them to move."

James laughed a bit. "You're kidding me. Is this the infamous code-switching the members of Switch be doing? What is the language of the day? Spanish?"

Oh, Xan wanted to throw hands at James, but Leo took action quickly.

"We are not trying to cause any problems," Leo reassured back in English.

"Nah, you are the last person I want to be talking to. You look like someone who got skeletons in your closet. I remember when you were in thousands of scandals left and right. But you think you are a changed man, huh," James said, moving closer to Leo.

Leo tried to keep his composure and not show any emotion. Save by the bell, an usher came by with a walkie-talkie in their hands.

"I want to apologize. It seems like the seating arrangement got messed up. Though we can spread out the members of Switch in the other rows. Maybe in pairs of 2s and 3s."

Split up the group? That sounds insane. We just gave a world-class cinematic performance, and now we can't even get the luxury of sitting next to each other? I turned around to look at the rest of the group, and they were against us splitting up.

I asked, "Is there a place where we can sit by each other?"

As the usher talked on the walkie-talkie, Leo looked around the crowd and noticed a familiar face in the audience.

"Ma'am, there is an option," the usher said, pointing off in the distance.

It was to the very back. 30 rows back, to be exact.

"We'll sit there then," Leo randomly said. Xan was shocked by Leo's quick response.

The usher then showed us the way to what could be seen as an embarrassment stunt to the back.

In Portuguese again, Xan said under his breath, "Why did you do that??? They should be at the back of the row. Not us. Especially that James guy and his band. I don't even know how they got in here."

"If you cared to look at the people in the third row, you would have noticed that Ex-S Records executives and our old manager were sitting there. Same people who try making us sign another 360 contracts. Not to mention the anti-fans who are here. Not good to make a scene."Leo then rushed up to Sammatha.

Xan looked back in alarm and saw Mr. Smith looking right at him.

Jumpscare by the tap on his shoulder, Mazen asked, "Why are we walking to the back? What about our front-row seats."

"Don't worry about it, okay. Do me a favor and tell the rest of your line not to be looking around when you called to the stage," Xan said, worried.

Xan realized that his mood was worrying Mazen, so he switched it up.

"Uh, because when we all receive our reward, you have to own the moment and not look like a lost puppy."

"Man, who cares about the award. The performance is done, and I vote for us all to go home while we are on our feet," Mazen joked.

Finally, we sat in the back row where the camera team was, interestingly, parked directly behind us. Theo looked down the row, then at the stage.

"You can barely see anything from here," Theo said to Romeo.

"I know. We have been sitting in the same spot for years now. Why did that have to change?"

One of the perks, though, was the cameraman could stay within a reasonable distance to get us in the frame for when the nominations came out.

"And the winner for Best Performance... SWITCH!"

Not the stage camera panning all the way to the back of the crowd as we stood up. And it did that dramatic pan to the very back again and again when we won Best Music Video for Hot-Line and Best Group. Walking back and forth was not ideal, especially for us ladies, because we had on heels.

"For Best Male Soloist Album, our nominees are Harry Longue, Switch's Dice Hernandez, Switch's Simon Fischer, and Raymond."
Tension filled the stadium as the results were being awaited.

"Wait, I have been nominated," Dice questioned.
"What are you talking about? How could you forget?" Rebecca said.

Dice glanced at Simon, who seemed pretty relaxed by the nomination for Tainted Hearts. Taking a look back at the stage monitor, the actress opened up her card.

"And the winner is...

Switch's Dice Hernandez for Solo About It!"

Dice rose up a bit, shocked by his win. He was very confident that he would lose to Raymond or Simon.

"Congrats, man," Simon said, getting up to dab him up.

"Thanks, though you should have won."

"I just wanted to win the best alternative album, which was accomplished. Go get your award."

Dice walk to that stage alone, and I mean WALK. Looking around at the other artists in the stands, they looked jealous and envied him. Didn't help that it took him a minute to get onto the stage, as it looked like he was taking his time. Luckily the fans on the upper level were screaming to help give the room some life. Like, give him his moment. It is a moment worth having for it being his first VVMA award with only his name on it.

Coming onto the stage, Dice was taken aback a bit when the person handing him his award told him that he only had 30 seconds to say what he wanted.

"Geez, I only get 30 seconds because I took too long to get up here? What was I supposed to do? Run?" Dice said into the mic.

Oh, the rest of us in the back sighed at Dice's comment. "Um, well, I like to not dedicate this award to Ex-S Records, for they saw me solely as a backup singer. I would like to dedicate this award to my Lord and savior Jesus Christ, and yea... That's all. OH, AND SHOUTOUT TO THE FLAMES OUT THERE!!!!!!!!!"

He signed to the camera to shout out his deaf fans before leaving the stage. Cheesing ear to ear, he left the stage. Nevertheless, it did not take him long to notice Mr. Smith in the third row staring at him.

Discreetly, Dice signed to him, "I hope you rot in a well," while walking back to his seat.

Judging by his expression, Mr. Smith was unhappy to see our wins.

In the following, I realized we didn't have anyone running for Best Female Soloist, where usually Cameron wins. So you should have seen the reaction when the monopoly on that particular award was free for someone else to win.

"Now for Album of the Year..."
   All the members grab each other's hands as the tension builds up and the stadium shakes.

"IN THE NAME OF LOVE BY SWITCH!"

Oh, how could I be surprised by that announcement? Anyone, hater or not, knew that was a great album. So off the group went to the stage. We all huddle around on the stage to accept the Victorian House shape award.

"I will give the speech," Carlos said.
   "I think I should," Jermany suggested.
   "You already gave one for Hot-Line. I will go," Romeo said, going up to the mic. He didn't make it far before Xan stepped

in front of him with his prepared speech.

As Xan gave his speech, Mazen's eyes wandered into the crowd.

"Code red…" Kyan whispered, a little frightened Mazen.

Mazen didn't get what Kyan was talking about until his eyes met directly with Mr.Smith. Mazen eyes open wide in terror.

"And we hope to see you all next year to pick up our next award," Xan said cocky.

Moving off the stage, Mazen and Kyan rushed over to Xan. "He's here???" Mazen said, scared.

"Everything is going to be fine. I won't let him come near you. Stay near Rap Line," Xan said quietly.

Without a thought, Kyan went over to LeeSung as we all walked back to our seats.

"He is here," Kyan said in Mandarin to LeeSung.

"Who?" LeeSung said, concerned.

"Smith…"

LeeSung turned around and noticed Mr. Smith was looking at the group.

"He can't get to you. I wouldn't let him," LeeSung said.

Mazen came up to them to join the conversation. Switching back to English, LeeSung told Mazen to not worry about the situation.

"Worry??? You don't know what happened in his office," Mazen said, trying to not raise his voice.

"We'll talk about this later," LeeSung said when he noticed some people were catching on to their conversation.

We didn't get the chance to sit down because we had won Artist of the Year by the time we returned to our seats.

So we had to walk past everyone again to go receive the award. Kyan and Mazen did not want to go up, though, since Asia and Alanna didn't know what was happening; they didn't want to draw suspicion.

Once on stage, I had to give a speech for our award. Taking a glance at the Ex-S Records executives, they seem pretty mad at our winning streak. But can someone give them a reality check because you can't sabotage an award show based on fan voting?

"Oh my. I want to speak on behalf of the members of Switch and saw that we are very grateful for the Artist of the Year award. Firstly we want to take the time and thank and honor God for what he has done for us and wouldn't be possible without him. Thank you, our Flame fans and stans, as well as our family, for the love and support. Thank you!"

What a night. Seven wins, though, could have been more but let's not get greedy.

39

09/02/22: The VVMAs. Part III

Traffic must have been really backed up after the show because we got a call that the bus driver was running about 45 minutes late. Luckily, David was kind enough to buy us some pizza for our accomplishment, while Kendrick just kept blowing up the group chat asking if someone could mail him his awards. I said, "No, it is going straight into the Hall of Fame room."

"Apparently, there are some snacks out there if anyone wants to grab some," Saige said, entering the dressing room.

Mia tapped on Maxwell's leg to get his attention.

"Do you think you can get me something there? I don't care what it is. I just can't eat this pizza."

Maxwell was quiet the whole day, as usual. I mean, the guy was holding a book during the red carpet. Just waiting for the perfect opportunity to sit down and drown himself in his imagination.

Putting down his book, he agreed to grab her something to eat. Simon and I were by the door, ready to go, when we saw Maxwell getting up.

"Maxwell! Maxwell is coming!" Simon cheered.

"Yeah, yeah, I'm coming," he said, letting out a little smile. "You seem to be in a great mood?" I said, opening the door.

"Did you forget that I won best alternative album? A win is a win, and it's worth being happy about!"

The three of us walked down the hall to where all the treats were. Surely enough, they were given goodie bags. We grab a few bags and then head back to the room.

Maxwell looked inside his bag to see what he got. "Pretzels sticks, oranges, and a juice box. Its not even name-brand."

"Food is food," I said.

Suddenly we slowed down in our steps. Some artists from earlier at the show didn't look too happy when they saw us passing by. Like, what did we do? One would say they are haters, but why hate on us? We have done nothing but sing and dance.

Walking past, Maxwell briefly looked back. "What's wrong?" Simon said.

"I could have sworn one of those people said they saw Kylie. You don't think she is here?" Maxwell asked.

Simon's mood got a little down. "I'm not sure, but I did see

Jordyn's car earlier today in the parking lot."

"How do you know that it was her car?" Maxwell questioned.

Simon sighed a bit, "Because I bought it."

"I saw her car too. But I didn't see Jordyn or even Zachary in the crowd." I admitted.

Finally, we arrived back to the dressing though Maxwell paused before he opened the door. "If my sister finds out that Kylie is in the same building as her, she will flip out."

Judging by Maxwell's worries, I can tell and understand why he brought his book with him because I can see his anxiety levels rising.

"You have nothing to worry about. Let's say she is here. It's her against the rest of the group in a public space. And last time I checked, she needs us if she wants those royalty checks to keep coming in." I said.

Oh, I was undoubtedly worried about Kylie being close to the group. She had too many strikes and you're-out moments to the point I want to personally blacklist her. On the other hand, I'm curious about whether or not Zachary and Jordyn are in the area. Even though they went MIA, it doesn't mean they aren't on the Switch roster as affiliates.

We returned to the dressing room, hoping to not give off any vibe that something might be wrong. To deflect the situation, I offered the group to play some card games with those who weren't knocked out from tiredness.

"Game?" I suggested to Kyan and Mazen, yet they passed on the offer to play with the big kids.

"I will pass too," Asia said.

I didn't bother to ask Alanna for obvious reasons. So I left them alone to go play a round with JV Line and Duo.

Asia looked at Kyan and Mazen in question. "Why are you two so down? You two were such a chirper earlier," Asia said.

"We saw Mr. Smith, but everything is going to be fine," Kyan reassured.

Asia did not like the sound of that.

"We will be fine. He probably is long and far away from here," Mazen said.

Looking up they saw LeeSung pulling a chair up to them.

"Hey, I talk to Xan and Lisa. Mr. Smith had left the area. So you have nothing to worry about," LeeSung said.

"What happened to the restraining order," Asia asked.

"It's still in full effect. I wouldn't allow him to get near you four. You have my word and everyone else in this group." LeeSung said.

45 minutes went by. Finally, the tour bus arrived to take us back to the BFF stadium. I wish and, honestly, wanted to beg the driver to take us to the actual house and not to Brooklyn. Since our regular guy is off the clock, we had to get a substitute to fulfill the duty. Plus, for security reasons, we can't let the new guy on the job drop us off at the main house. Especially when it is so hidden that it is not even on the GPS.

Packing up all our belongings, we headed out to the bus one by one.

"I think today was a success!" Dice yelled.

Brittany and Courtney were walking beside each other as they watched Carlos and Jermany chat.

"What do you think they are talking about?" Brittany questioned.

"I don't know, but Jermany has been acting pretty tense since we got here."

"Same with Carlos. But like Dice said. Today was a success. Rather long and tiring day, but I think it was fine."

Courtney couldn't stop looking at Jermany.

"I don't know Brittany. Something got to be up. Maybe something happened earlier today, and they are hiding it from us. There were a lot of people who didn't want to see us win today."

Coming up behind the two was Brionna. "Hey, have you two noticed something strange? Why is a part of the group acting up like they won the lottery, and the other half is all tightened up?"

Brittany looked at Brionna and then at Courtney.

Brittany said, "Usually, I would say this is a great example of the delusional and overthinkers, but judging by what happened today... Think about it. The jealousy on the red carpet. Xan's shirt being ruined. Mr. Smith was in attendance, plus us sitting in the back row? We have been coming to the

VVMAs for almost a decade now and rarely had any problems here."

"So what changed? You think we are being tested?" Brionna questioned.

The three didn't know what to say, but Brionna's theory didn't seem too far-fetched but rather in the right ballpark.

"Okay, Simon, how are we going to celebrate?" Leo asked.

"Celebrate!?! I figure you guys made plans already," Simon said.

Sammatha and Cameron were by the respective sides of their man, shaking their heads.

"Simon, leave me and Sammatha out of this," Cameron said.

"Exactly. Plus, the girls have a plan to do a movie night." Sammatha chimed in.

"Movie night?" Simon questioned.

"No, I am just kidding. I'm going to bed when we get back," Sammatha laughed.

Leo started to cheese really hard as he watched Sammatha smile. "Hey, let me carry your dress," Leo requested.

Sammatha glanced up at Leo. "No, I got it. It's not even heavy."

LeeSung shrugged. "Eh, I'm still here. Haru is out at her cousin's, so I'm free tonight."

"And what do you suggest?" Jean asked LeeSung. "We do what Simon wants to do. The guy is on fire right now!

Honestly, we should take him to the studio so that he can work on part two of Tainted Hearts," LeeSung suggested.

Leo wasn't even paying attention to the conversation anymore as he got lost in small talks with Sammatha. "You are already carrying my performance and backup outfit. That does not already include yours too. I can carry mines," Sammatha pouted.

"You might trip over it," Leo said softly.
"I will not."
"Well, you mention that you are tired."
"Tired of traveling and singing. But never too tired to carry my dress," Sammatha blushed.

Simon took notice and rushed in front of Leo and Sammatha. Walking backward, he asked, "What are you two love birds talking about?"

"Nothing," Leo blushed.
"Just Leo being Leo. Always trying to help out in the best way he knows how," Sammatha smiled.

Time slowed down immediately. Simon slowly watch Sammatha look behind him, and her smile turned into anxiety and fear. Eyes wide open, she then looked up at Leo in distraught.
Everyone halted right before we reached the exit.

"Well. Glad to see you all again. BFF, Switch, still not sure which dumb, didn't age well name you all decided to call yourself. How do you do?"

Brittany was shocked to see who she was seeing.

"We are being tested. Oh Jesus, the trials… the trials have begun." Brionna said, worried.

Quickly Brionna looked behind at Sammatha, who didn't look too happy.

Standing right before us was Grace and she looked a lot like Alanna. Maybe could qualify as a second cousin, just a little older. The 35th original member from when the group used to be known as just BFF, and surely enough, she was my former best friend.

We don't ever talk about Grace. She was only in the group for about a year or so until, one day, she decided that she loved drama. She loves to waste people's time and pull on heartstrings, but she was young back then. She was 13. How could she know better than to not start fights? Ex-S, though, didn't like her attitude. Didn't last long before she got kicked out of the group after a breach in her contract.

But us members didn't think less of her. Until she made it her goal in life to associate herself with anyone who had been on our blacklist. She unapologetically tried to dox the entire group and sell our insider drama to news blogs and our rivals for cash grabs. So I was surprised when I saw who was next to her.

"I think they call themselves Switch now," Kylie said, looking straight at Sammatha.

Leo quickly grabbed Sammatha's hand and held it extremely tight as if his life depended on it.

Kylie made sure to look photoshoot ready. Lashes done, nails done, eyebrows plucked, with extensions to fluff up her hair and a spray tan. The tension between the Mexican ex-member versus Sammatha's Italian/Moroccan identity for Leo, who is Brazilian, is intriguing to see. Love the diversity.

Simon slowly turned around and saw a woman, age 25, with long platinum blond hair and pale white skin. She was a little shorter than him, and immediately he knew who it was. His twin sister, Jordyn.

Lily moved up to the front. Questioning what was going on. Then she froze in her steps, baffled by who she saw standing in front of her.

"Zachary??? What...What are you doing here"
   Zachary looked a lot different with a new soft muscle build, a little tease of facial hair, and seemed to move away from the dirty blond hair color to hazel brown.

Varsity guys were, most importantly, the most disappointed to see Zachary, especially Carlos and Jermany. The same guy who used to sing lead with them is now on the wrong side of the fence.

Standing side by side, Grace, Kylie, Zachary, and Jordyn stood before us as if they wanted to get back in blood. Envying the "what if I stayed" conversation.

Simon's demeanor was shattered into pieces.
   "Jordyn! No call, no text! I woke up one day, and you're

just gone. It's been two years, and you've been ignoring any conversation I try to bring up to you."

Jordyn had their hands folded, trying to avoid eye contact with her brother.

"I figured you were busy."

"Busy??? That is the cheapest answer you could give. Clearly, I'm not busy if I have enough time to send a letter or call you!"

"UH SIMON! Hush! She doesn't want to talk to you. Or any of you stuck-up, entitled folks anyways," Kylie said with an attitude.

Walking up to the group was Jackie, Mia, and Maxwell carrying their belongings.

"Oh my goodness, she can't be here," Mia said as she noticed Kylie and Simon were going back and forth. Putting her stuff down, she walked up to Kylie, wanting to slap her.

Meanwhile, Jackie froze, getting one quick exchange of eye contact with Jordyn. Slowly she turned around and quickly hid behind the corner wall.

Looking over the edge, she noticed that Zachary was looking over at her.

"This can't be happening right now," Jackie said under her breath.

"Nice to see you again Mia. Still mad at me for being a homewrecker. I mean, so I did something I shouldn't have done, but you got Maxwell right?" Kylie smirked. Mia wanted to say something so bad, and Maxwell took notice of it too, because had Kylie not hooked up with Leo, Mia would have still been with him.

"What, is there something you want to say? Because the floor is yours," Kylie said. Before Mia could say something that could get us thrown into another scandal, I stepped in to dismantle the tension in the room.

"Okay, the party is over. Congratulations, Kylie, you still got that fire inside of you," I said. Suddenly the four let out a little laugh.

"Sorry. But, like, how are you even still in this group Valen. The weakest link is still the leader of BFF. Okay," Kylie laughed. I raise my hand slightly, signaling for the members to not say anything in my defense.

"It's called singing lessons. Have you heard of that or not? Cause you were the weakest link in the JV line, lower than me. Spent more time worrying about other people's business instead of figuring out how to dance. And Jordyn, I know you ain't laughing. You never did anything. You are neck and neck with Kylie for the bottom of the food chain. God forbid you actually volunteer to help around the house. Learn a skill maybe, or write a song, or clean your mess. Even Maknae Line put in more effort than you. And Zachary. You know you shouldn't even be standing next to these three. You were once a lead singer who simply needed to learn that he was not a soloist in a group full of backup singers. Thinking taking a hiatus would have us begging you back. And Grace. YOU WERE NEVER ON THE ROSTER! The group has 400 songs in creation, and you made it on to only three, and that's from the debut album that was considered a flop until you left. But last time I checked, I am the person who has the right to not give you all your royalty paychecks for the month because y'all didn't _______________?"

"Read your contract," the group said in synchronization.

"Thank you class. A+ for the day. And Zachary and Jordyn. Last time I checked, you two are still affiliated with the group, associating with Grace, who is on the blacklist is an ultimate rule breaker. I see you no longer care about Switch laws and regulations. Though since the group just won a bunch of awards that you could have had too, I will let this slide. So it would be advisable that you four leave. Say any comment about any of the current ACTIVE members of Switch, and I will give you a new insecurity that will have you first in line at the plastic surgery office at sunrise. Bien? Bien. "

"Wait. I'm not on the blacklist?" Kylie said, shocked.

   "Well, we are taking applications if you want to apply," I said sarcastically.

Side-eyeing us all, they left the area. Leaving us alone. I turned around and sighed in frustration. Looking behind, I saw Xan coming up to the group.

"Where have you been," I said.

   "I went to change my shirt. What did I miss?"

"Everything," I said.

40

09/02/22: The VVMAs. Part IV

It was a mandatory house meeting.

Packing all the members into the main living room with Kendrick and David on a video call was chaotic while everyone was talking over each other.

Coming in from the garage, Simon pulled Lily out into the hallway where all the recording studios were.

He said, "Do you think everyone is upset with me? I didn't even know my sister was in town. I mean, I saw her car in the parking lot, but I didn't see her in the crowd."

Lily looked down the hall and could tell how upset the other members were.

"I didn't know Zach was going to be in town either. Actually, I haven't been in great contact with him. I would get a Merry Christmas text or something equivalent but that's all. I don't know what his deal is?"

"Doesn't help that both of our siblings have to be dating each other...." Simon sighed.

"A relationship I never understood," Lily sighed.

The two's cover got blown when they saw Lisa signaling for them to come to the living.

"Okay! Okay! Quiet down!" I yelled.

"What was even that," Jackie questioned.

"What is Kylie planning now?"

"Switch 2.0"

"Out of Jealousy"

"FOMO! It has to be."

"Probably, they just miss the spotlight."

"Or miss living here?"

"My question is, why isn't Jordyn or Zachary here? They are still in the group."

"I think they should be kicked out."

"Kicked out?"

"They bring no value to the group anymore. Weren't even on the last two albums."

"Can't kick out someone who goes on a hiatus."

"Why not."

"What about Grace?"

Everyone rolled their eyes before continuing the discussion. Grace was in wave one, so technically, she was one of the original members. However, she needed to stay longer before the 2nd wave got their acceptance letters.

As the back and forth continue where the Varsity guys and Lily keep defending Zachary, and while the JV girls dog down on Kylie and Jordyn, Leo, Maxwell, and Xan when into the kitchen to talk in private.

Maxwell looks so heated and pissed off and Leo immediately knew he was in trouble. Maxwell started pacing around the kitchen before circling back to Xan and Leo.

"My sister has been doing so much better since we returned from California. So if I may ask Leo... WHY IS KYLIE ALWAYS ATTACKING MY SISTER?!?!? Why does it always have to be tied back to you?! I ask Sammatha, "Why are you crying" and it always stems back to Kylie's crush on you. Are you doing something that I need to know!"

Xan in panic, intervene. "I don't think Kylie is trying to just troll with Sammatha. Those four were on some kind of plan. I don't think it's fair to blame Leo for Kylie's actions."

Maxwell wasn't buying it though. "Oh really, 'cause this is the same guy who hooked up with Kylie."

Leo's face was full of shame. Rushing to Leo's defense Xan said,
    "For all we know and what the facts state, it only happened ONCE. YEARS AGO. As for Jordyn and Zachary. They get decent royalties, but since we stop including their singles for commercial usage opportunities, their check is significantly lower. Grace though. I don't care about her. I heard a rumor that she besties with Kylie but she should be smart enough to know that Grace is just using her for clout."

Xan looked at Maxwell and Leo, hoping that he had deviated from the conversation about the cheating scandal that happened with Mia which would eventually lead to the 2018 incident in Miami.

"Maxwell. I am sorry for everything, and I will try to fix it all," Leo said sincerely.

Though Maxwell wasn't buying the sales pitch. "That's all you ever say Leo, and nothing changes. All you do is make everything worse. You think you can just get away with anything by doing all these movies and taking your shirt off to get all your brownie points back. Still, last time I checked, you're the same guy who got checked into a rehab facility for anger management."

Xan quickly jumped in to de-escalate before anything got forward. "Okay, okay, let's change the subject."

"Hey can you three come out here," Lisa said peeping into the kitchen.

Giving in, the three went back into the living room to see what was going on.
    "I say we do a diss track," David said over the phone.
    "We should do a whole EP, actually," Jackie suggested.
"Wait, can't we just ignore them," Dice asked.

"It is too late," I said.

DING.

All at once, everyone's phone pulled out as I sent an article that was trending over the internet.

[BREAKING: Jordyn Fischer and Zachary Dion announced their disassociation with Switch.]

Looking up, I saw Simon quickly head upstairs to his room. Saige looked at the stairs, debating if she should go up and talk to him. In the few moments of thoughts, her eyes gaze briefly at Theo who was looking at her. Before she knew it, Lily passed her.

"Simon, wait," Lily said, rushing up the stairs.

The room was speechless and confused. Theo then glimpsed over at Jackie and knew something was up because she kept looking around.

"Does the article say why?" Jackie asked.

Reading through it, there was something about how they didn't like the members. But fail to go into any details.

Xan moved over to the center of the room where Lisa and I stood. "We just need to call it a day. No tweeting, no story posting, and don't even go into the city with the exception of LeeSung because your house is there. But for the rest, I don't want any of you to run into any paparazzi."

My eyes were wide open. A lockdown? A lockdown when we should be celebrating our wins from the VVMAs? Best Album of the Year? Best Artist of the Year?

Xan turned to Lisa and I, waiting for our decision to agree

for a lockdown to go through. Giving in, we agreed, followed by David. Lisa advises everyone to detox for the night before leaving for the office to get in contact with the legal and PR team.

As the room dispersed, Sammatha walked over to Leo as she noticed he was upset.

"Are you okay?"

Snapping back to reality, tapping into his acting face, he played it cool.

"I'm fine. How are you holding up? I - I didn't know she was going to be there. I promise," Leo said.

"I don't want to pay her any attention. But you seem off. Did my brother say something to you?"

Leo denied everything. "Nothing happened. Just a concerned brother, making sure everything is okay."

As Leo hugged Sammatha, he saw Maxwell mean-eyeing him before walking off with Mia upstairs.

In Simon's room, Lily watched Simon pace back and forth, trying to call Jordyn, but it kept going straight to voicemail every single time.

"Try again," Lily asked.

So he did.

"Sorry, but the person you are trying to reach is not -"

Lily jumped when she saw Simon launch his phone at his wall. The screen shattered into pieces as he walked into his bathroom to cool down.

"Maybe her phone is dead," Lily said.

Suddenly there was loud rumbling coming from the bathroom, which made her get off the bed to go investigate what Simon was doing. Slowly she walked over and saw that Simon was looking around for something at a quick pace. Opening every drawer, he started taking stuff out, creating an entire mess on the floor.

"I threw them out...Your pills." Lily said.

Simon froze before falling to the ground. Getting down to Simon's level Lily sat down by the door as she watched Simon cry. Simon was really emotional because he felt that his sister, Jordyn, had abandoned him. I mean, he was already taking it hard when Jordyn was no longer active in the group. However, her stepping down from her affiliation is at a whole different level. Kendrick may not be the most present member, but he is still an affiliate and stays well-connected with the group. He was done with the whole everyday practice routine, but that doesn't mean he doesn't want to eventually come back to do a performance or contribute to the album.

The two locked eyes as the two held each other's hands.
    "Where those needles," Simon choked.
    "NO! No... we are not doing this again," Lily said as she held Simon close.

"You don't feel upset about Zachary? We can do it together,"

Simon said, emotional.

"We are not doing anything. And Zachary does a lot of things I don't agree with, but I have a feeling he will be back."

"What if he doesn't come back?"

She was not a big fan of Simon's question. She let go of Simon and placed her hand to her side when she felt a ball of hair. Looking down, it was some red hair.

"You're still seeing Saige?" Lily said, getting overwhelmed. Simon looked at Lily as if he didn't know what to say once again as his eyes were bloodshot red.

"Don't worry. You don't have to tell me if you don't want to," Lily said, heartbroken. Leaning in, she gave Simon a kiss on the cheek before getting up to leave the room. Though as she was leaving, Simon got up to give her a hug from behind.

"Please don't think too much about it, okay," Simon said. Lily turned around, and the two made out briefly before Lily pulled away. Walking over to the door, she was just about to open it when she felt a wave of emotion rush to her.

"You can spend the night here if you want," Simon suggested. Taking her hand off the knob, Lily went to the bed to lie down.

There she started crying. Simon couldn't tell if Lily was upset about him seeing Saige or Zachary leaving the group. Simon went around the bed and lay down beside her. Having her roll over, he let her rest her head on his heart as she cried her eyes out. Tear by tear.

41

09/03/22: No purpose.

Today was the first day of lock down, and the main house was quiet as everyone was off in their respective corners, trying to move on from all that had happened yesterday.

Theo was leaving the recording studio when he saw Jackie passing by.

"Hey, wait."

Though she was uninterested in talking. Jackie tried to avoid Theo at all costs as she headed into the laundry room by the front door. Theo follows suit, closing the door behind him.

"Theo, I don't want to talk right now."

"But you are hiding something," Theo said.
    "I am not hiding anything. Now can I wash my clothes in peace," Jackie said.

"Have you been in contact with Jordyn since she left a while back?"
    Jackie nervously looked around for the detergent as she looked through the shelves. "Jackie?"

"No. I haven't heard from her."
    "I thought she was your best friend?"
    "Former." Jackie paused, looking at Theo. "Stop pressing me about this. Don't you have a lot of things on your plate right now?"

Giving up, Theo backed up to give her some space, and suddenly Jackie's phone started ringing.

"Who is that?" Theo asked.

Jackie pulled out her phone and noticed it was no caller ID.
    "No one."
    "But you look like you want to answer it."
    Jackie threw a hand towel at Theo in frustration.
    "Leave me alone!"

Respecting her request, Theo left the laundry room. Once the coast was clear, she went to lock the door before calling back the unknown number.

"Hello?" Jackie asked.

"Do you think we can meet up?" Jackie was surprised to hear Zachary's voice. Lowering her voice, "Are you calling me on your burner? And no, we can't 'meet up.' Even if I wanted to, the group is on lockdown."

"Not even for 30 minutes?"

Jackie ignored Zachary as she started the washer machine.
   "Hold on," she said, leaving the room to go outside for some privacy.

In the front yard, she crossed the driveway to the water fountain that was rarely on.
   "Why are you calling me? Have you even called your sister? Or even better, why did you leave the group," Jackie asked as she sat down.

Zachary was out in downtown Manhattan, looking out the tall windows from his hotel room. Right before he was going to say something, he noticed that Jordyn was coming out of the bathroom from washing her hair.

"Who are you talking to?" Jordyn said as she started drying her hair.
   Trying to find an excuse, he came up with the idea that he

was talking to his great-grandmother.

"Oh well, tell her I said hi. I should be dressed in about 20 minutes. Then we can head down to the Lunch Hour for that interview. I just need to do my hair," Jordyn said before returning to the bathroom.

"You leave the group and are now going on a press tour?" Jackie said, shocked. To keep the conversation private, Zachary switched over to French. Though Jackie's not the best at speaking French, she can surely understand it enough.

"I didn't want to leave the group, okay, but I had no choice."
    "You had no choice??? So you had to share your lines with the rest of the Varsity Guys. That doesn't mean you get up and leave. Now that you have announced your disaffiliation with the group, are you going to start your own solo career?"

Zachary took a few steps back to check on Jordyn. Making sure she wasn't eavesdropping. "I am not sure if I am doing a solo career just yet. But I was sick and tired of the whole group work, especially when the pay wasn't adding up."

"You are so entitled and spoiled! What do you mean the pay wasn't adding up. You're a nepotism baby with a 50-million-dollar trust fund. Plus, you were getting paid over half a million dollars per year after taxes."

"Xan and Lisa were taking 300k out of my paycheck every month."

"They were taking that out of everyone's checks unless you have a great boyfriend who could flip the bill for you, but I forgot you would never do something like that for Jordyn."

"300k each from 33 people as an excuse for 'members dues?'"

"You must have blacked out from 2016 to 2019, but if we had to pay out of pocket to build the BFF stadium in, I don't know, DOWNTOWN BROOKLYN! All so we could host BFF World here in good ole New York City and have a place to practice on a stage instead of relying on any free days we could get at Madison Square. Plus there were the complaints about the house being too small so we needed to build a new wing so that everyone could POTENTIALLY get their own room. Which I recall, you voted for that to all happen."

"It didn't need to be 300k per month," Zachary sighed.

"Oh well, that's what happens when you want a traveling orchestra and band. Someone got to flip all these bills. But for your information, are dues have to drop down significantly after paying off the house. Plus, the stadium pays for itself now that other acts want to use the stadium for their shows."

"How much are dues right now?"
    "I don't know, 30 to 40k. Unless we do a charity event, then it goes up, but it doesn't matter because no one is out here living the luxurious life that you love to flaunt to the world."

"Well, I'm not interested in the group anymore anyways. I

need to move on with my life."

"You need to move on with your life because the money got split multiple ways. You left the group because you wanted more money??? Why are you even calling me???"

"You're the one who calls me."

"Well, congratulations Zachary. In the biopic, you will be known as the Nepo EX-Switch member who loves to be a cheater and only sees his bandmates as cash cows and not once as his actual friends. But right, deep down in your heart, you know that's not true, but you can't admit it. Already bad enough, you have to pull the French to code your conversation with me. Something only a BFF member would do."

Zachary didn't know what to say. Turning around, he saw Jordyn signaling to him that she was ready to go.

"I will call you later," Zachary said over the phone.

"Right. Go public, humiliate the same people you spent your childhood with, who did nothing but support you along the way. Don't call me again."

Jackie hung up and then proceeded to block Zachary's phone number. Hovering over the block button, she hesitated to do so.

Instead, she turned off her phone and went back inside the house.

"AYE, AYE, HEY! Welcome to everyone's favorite podcast

coming to you live from the Bronx is THE LUNCH HOUR! In the house, we have some rather controversial guests. We have someone who is no stranger to this show Miss Kylie Torres but joining her is Grace, Jordyn, and once lead vocalist Zachary from Switch."

The four came into the room and sat down around the long table, each in front of a microphone and multiple cameras pointing right at them. The interviewer, Tim Johnson, a world renounce instigator born and raised in the Bronx, was ready to get down on the drama that would boost his rating score to levels he couldn't imagine.

"Thank you for having us here," Kylie said into the microphone.

"To start, my first question is to Jordyn and Zachary. Why did you guys leave Switch?"

Jordyn leaned in to answer. "We felt like the group was holding us back from expanding our career and life."

"What was it that you wanted to do?"

"Well, when you are a Switch member, you can't go do whatever you want. What people don't fully understand is that the group all pretty much lives together, and it's like living in one big college dorm. And dorms have rules, and they treat it like it's the end of the world if you break that rule," Jordyn said.

Zachary pulled the microphone closer to him. For a second, he thought about what Jackie said but disregarded everything.

"I hated the rules in the house too. But more importantly, I hated the lack of opportunities there is to grow as an artist. I remember asking multiple times if I could do a solo album and got constantly rejected and eventually just kept getting stuck working with the Varsity Guys, which, let's be honest. Other than Carlos, the rest of the guys are just noise. Especially Maxwell, who was my "singing pair." How are you going to pair me, one of the best dancers in the group, with Maxwell, who is terrible at dancing. I mean, have you really ever seen Maxwell ever do anything but wear a turtleneck and sing ballads??? I had a great time being paired with David until he was promoted to External Leader. Which, let's be honest, half the time, he is just partying in the name of business."

The room started laughing.

"So you felt like leaving the group was the best decision?"
    "Oh, 100%. My sister will be alright. She is satisfied with the bare minimum, but for me personally, I am not interested in having 4 am practices or dealing with Varsity Guy drama. Each and every one of those guys is messed up in the brain, and these so-called Flames fans need to understand that they are not perfect. If Ex-S Records didn't look at their files, Carlos would have gone down the same path he went through like before as a teen dad. Jermany, who is carrying the line right now, would probably have off himself in college from his poor stress management. Theo would be someone drunk in the alley for a thousand reasons that I don't even want to go into, or we would be here all day. Maxwell would probably be living back in Jersey as an incel, working minimum wage because he doesn't know how to talk to anyone. And Romeo would

be much further in life or in the music industry if he wasn't with Brionna. He knew that girl was holding him back. After that whole "I am depressed" episode she had back during the Around the World Part II tour in like 2014-2015. She had him wrapped up all around his finger, and now he married with a kid in his prime."

Zachary leaned back as if he had done something. On the internet, the anti-fans were living for this content. Popcorn and a soda. They saw this as prime-time television.

Kylie scooted her seat up to add on to Zachary's comment. "Yes, that is a way of exemplifying how fake and artificial Switch is. They just think they are better than everyone else. I mean, congratulations on last night's win, but we four here know that those wins mean nothing to them because they are the same group of people lying to their fans and the world about their persona."

Tim pulled out his speaking notes before continuing the interview. "Speaking of last night, it's been a rumor that you four ran into the group. If I may ask Kylie, the viewers want to know your reaction when you saw Leo and Sammatha."

Kylie rolled her eyes in the most dramatic animated way possible.
   "Oh, my goodness. I'm sorry." Kylie started laughing before continuing.

"I'm so sorry to anyone who actually thinks they look cute together. You could just tell that Leo doesn't really want to be in a relationship with Sammatha. He just uses her for the show until he finds a real one who actually has a figure. Some curve appeal. I mean, did we not forget that this was the same guy who was known as a certified playboy. Yea, we hooked up before he was with that Sam girl, and trust me, he is the experience type. I didn't say much to him, though, because I didn't want to watch Sammatha get all insecure and emotional. But like what Zachary said about Romeo and Brionna applies to Leo and Sammatha. That girl is holding him back."

I am not going to entertain and recap Grace's part of the interview because it's so irrelevant and pointless. She had no talking points other than saying how she felt like she found community with the three members, as if she got anything in common with them other than drama.

Wrapping up the Let's Talk Trash for an hour-long podcast, Jordyn said something that surprised everyone in the house.

Jordyn said, "Switch serves us no purpose. The entire group is nothing but broken souls that have abandonment issues. Why do you think they all live with each other? Why do you think they hide so much from the public eye? It's because they are hiding something and are too ashamed to tell anyone about it. But you 'Flames' don't care. All you see is some chick or dude that you fantasize about, wanting to marry and have your babies. Though you don't even know half of what you are signing up for."

"And what's the secret? What is hiding behind the doors of the Switch Estate," Tim asked.

The camera zoomed into Jordyn as it waited to capture her response. She turned to look at Kylie, then Zachary and Grace wondering if she should expose the group's secret. Sure, they had been hinted at or scratching the surface level of the itching question. Still, they had yet to say the actually questionable cancel-culture-worthy secret.

Worried about what to say, she noticed Zachary slightly shake his head 'no'.

"I- I- I can't say what it is. Legally it's apparently impossible. Unless I want to be in a courtroom tomorrow," Jordyn laughed nervously. Grace scratched the back of her head in disappointment.

"Well, that's all the time for today folks. We have dropped a new line of merch available to purchase below. Make sure to like the video and the stream, and make sure to follow us on all our social media at LunchHour. Comment who you want us to talk to next in the comment section. It's your host Tim Johnson from the Bronx, and I hope you have an amazing weekend."

Leaving the studio, out to the hallway, Grace pulled Jordyn to the side to talk.

"You folded," Grace said.

"Yeah, 'cause Zachary and I are under an NDA. There is only

so much we can say."

"That was the perfect opportunity to expose them," Grace said, getting upset. Though Jordyn stood ten toes down in front of Grace.

"You do it then," she said.

Grace looked fed up with Jordyn. "I would, but you haven't told me what had happened in that house or about what happened in Miami or on the tours. All you and Zachary do is tease around information that can already be found on the internet."

"What about Kylie then?" Jordyn said. Grace laughed a bit.

"Kylie? You got to be serious. Kylie didn't pay attention to anything but Leo's abs. Plus, last time I checked, she was part of the problem with Switch anyways. A tumor that did nothing but make things worse."

Jordyn was shocked by Grace's comment.

"What??? Why would you say something like that? I thought you two were cool?"

Grace looked to her side and saw Kylie and Zachary coming out of the studio.

"My ride's here. Chat later?" Grace said before she gave Jordyn two les bises before leaving for the elevator.

Jordyn was astounded as she watched the elevator close.

"Well, that was fun," Kylie said, energized.

"Glad you enjoyed your therapy session," Jordyn said before walking off.

"What's her problem?" Kylie questioned.

42

09/10/22: Questions. Answers. But the truth doesn't matter.

A week had gone by of being stuck in lock down as we all witnessed the sheer embarrassment we received from the ex-members. During the lock down, we still had rehearsals and practice for today's live showcase, The Switch Experience.

Walking out the backdoor, I headed to the studio off the side of the house. That is when I notice Leo laying against the wall, looking visually upset.

"Oi, como vai?" I asked.

He looked pretty down and had been like this since the 2nd. "Tudo bom Valen. I'm fine, just want to get this show over with," Leo said. At my notice, I saw his hand shaking and a large cut on his lower arm. Taking to awareness, he hid his arm from my eyesight.

"Are you sure you are okay? You don't have to perform today if you don't want to," I said.

"I have to perform today."

"No, you don't."

Leo looked at me, and I became very concerned with his mental health.

"Valen... Do you think I should be in the group?"

What? I didn't understand where this comment was coming from.

"You single-handedly wrote some of the best-hit songs in the Switch discography, and you're the reason why we were able to tap into the South American market and you asking me if you should be in this group?"

Leo wasn't buying it. "I am walking around here thinking I am captain peacemaker when I am a mess and always been a mess. None of this ex-member drama would have happened if I hadn't slept with Kylie, and I am sure Zachary and Jordyn know what happened in Miami."

"Do you think they will expose you?" I questioned.

"Why wouldn't they?"

"They wouldn't expose you 'cause, one, they were out of town when the situation happened, and two, they know the truth like everyone else in this house. But you let Maxwell control the narrative around here. Got all the muscle and physic but let scrawny little Maxwell run you over like a dog every time."

"But what he is saying is true."

"What? That after you got pretty much disowned by the

group for cheating on Mia, you fell into a deep depression. I mean, you turned into a mess-up drunk who loves to punch walls as a way to let the anger out. Plus Maxwell thinks anyone who likes his sister is automatically a bad guy. But, of course, you have a lengthy resume and cover letter, making you the most disqualified guy in the entire group to date the girl. And now you are upset because Maxwell won't drop the whole Miami thing and will hold that grudge till he dies. Not to mention what happened with the scar on his face. It's something you will have to be constantly reminded of because your past actions keep catching up to you. So you try to be a good person, trying to serve everyone. Plus, you're telling me you want to become a BFF leader as a way to impress your future brother-in-law, right? And..."

I pause a minute, realizing I had done one of my ramble rants.
  "Sorry... I didn't mean to -"

Leo kept his head down. "No you good. I'm going to go inside and get ready for the show."
  "Wait, Leo. I didn't mean to come off mean or anything."

"Even. Even if I didn't do anything wrong. The truth doesn't matter because it's easier to run with a lie the people want to hear. You're right. I have a past, and it's something no one will forget," he said.

Right before he opened the door, he paused in conviction.
  "Hold on. I want you to know that you are a changed man. I know Kylie likes to play this narrative that you are the same alpha type of guy, but you are not. You turned to a better leaf,

heading in the right direction."

Leo glances at me briefly before going inside. Alone in the cloudy, misty weather, I looked up at the sky in reflection. For a second, I thought I heard something, though maybe it was just the wind or a figment of my imagination. So I proceeded into the production room as if nothing happened.

Sometimes I hate this room. Full of the convenience of work-home and the annoyance of work being at home. This estate is half residential, half commercial, and it's starting to not be as cute as I thought it was back in 2020. Today's attire was beige and black. The choice was up to you on what color you wanted to pick, and of course, anyone who wasn't walking around with a big ole smile wore black to suit the mood.

As Xan and Lisa went to set up the cameras for production, I went to take my seat with the others like it was a class photo. "Geez, Valen," Mazen said, pointing at my arm. Kyan, who was beside him, looked over and immediately cringed. "Valen... Your welts are back...."

Looking down at my left arm, I saw that my dermatographia returned to full effect. Thick welt scratches that look like a raccoon or a wolverine claw me in seven different ways. Sometimes I blame my sharp nails, hence why I cut them down so low, but it doesn't matter because my skin is so dry; even the smallest nail can cause a cut.

"I think I will be fine. As long as I don't see, then it doesn't hurt."

Mazen got up and went to fetch me some lotion, preferably shea butter to help relieve the itching for continuing for the day. Sometimes I forget I had thousands of scars and cuts around my arms, legs, chest, and back. The attention only becomes aware to me when I take a hot shower from time to time, but I get the redness on my skin, making my fresh new cuts readily available to view for anyone with the naked eye.

"Here."

Taking the shea butter, I apply it to my skin when I notice Kyan staring at me in the process.

"What are you looking at?" I questioned. "Nothing. Just surprised to see you putting on some lotion," Kyan jokes.

I wanted to hit him on the side of the head, but I noticed that Leo and Sammatha sat down right in front of me, and Leo put that actor's smile on full effect. As if our conversation from earlier never even happened.

"Well, here, I put some lotion on. Now can you put this up," I said, tossing the lotion to Kyan. Taking the lotion, he went over to the makeup station, where some of the Varsity Girls were fixing their hair.

"Do you need any lotion by chance?" Kyan asked

"Not really," Brittany said as she put her massacre on.

Brionna took the lotion and placed it on the counter. Then he left Brionna, Brittany, Mia, and Courtney alone to chat.

"I do not want to do this show today," Mia said, applying some blush.

"Tell me about it. All Jermany kept talking about these last couple of days is how much he helped Zachary get to where he is today. Now he feels betrayed by his own childhood friend," Courtney said.

"Romeo feels that same way too," Brionna said.

"Same with Carlos," Brittany chimed in.

Mia looked through the mirror and saw Leo and Sammatha hanging out with each other as they waited for the stream to start.

"Those two seem to be handling everything pretty well, shockingly."

"Who?"

"Sammatha and Leo."

Courtney slightly and discreetly turned her head a bit to look at the two. "I guess they are. But surely they feel a certain type of way with all the Kylie slander."

"If I were Sammatha, I would have pressed charges on the girl, and honestly, Mia, you should have to," Brittany said.

Mia didn't get Brittany's comment. Brionna said, "She can't sue Kylie for being a man stealer."

Courtney shook her head in agreement. Continuing on, "If Mia sues Kylie, she has to sue Leo. No double standards cause it takes two to tangle."

Walking over, Cameron came in to join the conversation. "What is the topic of the day?"

"Brittany said I should press charges on Kylie for being a man stealer, but Brionna said I can't because being a man stealer is not a case," Mia said, grabbing her flat iron.

"Oh well, I would sue for emotional distress and call it a day," Cameron said.

"Of course, that was your go-to case," Brittany laughed.

"It sure is, and you all need to be ready-set-go for the stream. I do not plan on covering any of your lines for today."

The girls started laughing at Cameron's statement.

"Girl, we do not ask you to cover our lines. You are the one throwing up the four fingers so you can take our lines. You and Sammatha, that's all you two do lately," Brionna said, fixing her shirt. Courtney grabbed the hairbrush and started mocking Cameron playfully.

"I will be singing my lines like, *I just want to be with you.* Then here comes Cameron out of nowhere, BREAKING formation throwing up the four fingers pre-maturely to take my lines right when I get all warmed up." Cameron denied the claims, but the rest of the line couldn't agree more.

Mia went to fix Cameron's hair a bit cause the hair does look a little too frizzy occasionally. "Don't worry, none of us really care. Just you trying to get your man's attention, that's all," Mia joked.

Cameron opened her mouth wide open as if she had been exposed. "I- I- I- I do not. I do not know who told you that, but that is not true."

"Oh really, 'cause it couldn't be more obvious," the four girls said at the same time.

"Oh, whatever. Each and every one of you had your phase too," Cameron said.

Asia and Alanna did warm-up stretches and vocal exercises in the back of the room.

"Do you think those ex-members are going to be watching the stream?" Alanna questioned.

"Maybe. There is no paywall, so they might as well. Though I am already fed up with all this drama."

"Same. I used to really look up to Jordyn. Wanting to be a dancer like her, and now she turned into a sell-out."

Asia took a 180 look around the production room. "Let's just sing back up for the stream. I want to fly under the radar."

"So you and your boyfriend can live in peace and harmony?" Alanna said, cheesing from ear to ear.

"We live in peace and harmony when Mazen asks you out."

Alanna's smile went away in despair. "Well, dream on. He may act like Dice 2.0 at times but is not interested in any committed relationship."

"Have you brought it up to him?"

"Yes, back when we took those ASL classes."

"Uh..."

"What?" Alanna questioned.

Asia placed her hand on Alanna's shoulder as if she was a lost soul. "Alanna. Alanna. ALANNA.... You guys took those classes three years ago. I am sure Mazen's views have changed."

Alanna took Asia's hand off her shoulder. "Well, even if it did. The truth is that he doesn't want to be with me."

"He lets you lay next to him while you watch movies in the Maknae lounge. You guys exercise together, go out to restaurants with each other-"

"We don't talk about the cuddle stuff, but the other things you mention. You and Kyan are there right beside us."

"And you're not a third wheel. Your date is right beside you."

The conversation had to come to a close because the stream was about to start. After a final stretch, the two join in with everyone else for the show.

"SWITCH LIFE. IT'S IN EXPERIENCE!" Lame intro, but okay, cause the fans and stans eat it up like it's caviar. Got this sky, backdrop, and lights beaming down on us. Had we not dished out a great load of money to this black box, it would look real DIY.

"Hey, Flames. I hope you are doing well. Breathing well. Eating well and having such a blessed day today," Jermany said into the microphone.

"Woah. Jermany out here already trying to win our viewers' hearts," Carlos chimed in.

"Oh, I am only getting started. Today is a rather long show, two hours of your favorite songs, requested by you, our lovely fans and supporters."

"Wait." Romeo raised his hand. "The chat is asking how everyone is doing."

Brittany looked down the row at Carlos, wondering if he would say something mean and ill about Zachary.

"Well, on behalf of Varsity Guys, we are all doing really well. Healthy and breathing. We are... disheartened by our old friend leaving the group. Zachary is an amazing singer and an absolute piece of -"

"Wonder and full of joy. He will be missed," Jermany said as he quickly lowered Carlos's microphone, signaling to switch to a different camera.

Varsity Girls looked at each other, wondering who was going to talk when suddenly Courtney decided to say something. "Do some aegyo or something," Cameron whispered to Courtney. "Um, Varsity Girls are doing great." Courtney looked at Sammatha, trying to get her to say something.

Xan and Lisa, were standing behind the camera and were so frustrated with how the stream was starting off.

Holding the microphone closer, Sammatha said, "Yes, I agree.

We are all doing great. We are healthy and breathing."

Once the camera was off of them, the Varsity Girls all turned to Sammatha. Turning off their mic, Courtney whispered, "That was your chance to address Kylie."

The rest of the girls agreed. "I- I can't. Sorry," Sammatha said hopelessly.

The girls sighed.

Brionna gave the poor girl a side hug, reassuring her there was nothing to be sorry about.

"Hey everyone, it's your favorite member Valen!"

"Girl, I am the favorite member," Rebecca said.

"Ladies, it's not a competition even though some folks may have thought it was," Jackie slipped in. Rebecca and I looked at each other in confusion because that was not part of the bit we had practiced earlier.

"Yea. Uh, the JV Line is doing amazing. We are healthy and breathing," I said.

Next in line were Dice and Toran. Dice said, "The one and only D n' T or T n' D duo is doing great. We are healthy and breathing."

"D n' T? I think T n' D sounds better? Have a nice ring to it," Toran joked as he looked over at Vanessa, hoping to get her to laugh or smile or even look at him, but she didn't even try to look in his direction.

Once the camera was off-screen of two, Dice leaned over to Toran. "Did she look?" Dice asked. "Not even for a second,"

Toran whispered.

Dice scratched his neck and tried to discreetly stretch to get a glimpse at Vanessa. He saw from her body language that she wasn't even facing slightly in their direction.

"Everyone in the rap line is doing just fine. Carrying on with life as if nothing ever happened," Leo said in the mic. The way Jean and I looked at each other like 'what'. Simon, who looked so high and faded, wasn't even conscious of seeing what his homie said. Leo looked at the guys, and judging by their expressions, he knew he had messed up.

"What he meant to say is that we are healthy and breathing," LeeSung said. Jean then wrapped his arm around Leo's shoulder, "Exactly, healthy and breathing. We are all ready to get the show on."

I patted Simon's back to signal for him to straighten up. Especially when he is front and center. Turning over to Maknae Line, the four stood up beside me and did their little chant.

"Its Mazen."
  "Kyan."
  "Alanna."
  "And Asia."
  "AND WE ARE MAKNAE LINE!"

"We are doing great. Laughing and smiling as we promise to you all," Kyan said.
  "In addition, we are healthy-"

"AND BREATHING!" They all said together.

Clap it up for that correlation. We older folks need to be more like the younger ones. All ready and prepared to say a couple of words.

Xan and Lisa walked over to the front of the camera. They did a quick wave before getting out of frame as I went in to say my stuff.

"Last but not least, Leader Line is doing great. The same goes for Kendrick, who wants to wish everyone a blessed weekend. We are all healthy and breathing. We hope and pray that you are too. If you need any assistance, please check out the available resources we have to offer through our philanthropy non-profit. Don't worry about what region of the world you are watching. We should have a way to help assist you whether you have food insecurities, medical problems, or in need of therapy. Thank you for tuning in, and I hope you enjoy the show."

The Switch Experience went well. Everyone did their thing, whether they were helping behind the scenes or performing in front of the camera.

But it was overall good, as in no one threw up on the ground. It was lots of oohs and aahs with a dash of shade. Especially when Simon kept switching his lines to more targeting lyrics toward his sisters, which made him come off as extremely bitter.

Any fans watching could see that the group was not doing good and were starting to consider what the ex-members were saying during their press run. During the stream, the internet was beginning to become indecisive about which side to take. Anti-Switch or Pro-Switch.

"Healthy and breathing, but are they okay?"

"Switch looks so out of touch. They need Zachary and Jordyn."

"Seeing Sammatha and Leo dancing together got a whole new meaning after what Kylie said earlier."

"I don't get this whole Zachary should be back in Varsity Line. He hasn't been on the stage with them in over two years."

"I miss the old Switch."

"Who else is planning on leaving cause it's been about time, the group got a little smaller."

"Can y'all get off this app and just watch the show, geez."

That is a wrap. A quick two-hour shift was done.

Vanessa and Toran went to their ending poses and held their position.

The two were breathing hard and nearly out of breath. Looking into each other's eyes, Vanessa couldn't bring herself to look at him any longer.

"Aaaaaannnnnnnddd... cut", Xan yelled.

Vanessa quickly pulled away from Toran's grip and walked away to join up with JV.

"Hey, that was a great show," Vanessa said to the rest of us as we huddled together.

"Yeah. You and T over there were really selling that couple talk as girlfriend and boyfriend," Rebecca pointed over.

Vanessa turned around and glanced at Toran, who was talking to Dice and the rest of Rap Line. "We didn't sell anything. He has been my dance partner since I was 14, so don't be surprised if we get a little chemistry on the dance floor. We were groomed to do that. I mean, if I was selling it, then Saige must be married to Theo," Vanessa joked.

Saige's mouth opened wide in awareness.

"We have an image to uphold."

"And you guys have been holding this image for eight months now."

"Nine, actually," Jackie raised her hand, "And I think you two should get together because of it."

"What?" Saige question.

"What do you mean 'what'. You got to give him another chance," Jackie said.

"I am not interested in doing that. Theo is too indecisive for me. Never knows what he wants," Saige said, folding her arms.

We all turned to the other corner of the room to get a look at Theo.

"Never know what he wants? Girl, I could have told you that before you got with the boy," I said.

"Oh, don't worry, Miss Queen. He will come around wanting to be in a relationship with you," Rebecca said. Saige looked at Rebecca as it picked her interest. "When do you think that will happen?"

"New Year's Eve," Rebecca said.

"NEW YEAR'S EVE!" Saige yelled.

"Shush. We don't need the whole world to know," Rebecca said.

We slowly looked back at Varsity Guy's line and saw Theo looking at us.

"Not him looking over here," Jackie said.

"We are looking at some old pictures," I yelled over.

We moved into a tight huddle. "New Year's Eve. That's a little too niche?" I questioned.

"The 31st of December is not a little too niche. The 17th at 8:34pm Central Standard is niche." Rebecca said.

"I think Rebecca doesn't seem too off. Maybe Theo will be a changed man by then and will want to go into the new year with you," Vanessa said.

"I guess," Saige sighed.

Joining in the conversation was Lily.

"How is Sammatha?" Saige asked.

"Fine. Healthy and breathing and, most importantly, won't budge. I wonder how she is holding up with the hate train always stopping on Itoni Avenue. I talked to some of the girls in Varsity, and they said that Sammatha hadn't opened up much as usual," Lily said.

Saige lightly cleared her thoart a bit as she looked up at Lily.
"Um... How's Simon?"

Lily was confused by Saige's comment. "He will be alright. Why do you ask?" Lily questioned.
Rebecca and Vanessa looked at each other wondering why Lily was being so hostile.

"I- I was just curious, as a friend and -"
"He fine. I really like to keep stuff between Simon and I private." Lily said walking out the building.

Saige looked at us all in question as we back out of the huddle.
"Did I do something wrong?" Saige questioned.

We all shrugged for we all knew the reason for Lily's jealously. Saige should know too, as a JV sister. Sneaking around with Lily's best friend/ex-boyfriend is not the way to go.
"Just give her some space," I suggest.
"How much space?" she asked.

"Your not still seeing Simon are you?" Rebecca blurted out. Vanessa gasped at Rebecca with utter shock.
"Sorry but I had to asked," Rebecca said.

Saige started to blushed a bit. "No... No, no, no. I mean we made out a couple of times but that its. I'm a free woman."
"Well, technically-"

"Within these walls I'm a free woman. I should be able to sneak into Simon room for five minutes and chat with him," Saige corrected.

"Chat?" Jackie said nearly chocking on some water.

"Yes chat. You do it all time. I wouldn't be surprise you still chat with one of the members in the group like... uh... David. Yeah David." Saige said.

Jackie nervously laugh. "Yeah definitely hooking up with my old fling David. Definite nobody else. Single or plural am I right? You know what? I'm going to take a shower and call it a day. Super tired."

"You sang back up the entire show?" Rebecca said.

"Yep and it made me super dehydrated."

Just as Jackie was backing away she notice Theo signing to her to see if she wanted to meet up with him later in the day. Quickly she threw up a 'X' sign with her arms.

"You can't be serious right now?" She mouthed over.

"Please?" Theo said as he looked at Saige.

In panic, Jackie quickly rushed out the studio.

43

09/14/22: A bad way to cope.

Rebecca and Sammatha were relaxing in the lounge by the movie room, doing some crocheting cause why not, I guess. The house is no longer on lockdown, but it doesn't matter because no one wants to be spotted in the public eye because the drama still continues.

Rebecca was lying down on the couch while Sammatha sat on the floor while they listened to Kylie guest star on yet another podcast.

"Sammatha, why do you keep entertaining her? It's like you're her biggest fan or something," Rebecca said.

"I need to keep tabs on her," Sammatha said as she knitted a dark red and white scarf.

"What's to keep track of? How many times has she said she is going to steal your man, or how many times has she body shames you?"

Sammatha ignored Rebecca and continued watching the

podcast video.

"And thank you, Untitled Projects, for sponsoring the podcast. Now Kylie. My audience is dying to know if you are seeing anyone?"

"Me? I have someone in mind, but currently, I am not looking to be in a committed relationship as of right now."

Kylie was cheesing extra hard, her hair done again to perfection and pulled out in the most skin-revealing dress. Some would argue she got a breast job, but I doubt it.

"See Rebecca. She said that she had someone in mind. Who do you think it is? I saw that, according to Harry's fandom, he might have a crush on her. Or what Trevon Jones? He is big right now. Or Li Zhang's brother from that one drama."

Rebecca rolled her eyes.

"Nooo. Nooo. None of the above."

Rebecca sat up from the couch and reached over to Sammatha's tablet to turn it off.

"Sammatha, the guy she has in mind is Leo. It's always been Leo, and you can't fill up your watch history with every single appearance she makes. You need to put your foot down and say, 'KYLIE, BACK OFF MY MAN, YOU DESPERATE CHICK! HE'S TAKEN!'. I mean, it needs more work, but it's a starting point," Rebecca said.

"I'm not doing that. Many people want to get with Leo. Even your fans want to get with Leo. What makes Kylie any different," Sammatha questioned. Rebecca sighed in frustration as if things weren't clicking in Sammatha's brain.

"The difference is that she has actually hooked up with him."

"Once and it was a long time ago," Sammatha said.

"Honey, most members think 2018 was last year and that we only lived in this house for about three years. Time doesn't exist here. That hook-up incident technically happened recently, and Kylie still thinks it did happen recently. Unless...
"

Sammatha looked up at Rebecca in seriousness. "He didn't Rebecca. And I trust and believe that he won't do anything like that, especially with Kylie. I get it. Mia got the shorter end of the stick with Leo. But he is a different man. A much more gentle and caring guy. He writes me all kinds of love songs, buys me nice gifts, and treats me so well. "

"Oh, don't forget about your sleepovers in Manhattan," Rebecca laughed.

Sammatha started to panic a bit when she mentioned it.

"Itty bitty apartment. How do y'all even stay there? One bedroom with max two windows. With Leo's millions of dollar movie deals and you being the JV girl turned Varsity Girls lead singer, money should be flowing like a river. So why isn't your rent like a minimum 10k or even 30k?"

"I don't like big living spaces..." Sammatha said, trying to deviate from the conversation. Though Rebecca kept pushing it.

"What's the difference between staying in this palace or in a 5-bedroom penthouse?"

"Well, this palace is occupied by many people. A five-bedroom penthouse for only two people is unnecessary. Too many rooms, not enough people to stay in. I feel safer when I am in smaller places anyways. No one can sneak up on me."

Rebecca felt guilty for mentioning the size comparison as she saw that Sammatha's mood became more depressing. Her focus on crocheting became more intense as she added more yarn.

Coming into the room was Jean.
   "Hey Sammatha," Jean said cheerfully.
   "Hi," Sammatha said down.

Jean went looking through at the shelves of books that many use as a storage unit.
   "No, hello?" Rebecca said, offended.

"Hi Rebecca," Jean said with an attitude.
   "Hi to you. What are you looking for?"

"My notes from Portuguese class. Leo had a song he wanted me to work on with him, and of course, he wanted me to rap in Portuguese."
   "Your Portuguese sucks though," Rebecca laughed
   "It doesn't," Jean claps back.
   "If it didn't, why are you pulling out your notes?"
   "So that I can be grammatically correct. Geez Rebecca like hop off my -"

"You talk to Leo today?" Sammatha questioned out of nowhere.

Jean didn't know what to say.

"I... received a text message not too long ago, but I haven't seen him around since the show," he said.

Sammatha started to become more concerned.

"Did he say anything about meeting up with you?"

"Not really. He just sent me a beat and some lyrics. Told me to complete the other part of the song though I am about to just do it in Spanish if I can't put any words together."

In a change in tone, Jean asked, "Is he okay Sammatha? The guys are pretty worried. I tried knocking on your door, and he didn't answer."

Sammatha started to feel overwhelmed because it was true that ever since the 10th, he had barely left the room. Now, he did give me the courtesy of a happy birthday card yesterday, but other than that, he barely leaves his room.

"I'm sure he's okay. He just needs some alone time."

Sammatha got up and packed up her things before leaving the room. Worried and concerned, she quickly walked past the office, the dance rooms, and the recording studios. Making a left, she made her way to the stairs, and up she went to her room.

Upstairs is always dark, but her room was depressingly dark, with a little bit of light trying to come inside as it peeped through the long maroon curtains. Sitting on the edge of the bed was Leo staring at the wall. The room was silent. Pen drop quiet.

Putting her belongings down, she sat down by Leo on the edge of the bed.

"Hey, I made you a scarf. It's not anything fancy or long enough to wear, but it's something." She handed over the small scarf to Leo, hoping it would cheer him up.

"Thank you," he said as he held the scarf in his hand.

Sammatha leans in to give Leo a kiss on the cheek. "Have you taken your meds for today?" Sammatha question. It is a list of antidepressants, stuff for anxiety, anger management, stress...

"I took them already," he said. Leo finally looked at her, and her heart sank when she noticed that his eyes were red. It is best to explain that his past thoughts were catching up to him. All the bad things he had done in his past were hitting him like a tidal wave, and the silence and loneliness in the room made the strongest guy in the house cry in shame. Shame that it hurts to feel and hurts to be reminded by.

Fans, family, friends, even Kylie all have very different outlooks on Leo, but as he looked at Sammatha, he knew that she saw the real him. Some would say that is a good thing, but he felt awful for her to witness his downfall and low moments.

"It's okay. I'm here," she said in a soft voice.

Slowly she got up and held Leo's hand. As he rose up, it was like the world was moving in slow motion. Everything became blurry and concerning as Leo followed Sammatha into their walk-in closet. Slowly she closed the door, and their vision became blurry as their hearts raced and cried in vain at the same time.

It was 2 am in the morning the next day. Laying on the ground, side by side, Sammatha noticed that there was a blanket lying on top of her as she noticed Leo was sound asleep. Staring at the roof, the silence was there once again. A tear fell down the side of her eye, hoping that Leo would feel better in the morning. But something in her spirit felt weird. She took one more glimpse at Leo before closing her eyes to go back to sleep.

They weren't at their apartment like usual. They weren't in their small escape room where they could escape from the world and its judgments. They have a bad coping mechanism. A bad one indeed, and they know it is. Why do you think they went in the closet?

Well, if you're in a tornado warning and you don't have access to a basement, you have two choices. The first option is a bathtub because of how sturdy it is, and the chance of it going flying is slim. And the second option is a closet, ideally, somewhere in the middle of the house or apartment, if possible.

Why? Because the more walls between you and the exterior, means the safer you are from danger. With that information, why do you think they went into that closet? Something to keep in mind. Respectfully.

44

09/15/22: Sailing Away.

Maxwell was sitting by his car, listening to the waves as the sea breeze blew through his long black hair. By the coastline, as the golden hour hit, he looked down at the beach, where he saw Toran and Leo talking.

"What are we going to do now?" Toran asked.

Leo stared off to the sunset as he took a sip of his drink. Far in the water, off to the distance, was a large ship sailing away off to the horizon. "It's game over. We lost the game. We failed." Leo stood up and started walking away from Toran.

"Maybe we can get a second chance? The ship may come around!" Toran yelled. Leo continued walking away, ignoring Toran. Toran glimpses up at Maxwell at the top of the hill, looking down at him.

Leo hops into his red top-down car and signals Toran over. "Are you coming or what?"

Toran rushed over and got inside. Leo then pushes the button for the sunroof cover to their heads.

"Where are we going?" Toran questioned.

"Just a place to blow off some steam. Tell the rest of the team to follow me," Leo said. As he started the car, Toran stuck his head out the window to signal Maxwell to get ready to leave.

"Okay, let's head out," Maxwell said. Alongside him, Saige, Lily, and Mia got inside the vehicle.

"Where are we going?" Lily asked, worried. Maxwell said nothing. As he turned up, his 60s music and started the car.

They went to a shady building off the corner of town as the sun went away and the moonlight came out. Entering the underground casino, there were coin slots and card decks flipping and turning. Smoke filled the air, and the music was bumping. Suddenly, it all stopped as all eyes turned to the members.

"Maybe we should leave," Toran said to Leo. But Leo didn't care and went to walk up to a random person who was minding his business. The man, who looked no older than his 30s, turned around and looked very irritated.

"Ahhh. Why did the music stop? Oh. It's you guys. Are you here to join the rest of us in our festivities? Party, drink, gamble your life savings? I have a friend who can hook you up with a quick loan if the money is low? Or maybe you're looking for something to take off the edge?"

Toran, Maxwell, Mia, Saige, and Lily came up behind Leo, all looking uneasy. "So you brought the whole family. So I guess you failed the Birthright Challenge. You failed the trials. Each and every one of them flawlessly. Well, if you head over to the bar, you can find a wide range of selections to choose from to numb the pain. We got weed all the way to heroin. Xan to crack."

Saige looked concerned, "I can't do this. I didn't know. WE DIDN'T KNOW-"

"That it was a test?" the man said. He pulled at a cigarette and slowly lit it up.

"You didn't know it was a test? Have you heard the saying *Life is a Game*? Well, games are made to test your smartness, your senses, your wisdom, confidence, and bravery. You guys are pretty successful as a team and as individuals. With all the money in your name, you would think you would be the first person on that boat to leave. But you're stuck here with the rest of us."

The man stood up, headed over to the bar, and pulled some cocaine out of his pocket before laying it down. The entire room was still staring at the group as they watched the man walk over to the poker table to grab a Joker card. Then he went back to the bar to set up his line. Just when he was about to lean in to take a sniff, Leo cleared his throat.

"You must have failed your test too?" Leo questioned, trying to act tough.

The man froze in conviction. "I actually passed them all. Every single one of them with ease." The man walked up to Leo until he was eye-to-eye with the guy. "But then I was sold a dream. A false dream. My life was full of sunshine and wonders until someone handed me this card," Leo looked down and saw that the man was offering to give Leo the Joker card.

"It's another test," Saige said. The room started laughing more and more. Then all at once, it stops. "She is right. If you grabbed this card, you would have already failed your second test while being here," the man said.

Maxwell pulled Leo away, stepping in front of him. "What do you mean we failed the second test already?" The man smirked and started walking away but then paused in his steps. "You didn't hear that voice saying not to come here?"

The room was so eerie as the dream core music started to play. Suddenly the lights began to flicker rapidly, and the room began to shake.

The group became terrified, not knowing what to do as the other people in the room went into a full-blown panic.

"SO! WOULD YOU LIKE TO TRY AGAIN!" The mysterious man yelled over the chaos.

Leo wasn't buying it and rushed over to the man. Fist, fully ready to tussle, he grabbed the man's shirt and glared at him.

"What's the point of trying again? You want us to relive all that pain again just to fail this game of life again," Leo yelled, trying to not get emotional.

Toran rush over to Leo. "Let go of him! It's not worth it." Toran anxiety was raised like crazy when the lights stopped flickering, and everyone stopped panicking. Looking over his shoulder, he saw the rest of his friends were terrified.

The man seemed unfazed by Leo's intimation but was rather calm.

"Sir, you and your friends have two options. You can either give up and spend the rest of your lives here having some worldly fun till the world crashes and burns, or you can try again."

Lily rushed over to the man and told Leo to let go of him. The man fell hard to the floor once Leo let go of his grip.

"How much does it cost to try again?" Lily asked.

"Cost nothing but willpower," he said as he got up.

"You guys can't seriously believe this guy," Leo said concerned.

The man checked his watch and realized his time was up. "Welp, I got to go. The reason why you all fail is because... you all refuse to change your old ways. I am going to do you a favor and have you all redo the Birthright Challenge. With that tip in mind, hopefully, I don't have this conversation with you again for the fifth time."

"THE FIFTH TIME???" Before any of the members could ask anything, the man snapped his fingers, and then a bright flash of the light beam was like a great reset. Breathing heavily, each team member woke up in their respective room, laying down, out of breath, as if they ran a mile in under four minutes.

Roll credits.

"What was that all about," I said, putting my popcorn down. "That's what y'all were filming last year?" LeeSung questioned.

Today's Birthright season four dropped today, and it was interesting. The BFF's household huddled up in the movie room to watch the showing. Cool to see some folks like Mia and Saige make their debut in acting. I see Sammatha must have pulled some bells to get Maxwell and Leo on the same show. Her theory was that the two would learn to get along, and being guest stars on the hit show, Birthright would be a way for the two to do some bonding exercise. And well, we saw how that turned out.

"Play the next episode, please," Rebecca yelled. Theo grabs the route to hit play and off-course commercials. Ad break.

Over in the back row, Leo and Sammatha were all cuddled up watching episode 14 on the lounge sofa. Just like in July, when Jean had all those feelings of insecurity and thoughts of breaking up with Cameron, Leo had the same thoughts running through his head. He felt uncomfortable around the other members and knew the isolation inside the house was getting to him.

Sammatha sat up a bit and noticed Leo wasn't paying attention to the show.

"Are you okay? We can watch it later," Sammatha whispered.

Leo looked to his side and saw that Theo was leaving to grab some snacks. Without thinking, he gave Sammatha a quick kiss on the lips before he got up to follow suit to the hallway.

"Theo."

Theo turned around in question. "It's the other 'Eo' in the house. What do you want?" Leo was a little amused by Theo's joke.

"Come on, you can laugh at it. I thought it was funny, at least cause you know. Theo, Leo, Eo?"

"Sure. I'll give you that point. I was wondering if it's okay if Sammatha and I could crash at your spot tonight?" Leo asked.

Theo was confused for a second, not understanding the math behind Leo's request.

"Don't you guys have an apartment? My place is alright. Nice three bed, 2 bath, but doesn't compare to a Grand Central Park view.," Theo said.

"I can't risk running into fans while being stuck in traffic. Yes, we are off lockdown-"

"But the hate train is still going on. I get that, but my place is such a downgrade. What about the hidden house? That should be open to stay at," Theo suggests.

"I have to get Xan or Lisa's permission to go there, and I would need a pretty good excuse to get the keys," Leo said.

"And your excuse isn't good enough?" Theo questioned.

Leo pauses for a moment.

"What are you doing?" Theo questioned as he watched Leo roll up his sleeve.

Theo was in shock when he saw a thick red scar near Leo's wrist, followed by smaller cuts that whined up his arm.

"Our apartment in Manhattan is a mess right now... There is glass everywhere..." Leo said, trying to keep calm.

"What... what happened to your arm?" Theo questioned.

"Don't tell anyone, okay."

"I promise," Theo said, worried.

Leo moved closer to Theo. Lowering his voice, he said, "Sammatha had been trying to cut her wrist lately, and every time she does it...I put my arm in her place..." Theo's eyes open wide.

"When was the last time this happened?" Theo questioned.

"The day after the VVMAs. She is fine now, but I really want her to take her out to get some fresh air. Same for myself... I just can't take her to Manhattan right now. I don't want these feelings to come back into her head." Leo said.

Taking into consideration how Leo's been acting the last couple of days, he reached down into his pocket to grab his keys. "Stay out of the primary room and the room upstairs to the left. Jermany got that room checked out, so don't be shocked if you see him and Courtney there. You know, just let them be. The room downstairs is probably up your alley anyways. I won't tell anyone about what you just told me. I still be getting drunk at 3 in the morning, crying over Saige, so your secret is safe with me. Just be careful," Theo said.

"OH MY-"

Leo and Theo looked at each other in concern. "What's going on in there?" Walking back to the movie room, they saw that the show was paused. Theo went to Romeo to see what had happened. Romeo stood up and handed his phone.

"I want to say from the bottom of my heart that I'm sorry for Switch. Just watch the new season of Birthright, and I can tell you right now they are going to fail their test once again like how they always do. I get it. It's just a show that is scripted, but in reality, they are nothing but a whole bunch of neglected children who got turned into industry plants. From my days of living in the BFF mansion, it was hard to witness any form of growth in any of the members. They had no character development ever. Yes, their music got better, and their popularity grew, but they never changed. They never have, and they never will because they choose to stay stuck in the past. Switch only cares about numbers, sales, and their careers. Jordyn, Kylie, Grace, and I are not apologetic for what we had said on the news outlets. Check yourself into therapy for once."

Theo went to the comment section and saw that Alanna had commented on the post. All eyes turned to her, and she raised her hands like she had been caught red-handed.

"What, all I said was 'you do the same.' I'm sick and tired of this narrative going on, and no one is clapping back at these guys. All we do is sit around and let them run over us."

"We don't respond because we are trying to be the bigger person," I said.

Alanna shook her head. Asia chimed in to defend Alanna.
  "No, we are always going into lockdown whenever someone is cyberbullying or trying to start beef in the group. All we do is run away from our problems. Then we forget those problems exist, and then boom. Out of nowhere, they are back again. I mean, those ex-members are right. We are selling a dream half of the time when it's a nightmare in this house. We laugh

a lot but are divided at times. There are so many secrets that we are hiding from not just the world but from each other."

Asia started to tear up, and the rest of the group started to get in their feels too.

Continuing on, she said, "Being one of the youngest in this group, I really look up to you all. Alanna, Mazen, and Kyan do, too, but it is hard to do so at a time when you are all a hot mess blinded by time. That mindset that everything happened yesterday when it was, in reality, weeks, months, or even years ago needs to end. But it is not being acknowledged or registered in this house. Zachary is right. No one ever evolved in this house. I'm sure God doesn't want us to sit here in vain and sorrow all the time. Drowning ourselves in practice all the time to numb our thoughts. We need to face our problems, insecurities, and trauma and stop trying to put the blame on something or someone else. I'm not saying that Zachary, Jordyn, Kylie, or even Grace is perfect cause no one is because they are clearly no different from us. They are just bolder to show their flaws out to the world compared to us... So maybe... we should try again. Like in the show. Face our fears to become a better version of ourselves."

Silences in the room as the show continues to play on mute in the background. Dice tried taking a step forward, but something kept pulling him back. It was like he became paralyzed. A tear fled down Asia's cheek as she noticed Dice was struggling to move his foot. He tried to lift it up, but his knees wouldn't give him the strength he needed until, finally, he stumbled forward.

"I have something to say... Believe it or not but I pulled out and read the Bible. I know it seems a little off-brand for me to do so, but I did read some pages." Dice started looking around the room before rushing out to the lounge room to look through the bookshelves when he found the big book.

No one moved from their spot or said a word as they waited for Dice to return. In he came with urgency, and he showed up the Bible, and it looked very familiar. "The Bible for teen girls. That was a gift I got when I was younger. Where did you find that?" I said. Dice looked at the cover and noticed that it did say that. "Oh. In the bookcase in the lounge," he said.
   "The hidden one?"

"The one by the movie room. I have my own in my room, but I remember seeing this one there. It doesn't matter. We are getting off-topic. I saw that verse in Luke or Matthew... John?"

We watch Dice flip through the pages trying to find the verse he remembers but couldn't find it. Couldn't find it at all until suddenly he paused. Clearing his throat, he spoke with volume and confidence to each and every one of us in the room.

"John 8:34-36 KJV

Jesus answered them, Verily, verily, I say unto you, Whosoever committeth sin is the servant of sin. And the servant abideth not in the house for ever: but the Son abideth ever. If the Son therefore shall make you free, ye shall be free indeed."

Then he quickly flipped over a couple of pages before continuing.

"1 John 1:5-8 KJV says,

This then is the message which we have heard of him, and declare unto you, that God is light, and in him is no darkness at all. If we say that we have fellowship with him, and walk in darkness, we lie, and do not the truth: but if we walk in the light, as he is in the light, we have fellowship one with another, and the blood of Jesus Christ his Son cleanseth us from all sin. If we say that we have no sin, we deceive ourselves, and the truth is not in us."

Dice closed the book and looked at the rest of the group. "Asia and Alanna are right. The ex-members are right. We all are a mess, and we normalize it to the point that we think it is no problem. We were doing so well as a team, as a group, and as a family, until 2016. The year we made it to the top of the food chain and broke free from Ex-S Records control. That was God setting us free. But what happened when 2017 rolled around, or 2018, 19, 20? We all fell into a deep sin. I include, and I take full shame and humility in it. But we thought everything was okay, cause the records were selling, and the money kept flowing, but no, it didn't matter because, at the end of the day, we are hurt souls that never got to heal from anything. So... I asked you all. Romeo, Maxwell, Carlos, Jermany, Theo, Cameron, Brittany, Brionna, Courtney, Sammatha, Mia, my best friend in the whole wide world, Toran, Lily, Jackie, Vanessa, Saige, Rebecca, Jean, Leo, Simon, LeeSung, Alanna, Asia, Kyan, Mazen, Xan, Lisa, and Valen... Walk with me in this journey of healing, recognizing our flaws, and fixing our errors."

The room felt so heavy with emotions. Something was pulling us back from reacting or doing anything. When suddenly, I looked over. Rebecca had stepped forward. "I want to start the journey."

"Same," Cameron said softly, looking at Jean.

One by one. Each member steps forward. Maxwell gave in. So did Xan, Simon, and the others. I took my step forward, and it felt scary. Dice looked up at the screen as the show Birthright was still playing.

"So the trials have officially started then. Let's be supportive of each other in this journey. I'm no expert in the Bible, but I do know that we humans will fall into sin, but Jesus loves and forgives us. Luckily, we are all baptized, so that step is taken care of. I hate to say that the next couple of months or maybe years are going to be rough for each and everyone one of us. However, we will be okay."

Leo looked at Sammatha as he watched a tear fall down her

cheek. She glances at him briefly, quickly wiping her tears away. Then a loud phone began to ring.

45

09/15/22: Sailing Away. Part II

Xan was confused to see who could possibly be calling him at this hour.

He slowly walked to his phone and saw it was a private number.

The room felt intense as the phone continued to ring.
RING RING!
Adjusting his glasses, he picked up the phone.

"Hello."
Xan quickly turn around to everyone in terror.
Quickly he started patting around his pocket, looking for something.
"What's wrong?" Lisa questioned.

Xan looked up and quickly rushed to the second row in the front of the movie room where he was sitting. Grabbing his notebook and pen, he promptly wrote down in his notebook. Then torn out three pieces of paper.

He handed one sheet to Lisa and one more miniature sheet to Leo and Kyan.

Leo looked down at the small handwriting that was in Portuguese. It read, [Get her out of here asap. Code red].

Leo didn't stop to question what was going on. Taking Sammatha by the hand, the two quickly left the room, setting off to Theo's house.

"What is this? Why does Maknae Line need to leave?" Kyan questioned.

"Mr. Smith is here," Lisa said concerned.

The room gasped at what they just heard.

Xan hung up and walked over to the group.

Cursing under his breath, he begged Maknae Line to leave the house. "On my desk in the office, there are the keys to the escape house. Go there for the night."

Mazen pauses in his steps. "He can't be here..."

"He is waiting at the gate. I had Leo get Sammatha out of here cause I can't afford to add another stress level to her plate. So when he leaves, Mr. Smith is coming in," Xan said.

Asia shook her head. "He cannot get past those gates."

Xan turned to Asia. "You said that we shouldn't be running from our problems. Maybe this is God giving us our first challenge."

Mazen looked at Xan in panic.

For a moment, all Xan could see was a bloody face embarked on Mazen from when he was younger.

"We aren't leaving then," Alanna said, ten toes down.

"Wait, hold up. Mr. Smith is HERE? Right now? I know we are allergic to 911, but this is a valid case," Dice said.

Xan ignored Dice. "Meeting in the living room," Xan said, leaving.

I was just absolutely confused about what was going on.

"Where are we going?" Sammatha questioned as Leo quickly helped her get in the car.

"We are just going to Theo's place for a bit," Leo said as he leaned in to give her a kiss.

Impatiently he waited for the garage door to open. "Leo... what's going on?"

"NOTHING!" Leo yelled. Leo's hand started to shake as he put his seat belt on.

"Sorry for yelling. I–"

"It's fine. Let's just get going," Sammatha said softly.

Driving out the side of the house, Leo drove for about three minutes until he reached the gates of the estate, surrounded by thick bushy trees.

There he saw a black, tinted window car that must have been worth over 200,000 dollars. The lights were flashing brightly at the two.

"Who is that?" Sammatha said.

"Mr. Smith," Leo said, getting out of the car.

Sammatha, in fright, got out of the car as well, rushing over to Leo's side as the gate opened wide.

"Leo, please, let's just leave, okay."

Sammatha stood before him to block his step as Leo stared down the car in front of him.

"Come on, let's just go," Sammatha said.

Taking him by the hand, she drags Leo back to his car.

He got inside the car without taking his eyes off the tinted windows.

"Leo, please..."

Leo took his foot to the pedal and drove past Mr.Smith.

As he left the estate, the enemy entered BFF's territory. Though it wasn't long before Leo made a U-turn to follow Mr.Smith.

"What are you doing," Sammatha asked.

"Something I shouldn't have done years ago."

Everyone else sat in the living room impatiently, scattered around the room.

Meanwhile, Mr. Smith got out of his car. Turning, he saw Leo's car parked right before his.

"Leo..."

Sammatha signals for him to move closer to her. Grabbing some of his hair in the back of his head, she started braiding his hair.

"What are you doing?"

Sammatha continued on before grabbing a small piece of hair from the back of her head to braid.

Leo watched her do this, not knowing what was going on until she grabbed his shaky, twitching hand. Gently she placed it on her braid, hidden deep in her thick dark brown hair.

"Whenever your hand starts to do that, place your hand on my braid," she said.

Taking off her jacket, she placed her hand on Leo's braid, also hidden deep in his thick brown hair.

Leo's heart sank when he saw all the razor scars that took up Sammatha's arm.

"He made them worse," Leo said, trying not to get emotional.

Sammatha shook her head. "Mr. Smith's impact on me is at a minimum scale. I'm just a broken person…"

"I'm just as broken Sammatha," Leo said, trying not to get emotional.

Pulling out his arm, exposing his cuts to Sammatha. "I have been trying to save you from harming yourself when, in reality…I have been trying to kill myself in the process."

Sammatha started making out with Leo, but it wasn't long before Leo pulled back.

"Don't you ever say that again? I'll stop it, okay. I'll stop cutting my arm," Sammatha begged. Tears started to fall intensely as she got out of her seat and moved on top of Leo. Once again, she tried to start making out with him.

Though Leo pulled back once as the tears fell down his eyes.

"Everyone hates me. It's all my fault. I brought nothing but pain to your life and disgrace to the group. Now Mr.Smith is here and -"

Sammatha started making out with Leo again, trying to get him to be quiet. "Stop talking, okay, okay. Please stop. Please."

Everyone stared down at Mr.Smith inside the house as he made himself comfortable in the center of the living room, right in front of the TV.

He was in his suit and tie as if he was working at the stock market in the 80s.

"Hello, my children. I see you have been holding up the place very well," he chirped.

Brittany was unhappy to see Mr.Smith, and Carlos quickly took notice.

Mr.Smith creepily waves to Maknae Line. "You all got so big. I remember when you were all barely 8-9 years old."

"You must also remember when you forced us to get emancipation from our parents," Mazen said.

"You're rich and famous. What is there to complain about?" Mr.Smith said.

"What is your purpose for being here?" Xan questioned.

"I can't say hi to my children?" Mr.Smith said.

Everyone cringed at Mr.Smith.

"We are not your children and never were, to begin with," Xan said, trying to stay calm.

"Really, 'cause I was the one who got you all out of really bad living situations. Simon. You and your sister were living in trailer park poverty. Jackie, you were homeless before you got signed. Jean and Rebecca, should I really mention what happens at your home in Miami? Carlos, your father beat you, or was that you, Jermany. Valen, you were so lost in your mind you couldn't recall what happened the day before. Poor Maxwell. You can't even walk around with a turtleneck. Plus Romeo-"

"Your point?" I said.

"I'm your father. I know I was a little rough on you all, but-"

"BUT?" Cameron said, upset, "YOU DOGGED ME DOWN AND CONSTANTLY CALLED ME UGLY AND WORTHLESS BEFORE HITTING ME!"

"And now you are the lead singer of Varsity Line. What doesn't kill you makes you stronger."

"You're a menace to society," Theo said.

Mr. Smith laughed. "A menace? Talk about the guy who had multiple DUI on your record."

"Key word being the past," Theo said, folding his arms.

"You know I can do that too." Mr.Smith started to mimic Theo's pose.

"What's your purpose here?" Lisa questioned.

"I want Switch to come back to Ex-S Records."

Everyone in the room was intrigued by Mr. Smith's boldness.

"You want us to come back to Ex-S? You're kidding me?" Xan laughed.

Mr. Smith pulled out his briefcase and pulled out a stack of contracts.

"Clearly the leader line can't take care of the members of Switch anymore. It seems that you are in the headlines for something new every week," Mr. Smith said.

Xan, in anger, left the living room to go into the kitchen.

Lisa quickly followed behind him.

"Hey Brittany," Mr. Smith said as he waved at her. Brittany tried to keep a straight face to show no fear.

"Where's your kid Kimberly?" He asked.

Coming inside from the front door was Leo and Sammatha.

"Hey Leo, do you remember seeing Brittany laying in front of the stairs."

Brittany started breathing heavily as Carlos himself was confused about the situation.

"I- I don't know what you are talking about," Leo said.

"It was the day before we all left for tour. Oh, how I failed to raise you all. Turning into delinquents with no care in the world. You know Carlos, I thought pushing Brittany down the stairs would save you two the headache and drama that would follow but I guess your kid's head is made of steel," Mr. Smith laughed.

Carlos looked at Leo and then at Mr.Smith. "Carlos, Leo immediately took me to the hospital with whatever money he had left," she said.

"You tried to kill my kid?!?!?" Carlos said, walking up to Mr.Smith. Though he was blocked by Xan as he came back into the living room with a lighter and oil.

Seconds later, he set the contracts on fire.
"That was a bad idea," Mr. Smith said, getting up from his seat.

As the flames started to burn the stacks of paper. Carlos came around and punched Mr.Smith.
In retaliation, Mr.Smith hit him back, causing Carlos to fall to the floor.
"Who let the dancer fight around here, huh? YOU ALL WILL BE COMING BACK TO EX-S RECORDS!"

"Is business hurting? Now that Ketrean is on the blacklist, it must be hard to have your biggest artist knocked off the charts," I said.

Carlos stood up and struck Mr. Smith again. With one blow, Mr. Smith's lip started bleeding.

"YOU ARE A PIECE OF SHI-"

Before Carlos could finish, a revolver was pointed at his forehead.

Carlos's eyes were wide as he was shocked to see what was pointed at him.

Leo, in quick reaction, slowly tried to move closer to Mr.Smith. Sammatha was resistant to letting Leo move, but he kept pushing forward. JV's line was tense as we sat, fearing what was happening.

"Wait. Wait, it doesn't have to be like this," Carlos said, getting emotional.

"You all ruined my life when Switch left Ex-S! And now you are hurting my pocket and driving me insane! Though I really should be saving this little bullet of mine for...."

Mr. Smith pivoted to Xan as he stood by the burning table.

"Alexander Oliveira. You threatened me for all I have and took my most valuable possession. You know I was planning to have you become a successor of Ex-S."

"Pull the trigger," Xan said with his chin up.

"You want me to pull the trigger? Alexander Oliveria, lead "leader" of Switch. You must be stressed out for the amount of work you took on as a manager. I heard you try to get hooked on heroin recently. Friend of mine saw you at Daisys. I should probably pull the trigger and help put you out of your misery."

"Pull the trigger, then."

Mr.Smith was shocked by Xan's boldness.
"PULL. THE. TRIGGER! ARE YOU DEAF? PULL IT!"
Xan grabbed Mr. Smith's gun and pulled it closer to his head.
Everyone in the room was scared.
"Xan! Stop this, okay! We can work something out," Lisa yelled.

"PULL THE TRIGGER, ANTHONY! PULL IT!"
Mr.Smith recoiled the gun, shaking in his boots.

Just when Leo is able to sneak up on Mr.Smith to put him into a chokehold, Mr. Smith shoots his gun. Some members looked away in fear, scared to witness a murder before their eyes, when we all noticed that we didn't hear a loud bang.

"Absolutely pathetic," Xan said. Mr.Smith took a look at his gun, wondering what was going on.
"You have done this skit with me all the time since I was little. Same script, with the same gun. You have tried to shoot me 35 times now for 35 different reasons."

Xan pulled out a pocket knife from his pocket. "Hold him down Leo," Xan said.
"WAIT! WAIT! I'M SORRY," Mr.Smith begged.

"No, you're not," Xan said, moving closer to him.

"HEY XAN, STOP," Lisa said, pulling him back.

Everyone in the room started to tell Xan to step down from his ground as the room got really loud. "I'M GOING TO KILL HIM!" Xan yelled at the top of his lungs, which got everyone to be quiet.

"I'm going to kill him for everything he did! He tried to silence me way too much while he ran with the group's money while we starved here. HE CALLS US HIS CHILDREN AS IF HE DIDN'T STRIP US AWAY FROM OUT CHILDHOOD! Neglected us and thought it was fun to play Russian Roulette with me!"

Xan went in to stab Mr. Smith's knee, but Leo pulled back, causing only a cut to occur.

"Xan, maybe we can work something out," Leo said.

"Don't defend this guy! He needs to be killed," Xan said, crying.

The fire on the table started to expand. I signaled to the JV line to find a fire extinguisher.

Getting up, I slowly walked over to Xan to get him to calm down.

"Valen! He deserves to die," Xan said as tears fell down his eyes.

"Murder isn't going to make it better," I said, slowly reaching over for the knife.

"YES IT WILL!" Xan said.

Lisa, in quickness, was able to fetch the knife. Grabbing it by the blade, Xan accidentally yanked it out of her hand, causing it to bleed.

The pain was delayed as Lisa looked at her hand in panic.

"AHHHHHHHHHHHH!" She screamed in terror as her hand was gushed open.

Xan immediately dropped the knife and quickly rushed to Lisa.

"I'm sorry!" Xan said. Not knowing what to do, he took his shirt off and wrapped it around Lisa's hand in panic. Tears of panic came from Lisa as she cried in pain.

Leo still had Mr.Smith in a chokehold, not knowing what to do.

Turning to me, he said, "What do I do with him."

"Let me leave!" Mr. Smith yelled.

Jean let go of Cameron's hand and walked up to Mr.Smith. With his rings on, Jean took one blow to Mr. Smith's face. "That is for hitting my lady for all those years," Jean said in Spanish.

"It was an accident," Mr. Smith said in pain.

Jean laughed. Grabbing the knife off the ground, Jean started moving to Mr.Smith.

"No, let me have this one," Carlos said.

"No one is having this one," Vanessa said, rushing over to Carlos and Jean.

"Leo let go of him," she said.

"XAN RIGHT HE DESERVES TO DIE. RIGHT NOW!" Jean yelled in Spanish.

"We are not going to do this right now," Vanessa said back in Spanish.

Cameron came to Jean's side to calm him down while Leo threw Mr.Smith on the ground.

"We expose him," Mazen suggests out of nowhere.

Mr. Smith looked up and noticed he was kneeling in front of Maknae Line.

"We have a whole secret lounge just to get away from you. You lied and cut communication with our parents just so you can make money off us," Mazen said, choking up.

Everyone in the room turned to Mazen as he started crying.

"You told us to not cry. But what do you expect when you take a kid away from the life they were supposed to live? You sold us a dream and milked it for all it had to offer. Do you know why we are all a mess?!? You kidnapped a school bus full of kids with bright talents and futures and told them to dance for 16 hours straight. If any of us mess up, you would beat one of us up. Though you... you figure Maknae Line needs the most discipline. YOU THOUGHT WE NEEDED THE MOST DISCIPLINE! AND YOUR ASSISTANT DIDN'T DO [REDACTED] BUT TURN UP THE MUSIC WHILE WE CRIED IN PAIN!"

Mazen started beating up Mr.Smith in rage. Simon, Romeo, and Theo quickly pulled him off of Mr.Smith. "I'm sorry!" Mr.Smith said in pain.

Then Mr.Smith looked up at Maxwell, who kept quiet next to Mia.

"So you thought you could have a field day with me once I moved in? That I was just damaged goods," Maxwell said.

"It was an honest mistake," Mr.Smith said as he coughed some blood onto the red carpet.

"You're the one who told the media how perfect our lives are. You're the one who has been controlling the narrative, never giving us a voice to speak. While we went days with no utilities, you told the world we were snobby rich celebrities living the fast life. But instead, we were out here in the middle of nowhere trying to survive, and we still are," Maxwell said.

"We don't need to kill Mr.Smith. Once the news about him comes out about what he did to all of us... He will end his own life. IN HIS OWN HANDS," Mazen said.

Xan examined Lisa's hand as her blood bled through his white t-shirt. Clearing his throat, he said,

"Sorry to break the news, but I have to say that you, Anthony Smith. CEO of Ex-S Records is now officially on the Switch Blacklist. If you decide to sue, you are guaranteed a losing case, for following suit is a waste of money. At spot number 1, your name may remain on the list for eternity. The news will break on September 22. That should give you enough time to pack up your belongings and resign from your position."

46

09/22/22: The Never-Ending Show.
Part I

The show must go on. Three back-to-back concerts. One could say it's a PR stunt to cover up the drama in the news, but that's such a cheap answer to say. From our point of view, it was more of a show that we felt drawn to do. Today was the day that we were going to expose the one guy who held us hostage and groomed us into global superstars.

With last-minute planning, it was decided to do an intense, powerful, over-the-top show that would go on all night. From sunset to sunrise will be nothing but performing and having fun with the fans and the group as an attempt to heal from our past. It will be like one big sleepover, except it is on a stage. With only a week's notice, we weren't worried about being unprepared. Why do you think we practice all the time?

"We are the first ones here?" Jermany sighed. Courtney and Jermany stood by the door, grinning their teeth slightly disappointedly. The first show is at the Pollo Theatre. Starting off with a smaller yet humbling venue. Courtney grabs her bags from the ground and walks into the room to find her a spot to step up. "We will be all over the place, just like back during the AAPI festival. Ready to be overworked as Switch's lead singer?" Courtney said.

Jermany walked over to give Courtney a hug from behind. "I don't see it as being overwork." Courtney looked at Jermany through the mirror and could tell his mind was preoccupied.

"How could you not? Zachary is now officially out of the group. Romeo and Carlos are trying to be more active outside of performing, but they do have father duties. Maxwell is barely present, leaving you with Theo as the only guy qualified to truly share the burden of lead singer at the moment."

Jermany let go of Courtney and went to the dressing dock that was right behind her. Just when he was about to take off his glasses, he saw through the mirror that Courtney looked concerned.

Pondering back and forth, Courtney asked, "Jermany. What are our trials going to be like? After what happen with Mr.Smith, I'm really scare of the future."

Jermany went into deep thought as he reflected on what the possible answer could be. His lips quiver as he tries to say his words but giving in he said, "I don't know what it will be like."

Opening the door, it was Carlos and Brittany, followed by everyone else.

"Let's go! Ready to conquer the world," Dice said excitedly, coming inside.

Carlos sat down next to Jermany, all happy and ready to get the show on. Opening up his bag, he handed Jermany a bento box. "Kimberly and Brittany stayed up yesterday to make everyone some dinner for today's show." Carlos pauses and switches to a more sincere tone.

"I also wanted to say thank you as well. For everything."
Jermany looked over at Carlos. "What are you talking about, Carlos?"
"For always holding up to being my best man," Carlos said. Carlos insisted that he opens up the Bento box. So Jermany did, and inside was some kimbap and seaweed salad and a little cookie that was decorated with an amateurish cartoon of Jermany's face.

Jermany picked up the cookie and admired it to its fullness. "Thanks," he said. Leaning in, he gave Carlos a brotherly hug. "No problem."

I was over at my desk when suddenly I got a call from Jackson. I picked up my phone and held it to my ear. The room was loud, so I took the time to step out of the room momentarily.

"Hey, what's up. Are you able to come to today's show?" I asked.

"I'm so sorry. I had bought my plane ticket and everything, but a business emergency popped up," Jackson said over the phone.

I rolled my eyes. However, how could I be surprised once again?

"Where are you right now?"

"Hong Kong, but I will soon leave for Singapore to meet with some contractors. Don't worry, though; I sent you some flowers your way to wish you luck." Look at that timing. Just when I turned a bit, a worker came up to me with a big bouquet of frozen red roses.

"Oh, you shouldn't have Jackson," I said as I grabbed the bouquet. After a short conversation, I returned to the dressing room to get ready. Sitting next to Sammatha, she was amazed at the flowers.

"Oh, my God! Did Jackson get you this?" she asked.

"He sure did. A gift for missing today's show, but I'm not mad at it. He is a busy man. My man works two jobs." I said, pushing the flowers off to the corner.

"Two jobs?" Sammatha questioned.

"Yep. A singer and realtor at the same time. I just wish he wasn't so busy," I smiled.

Incoming was Rebecca with her pen and paper. "Hey Sammatha, I got a diss track I can perform for you at today's show.

I got a couple of punchlines that could make the chick cry if I land them right."

"No way. I want no part of it," Sammatha said.

Rebecca whispers over to me, "I'm still going to perform it. Switch out a couple of my lyrics to slide it in."

I shook my head in disagreement. "Well, you go do that and let me know how that goes."

Looking up at my mirror I saw Lisa passing. Quickly I got up to chat. "So when is the news going to be release about Mr.Smith," I asked.

Looking down I couldn't help but notice that Lisa's hand was still bandage up from last week.

"Once the third show happens, we will release the news. For now just make sure everyone is having a good time on stage," Lisa said.

"That is something I can do but firstly how are you? How's the hand," I asked.

Lisa looked tired and exhaust behind her calm appearance.

Taking a look around she notice how excited everyone appeared.

Lisa said, "Ever since we left Ex-S Records, I barely got genuine rest. Its was always something coming up with the members. It is like the world doesn't want to see us win. Not once ever..."

"I think we have been the winner this whole time."

Lisa was taken back by what I said.

"Change your perspective on the situation. We opened our eyes and saw that we were drowning ourselves in our circumstances. Many people don't get that privilege of experiencing it in their lifetime. Whether they are too scare to admit how traumatizing their past is or too fearful to see how scared and damaged their souls are. We are winners because we though we all went through alot this past decade, we still have each other. Through all the ups and downs, we still have each other. Not many people can say the same," I said.

Lisa took a look over at Xan and noticed flipping through some paperwork. "Valen... What did Mr. Smith mean when he said you spend too much time in your head?" Lisa questioned.

I shrugged my shoulders. "Sometimes I think Mr.Smith just threw me into the group to meet his black people quota. That was my guess because he didn't really like any of my ideas I had to share. He thought I was a wasted talent and feared that my looks wouldn't have enough social currency to boast the group's popularity."

I looked at Lisa in seriousness. "He treated me like I was an employee working overtime for no pay and he says I spend too much time in my head. Yea whatever. I don't have the time or the privilege to even dream at night. Too busy making sure everyone else in the group is okay. Healthy and breathing they say. I'm fine Lisa. Don't worry about me."

Outside the venue, disguised in all black with shades and a mask, was Zachary, Kylie, Jordyn, and Grace. They were waiting in line to enter the building. The queue was long, and the sun was about to go down at any minute as the time reached closer and closer to 8:00 pm.

"I don't want to go anymore," Jordyn said worriedly.
  Grace wasn't buying it.
  "We are going to this show," Grace said with an attitude.
  Judging by Kylie, Zachary, and Jordyn's eye expressions, they didn't seem too fond of Grace's matter.
  "What's your problem Grace? Loosen up a little," Kylie said.

The line started moving up, and the four eventually made their way to the front doors when security stopped them.

"Ma'am, you can't bring that bag in here."

Grace got irritated with the security guard.
  "It's just a fanny pack?"

The security didn't care and wasn't going to budge. Giving in, Grace walked over to the trash can by the stairs. She took out some knickknacks and her phone before throwing away the bag. With the rest of the stuff, she places it into her hoodie pocket.

"Happy?"
  The security rolled her eyes before proceeding to check their tickets. In they went inside. Fans from different corners of the world, of all ages, were running around trying to find their

seats or wait in line to buy their merch.

"Think anyone will recognize us?" Zachary asked. "Doubt it," Kylie said. Jordyn walked up to the case of merch being displayed. Admiring the t-shirts, mugs, socks, and umbrellas one could buy, she felt a wave of nostalgia coming to her when suddenly the moment was interrupted by Grace.

"Come on, we need to find our seats. No time to sit here and entertain this nonsense," Grace said.

The four walked up the stairs to the 1st balcony where they would be seated. The room was loud as fans packed the room. Kylie wasn't amused by the large crowd but became more upset when she saw where she was sitting.

"You want us to be in the center? In the front row? Your joking." Looking down, she saw something was off with Grace.

Funneling down to their seats, Kylie taps on Zachary's arm.

"What?"

"Does she seem off and tense up," she whispered. Zachary sat down next to Grace and noticed that Grace still had her hand in her hoodie pocket. Looking over next to her, he saw Jordyn was made aware of the situation.

Zachary pulled out his German tongue, and in a cheerful voice, he said to Jordyn and Kylie, "What was in that bag?"

Grace looked at Zachary, annoyed. "Why aren't you speaking in English?"

Jordyn tried to get a look, and judging by her stance, she was holding something.

Jordyn then pulled out her German, "I don't know what was in the bag, but she clearly holding something." K

ylie immediately became alert, so she pulled out her limited word use of informal broken German. "That's not possible."

"I might have my problems with the group, but I don't hate them to that degree," Jordyn said.

Grace pulled down her mask a bit and was very irritated. "English. English. English. It's that so hard to ask?"

Switching back to English, Kylie glared at Grace uncomfortably.

"What's up with you three." As more and more people pack the room, Kylie signaled for Jordyn to go get security.

"Grace, what's up with you?"

Jordyn slowly got up and walked away.

"What are you talking about?"

Kylie laughed a bit before switching to a serious tone.

"What's your problem with Switch? I got kicked out because I apparently chose to have drama with a sensitive chick. Rookie mistake, I'll admit. Meanwhile, Jordyn and Zachary felt like they were being robbed of their time and money. What's your story? Because out of all of us here, you're the only one on the blacklist."

"Excuse me, ma'am. But I am going to need you to leave."

Grace felt so offended and betrayed when she saw Jordyn standing next to the security guard.

"What is this? A setup?" Grace said, raising her voice. That is when the people in the row behind them notice who the four are.

"Ma'am, can you empty your pockets?"

"My pockets??? All I have is my wallet and phone, and I don't know. Some lip bomb."

Grace emptied its pockets, and surely enough, that was all she had. "Did you guys really think I would have brought a weapon in here? You all are pathetic. Had an amazing opportunity to be in the greatest group of all time, but because something didn't go your way, you got mad and ruined it all for yourself, then played this dang victim card. Yea, you got me. I want to be a Switch member and not one of those rejected lost members. But after spending time with you three, you made me realize that I want no part of anyone in that family. Every single one of you has problems; the only difference is that you three are bold enough to be hypocrites."

Just when Grace was about to leave, she took one last look at Kylie, Zachary, and Jordyn. "You three claim you hate Switch. But it sounds like the complete opposite. Deep down, you still care for them," she said.

Grace pushed the security guard off to the side and left the three in the stands.

Screams filled the air as the members of Switch walked out onto the stage. Simon's eyes opened when he saw Jordyn in the stands. "They're here," Simon said on the inter-piece.

"Go figures. Just give them a show they won't forget then," I said.

Lights turned off and cue the group's theme song, "Dance." Goosebumps filled the air as the acapella of our voices harmonized. Then breaks out to this 2000s R&B/pop sound.

Grace was walking out of the venue when she heard the song playing and couldn't believe what she heard. The catchy rhythm and lyrics couldn't be ignored but instead sang along too. Kylie, Zachary, and Jordyn couldn't help but sing along under their breath, knowing they wanted to sing it out at the top of their lungs.

"You and I can stop and watch the moon dance away.
The sunrise will rise, and we won't stop shouting even when it comes our way.
Ohhh yea.
Can't you believe it when we are dancing away? The tears from my eyes are not drowning in sorrow.
But it's tears of joy when it's you and I when we watch the moon dance away."

Little tease of the song. The first show was great. Should have saw Kylie's face when Rebecca sent that diss message to her. I didn't even know, but Simon, too, handed a couple of words to exchange with his sister during another song with Rap Line. He made it sound like she was their deadbeat dad or something. But all was fine when it was the couple's dance portion. Of course, off to the side, the ones considering or not paired with anyone had to watch that whole thing go down. Though I wish Jackson was here to occupy some space with me until it was time to go back on stage.

Once all was done, it was quick moving. Grab everything, pack up the bus, and run over to CC Outdoor Football Area, where about 55,000 fans were waiting for us at 1 am. So technically...

47

09/23/22: The Never-Ending Show.
Part II

It's September 23, 2022, and the party has just started. We had some guest performers hold down the show while we went to Long Island from Upper Manhattan.

Coming inside the dressing room, I drop my bag in shock. I see this dark skin guy with a small buzz cut, all kicked up with the most outdated glasses of the century.

"Shut up!" This sucker Kendrick was chilling on the couch backstage.

"You late," Kendrick said, getting up. Rap Line rushed over to give him a big hug.

"Where have you been," I said, cheesing.

"Don't worry where I have been. I figure I show my face for once and perform with y'all. Plus, I got a contract to fulfill."

"You got it," Xan said, thumbing him up. David and his money gun was coming around the corner, spraying it all over the air. My man had finally decided to get the mullet haircut. "You guys should have been here earlier. I had this place like a rave party. Spinning the records like a true DJ."

The dream team was here, and it was time to have some fun. Our world tour theme, Around the World, inspired the second show. It was cool to see everyone sing and rap in different languages as the fans waved their home country flag in the area. Just from a quick glance, you could tell we had a lot of Dominicans, Puerto Ricans, Nigerians, Filipinos, Belgians, and Brazilians in the crowd, ready to dance.

Compared to the bland stage set design at the Pollo, the second show had the most elaborate set. It looked like a dollhouse, and everything was plastic.

Real metaphoric. It was Maknae's idea, so as creative director, it was my job to make sure I delivered on their request. Just know I took all the money it needed to put the whole set together out of their September check.

We performed some songs from the In the Name of Love album and some OG hits from Cold Weather, Kiss N' Tell, Under the Impression, Dreams, and Nightmares, and the list went on. We did some fun bits, like a dance battle between Varsity Guys and Varsity Girls. Some fans got to come on stage and pie the members of JV and Duo, which, uhhhh. The whipped cream messed up my edges. I felt bald at that point, and that was when I wished I had worn a wig instead of straightening my hair.

The rap line got a makeover by all the girls in the group. I think the ratio was about three girls per guy and yikes. Cameron made sure Jean looked like a hot mess while LeeSung, on the other hand, looked like the next K-Pop star. Then for the babies in the group, we had them go against four other fans in the crowd to battle out in a random dance challenge, and they got eaten alive. Probably because it was past their bedtime.

Xan, Lisa, and David did come out to share a little fashion walkway. Xan and Lisa come onto the field in this 50s top-down car, waving their hands like they won gold for the US. Though there was a potential disaster when David almost drove the car into a wall.

The second show started to fill less like a concert and more like a fan meet-up. But all good things must end because once it was 4 am, the show had to end so that the third show could start.

With an hour and a half to prepare, the group had to rush to the BFF Stadium in Brooklyn. Since it was late, though, we offer for our fans who attend the 2nd showing to stay and watch the live stream through the Switch Experience. Though some left to attend the third showing that would start at 5:30 am.

The third show was the actual concert, a true cinematic movie experience. You would have thought you were watching a Broadway show with the quality of the performance. You would think we were exhausted, but we were too busy cracking jokes and pulling pranks on each other backstage. Everyone put their differences aside for that one and had fun. According to my notes, class favorites for tonight's show were Theo, Toran, Cameron, Jean, Maknae Line, as usual, Dice, and Rebecca. But most importantly, the real excitement was to see Kendrick with his pearly white teeth. Every Nigerian in the crowd was screaming and crying as if he was their husband.

"Hey Xan and Lisa! Coming onto the stage" Jermany said into the microphone. In the sound box Lisa took a glance at Xan. "Are you sure about this?" Lisa asked.
   Xan nodded before leaving the room.
   Lisa took a look at the stage for the fans had no idea what they were about to witness. "Is the live stream still running," Lisa asked the staff. They all gave a thumbs up.

"Awesome…" she said before leaving the sound box.

On stage, all 31 members were front and center for everyone one to see. Xan signal for someone to give him a mic.

"Um. Hi everyone. The group has something that we would like to announce to the whole world. Our old manager Mr.Smith was someone we have vocally mentioned in past interviews. Surely you all know that we hate him but we never went into details for why…"

Xan paused as look around the room. In a stadium of tens of thousands of fan with the additional half million plus people watching the live stream, Xan was scared to continue his sentence.

We all looked at Xan as he trembled to say his words.
   "We like to announce that he will be on the Switch's blacklist."
   Without going into much detail Xan handed his mic over to Theo before exiting the stage.

Lisa signal to not play the video clip that had prepare before getting off stage.
   Theo panicked and without much thought he said, "Yes you heard that! MR.SMITH IS ON THE BLACKLIST! FINALLY!"

Then he signal for the final song to play which was more playful song. We ended the show with a ballad accompanied with the orchestra. As a group who didn't do the MP3 singing, it was chilling. We sounded like a church choir in that room as the entire stadium sang till the sun came up at 7:15. Each Flame puts their lightsticks in the air as they sway side to side.

"Xan!" Lisa said under the stage. Rushing to his side, she got him to stop.

"What was that all about?"

"Lisa its all done. We put him on the list. Now we can let God handle the rest. I'm not going to show videos of us getting abuse for millions of people to see. We make comfort music and when people have a bad day, they sing along to our songs. Putting that video there would do more harm than good."

"But–"

"He is gone and we can all finally start healing from the past. We don't need an audience for that journey right now. It not like the world like us anyways," Xan said.

A montage later, everyone was so tired, just wanting to crash on the floor. Shoutout to Kimberly for the bento boxes cause they carried us through the night. No one questioned why we didn't show the graphic video of Mr.Smith six years of torturing us. It was ultimately best to put him on the blacklist, followed by an official statement.

Fans tried to come up with their own theories for what happened but none were close to the actual reason.

Mr.Smith released his official resignation as he stepped down as CEO of Ex–S Records for his career was indeed over.

While waiting for the tour bus to pick us up, Jean noticed that Leo kept checking out Sammatha as she was chatting it up with Jackie and Brittany.

"Blink, Leo. Blink," Jean joked.

Kendrick shook his head, "The boy is in love."

"And that love is a drug indeed. Well, glad you're doing better, man." Simon said, tapping on Leo's arm.

"Same to you. Glad we all decided to do this show," Leo said.

"Yea, it was a great bonding experience that costs us a lot of money out of pocket to put together," LeeSung said, taking a sip of his orange juice.

"Okay, penny pincher," Jean laughed.

The guys started cracking up hysterically when suddenly a flash of light hit them. "Oops. Sorry. I forgot to do a countdown," Alanna shrugged.

On the other side, Carlos and Jermany were talking to each other off to the side, a little bit more exclusive and private.

"Bold for you to sing, "Raining for You," Jermany said.

In which this context, Raining for You is a blacklist song. It's about the time when Carlos and Brittany broke up back during the Around the World 2013-2016 era. Carlos tried laughing it off, but deep down, he was worried for Brittany.

"Say Cheese!"

The two quickly pose as Alanna snaps a shot. "Awesome." Alanna handed over the polaroid. "Cash or credit? And would you like to give a 10% tip," Alanna said.

Jermany and Carlos looked at Alanna in question.

"Last night's dinner is your payment," Carlos said, grabbing the polaroid.

Alanna was about to say something until she saw a perfect picture opportunity to get a picture of JV posing for an Instagrand picture.

"You know, today reminded me that I should be having fun with Brittany. I can't help but feel guilty about what happened back then. Had I done it differently, I should have been by her side. Never let Mr.Smith get close to her like that. "

"Hey, Carlos. It happens. Mr. Smith is out of the picture. Kimberly came out to be a healthy adorable kid and Brittany is okay. It is what it is. Can't go back and change the past."

DING DING DING!

Jermany and Carlos looked over and saw Xan was standing on a chair, clinking on a spoon to his mug. "ATTENTION! ATTENTION!"

Everyone quieted down and shifted their focus to Xan. "First off. I want to thank everyone for showing up today and hope you enjoy a fun all-nighter. Just got off the phone with our extended music team, and the great news is that we are making yet another album. So once we get back to the house, I need you guys to pack up cause WE GOT RESIDENCY IN MIAMI!"

Should we be excited because who wouldn't be? A chance to get out of gloomy backwoods, New York state and visit our other estate down on the beach that has been collecting dust since 2019. Not to mention the burnt table in the living room that I don't need to be constantly reminded of.

Jermany leaned into Carlos, "Maybe this is a sign from God. Couples therapy retreat. This should be fun."

Lisa raised her hand up high in the air. "We leave at 5 pm. Not a second later, okay?"

"Yes," Everyone said all together.

"Are you good, Leo?" Kendrick asked concerned. Leo looked distraught by the news. Jean and Simon looked at each other in worrisome. They went to look at Sammatha, who seemed fine with heading down to Miami, but Leo looked triggered.

The bus finally arrived, and it was time to leave.

Time flew by, and it was 6 pm at the JK Airport. Private entrance, in the back where another thing we owned was collecting dust, was our private plane. One of many toys we bought that raised our member dues to the five digits minimum. As the golden hour hit our faces, we waited outside to board the aircraft. I myself, like others, was sleepy. I didn't even know how much clothes to pack. Are we going to be in Miami for a few weeks or a couple of months? I grab whatever I can find, and for the rest, I am going to go shopping with Jackie cause I'm not about to sit here and figure it out. Cause the minute we got back to the house, I like many, went straight to bed.

Coming up the stairs to enter the plane. Inside there were couches and a snack bar to grab food from. Guys sat with the guys, and the gals sat with the gals. The plane ride was chill and smooth. Simon was in his little corner in the back, listening to music.

Jumpscare saw that Xan was standing in front of him with a mp3 and some wired earbuds. "Hey, here are some songs I wanted you to check out. You are on the production team, so I want you to review these demos and rough drafts and pick out anything that interests you."

Taking the mp3, he turned it on and saw there were about 40 songs on the list to go through. Looking through, he saw a song called 11:59. Giving it a listen as the plane took off, he waited for the long intro to play out. Out of shock, he heard Lily singing. Immediately he stopped the song and started the song over.

Not prepared to actually listen to it, he open his mind and heart to give it a fair listen. Little did he know that he ended up listening to the song on repeat the entire three–hour flight trying to dissect the lyrics one by one. Simon couldn't tell if the song was about him but also couldn't help but entertain that idea. With original plans to gaze his eyes at Saige the entire flight, Simon kept having his eyes wander over to Lily.

The song played out like a end credit scene to a movie as the Switch '' plane flew through the clouds down to sunny beach Miami. The Never-Ending show is over. No more fronting or continuing our old habits and cycle. But first, let's have a quick vacation in paradise.

48

??/??/??: XXX XXXXXXXXX.

"So what happened in Miami," the interviewer asked.

Each member sat in silence in the dark lit room for there was only one yellow light hanging above their head. One by one we took turns individually, alone, to speak our truth.

"Nothing happened in Miami. Nothing happened... ," Jackie said, trying not to be awkward.

"She said that?" Dice questioned in shock. He folded his arms as he rested on the stool.

"So something did happen in Miami?" the interviewer asked.

Suddenly the smile from Dice's face dropped as he became more reserved.

"I–I think we can skip over Miami," Cameron smiled.

"And explain what happened in January? Cameron, were you fully aware of the fact that you were being tested?" the interviewer asked.

The camera zoomed into her face as a wave of emotions hit her.

"I passed, didn't I? Didn't we all? Battle our Goliah like David," she laughed.

"How long did it take?" the interviewer asked.

"To give my life to Christ?" Simon questioned as his foot began to tap rapidly.

Xan rubbed his hands together and combed his hair back while Alanna straightened her back to look more presentable.

"To be a reborn Christian?" Lisa asked. Thinking it through she said, "Well it didn't take too long. Um God, Jesus, the Holy Spirit has always been by our side since day one."

"Even in the midst of you sinning?"

Theo tried his best to avoid making eye contact with the interview.

"It's... it's a battle against the flesh sometimes. Um... the devil... he... he can't be everywhere all at once. It's... not possible if you know what I mean. So he would get you hooked on a schedule," he said.

"I never said I was proud of my sins," Saige said confidently.

Jean said cheesing, "I came from a damaged family to live with other people who came from damaged families. It's a recipe for disaster. But everything is good. God saved his all by his grace."

"You say it like the conversation is over. As if the archives end after September 23rd 2022," the interview said.

"Well there's not much to talk about," he said.
"What happened in Miami Jean?"

"Nothing. I promise you nothing happened there. What is this a therapy session?"
Jean said, trying to not get frustrated.

"It's an unplugged session about the members of Switch's se-cret life before they gave their life to Christ," the interviewer said calmly.

"Well good luck trying to get Jean or Maxwell to talk. Or even Leo," Valen laughed.

Maxwell sat in silence as the interviewer waited for a response. Same followed for Leo and Sammatha. Same for the others.

Courtney smiled. Ready to explain what happened.
"Well we should probably start with what happened when the plane landed. You know, right where the archives pick from. Volume two right? Um, well the weather was nice. And-"

49

09/23/22: The Never-Ending Show
Part III: The End

A preview of Volume Two.

"Welcome to Miami," the flight attendant said as we all exited in the plane.

The weather is nice, though I wish we had arrived here before the sun went down. The sky was still a little lit with the dark blue, and purple haze off to the horizon. Walking down the steps I could tell that everyone was tired and the wind didn't help.

"Get me off this plane! My bed is calling me," Mazen whined as he waited in the line to get off. Just when Simon was about to get behind Mazen, he saw Lily getting up to exit as well. Freezing in his place he showed his hand out to give her the space to leave.

"You seemed pretty quiet back there," Lily said playfully.

"Just me listening to music as usual. Do you have any plans in the 305?"

Lily pondered and gave it some thought, "Not really. Though I will say it does feel weird to be back in the city. It's been a minute hasn't it. We did come down for like a day to perform at that university back during the 2021 HBCU homecoming tour but I mean we were pretty much in and out."

"Oh during Asia's 'I want to go to college' phase. Well yeah we came out then but also a couple of other times. I had my concert here for my Tainted Hearts album," Simon said.

"Sure. But not everyone went and the house was under renovations so we couldn't even stay there."

The two thank the pilots and flight attendant before stepping down the plane and into the shuttle bus. The bus ride to the house was quiet and loud at the same time. "Can't you believe it? We are in Miami!," Dice said before switching to Spanish. "We are going to make the best album that man will ever witness because WE ARE THE DREAM TEAM!!!!"

"Shut up!" Brittany said before going back to sleep. Rebecca glanced at Brittany then at Dice. Pulling out her Spanish she yelled, "Don't tell him to shut up!"

Then Brittany pulled her Spanish, "I'm going to tell him to shut up if I feel like it. Yelling like we haven't been up for 24 hours."

"We? YOU'VE been up for 24 hours! Should have taken a nap like everyone else if you were going to be this sensitive. Matter of fact I don't even know why you even came. You're the one on the next flight out in two days."

Jean, who was in the back of the bus next to Cameron and the rest of the Rap Line, called out Rebecca.

"Aye Rebecca. Calm down. It's like 10pm right now. And Dice sit down."

Before Rebecca could say anything Dice demeanor changed as he didn't want to upset Jean. Taking a seat, he zip his lips shut, locking the key.

Though the excitement couldn't hold him back so he started signing, "We. Are. The. Dream. Team! I already have a few songs already written, ready to be recorded."

Toran who was sitting across from him shook his head, sending him the thumbs up knowing good well he didn't know what Dice just signed.

After missing the exit twice and getting stuck in traffic we made it to our Miami House Estate. The house back in New York looks like amateurs built it compared to the

Mediterranean style mansion we have down here. Only downfall is that not everyone gets their own room.

Reality check but the chances of finding a home with 30 bedrooms is slim. This house does have memories, whether or not it was positive... or negative BUT... HEY it is another place to chill without worrying about a hotel bill.

Getting off the bus Leo heart started racing as the memories started to flood back to him. One by one.
   Though he came back to reality sharply to help Sammatha step down from the bus.

Maxwell followed behind her and you can tell that any mess up Leo does while down here is going to be a field day for him. He was just itching for Leo to make even the smallest error so he could feel like the big man.

As I watch Xan flip through the million keys that he has, trying to figure out which one opens the front door, I took a glimpse at Leo and Sammatha. Then randomly I heard a sea eagle crow loudly.

50

??/??/??

Coming up next. The Archives of BFF Vol. 2: What Really Happened in Miami?
The Archives of BFF Vol. 7: Before the Reign (A Prequel)
[Read before Vol. 2 is recommended.]

God Bless. – Valen

For more visit: thearchivesofbff.com